UNWILLING BRIDE

"Madam," Steven said sternly, "whether you want it or not, one fact remains; you are my wife."

"I am not!" Angelina answered vehemently.

"You are," he insisted and began stroking her.

She tried to pull away again. "Steven, please, have you no honor? Must you take me by force?"

"Madam," he answered menacingly, "How does honor enter into this? I am a man who wishes to enjoy his wife. And from past experience I know her to be more than just a willing partner."

"I told you, I am not your wife. A medicine man or chief, or whatever he was, spoke some ridiculous sounding gibberish I did not understand, and suddenly I am your wife? What nonsense!"

Sternly he answered, "It is useless to keep up this conversation. When it is possible, we shall stand before a priest."

"Steven, please," she begged, as his arms closed around her, pulling her closer to him. Now his mouth was on hers, working its special magic that caused her mind to slip out of focus and the room to spin about her.

His mouth strayed to her neck, kissing and nuzzling against the pulsating hollow at its base. Angelina closed her eyes tightly, fearfully awaiting the inevitable. With all her will power, she forced her mind to focus again, and demanded her brain to remain cool and indifferent to the onslaught of his lovemaking, her body remaining stiff and unyielding in his arms.

He laughed confidently as he pulled his face away. "You are going to give in, you know."

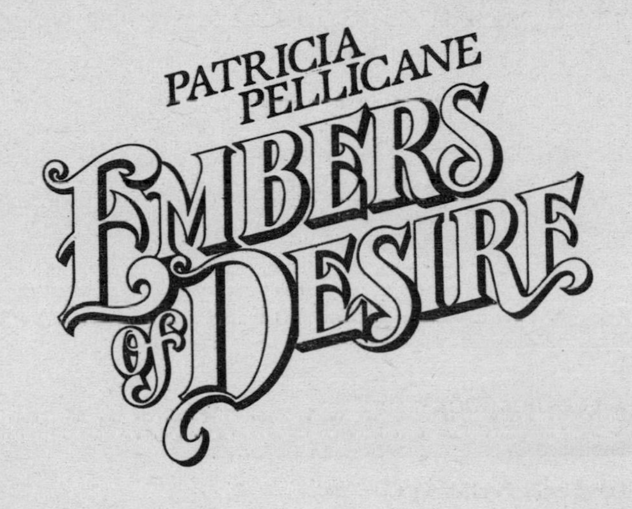

LEISURE BOOKS NEW YORK CITY

To my mother who introduced me to the world of books. To my husband who nagged me into writing one of my own.

A LEISURE BOOK®

Published by

Dorchester Publishing Co., Inc.
276 Fifth Avenue
New York, NY 10001

Printed in the United States of America.

1992 Edition
Leisure Entertainment Services Co., Inc.

Part One

Chapter 1

April 1770

"Father, please," she groaned in a heart-rending cry of horror. Her big blue eyes grew huge as they glistened and brimmed over with tears. Her lips trembled just enough as she allowed the enormous drops to slip pitifully down her golden smooth skin.

"Daddy Darling," reverting to a childhood name she had used when hoping to obtain a particular want, "you cannot mean this. Any one, anyone but him."

Stonily, he answered, "On this matter, I am adamant. As it is, you have remained unwed for too long. You will obey me. I want you well provided for. Even with your pretty face, it is not likely you would get a better offer." Softening his voice, he continued, "I can understand your feelings. I see the man is far from an ideal physical specimen, but physical beauty is not necessary for marital happiness and security. Mr. McCray has promised an enormous amount to be settled upon you. The day will come, Angelina, when you will thank me, for on the day you marry him you will become the richest and most respected young woman in this colony."

He felt some degree of guilt as he watched the sudden crestfallen look of despair gather and grow in her eyes, accompanied by the hopeless dejected slump of her delicate shoulders.

It almost worked. For a moment he wavered, but then knowing in his heart he was doing the best he could for his daughter, he turned and with a final authoritative look left her alone in her room. Feeling somewhat like a Roman offering a Christian to the lions, he quickly descended the stairs, heading for the haven of the library.

She waited for the bedroom door to close before she let a cry of frustrated rage escape her round lips, while diving full length upon her large high bed, and beating her pillows with unleashed childlike fury.

"I will not, I will not! He cannot force me!" she cried, but she knew in her heart, he could and would. She had to think; she was desperate and had to do something, or by this time next month, she would be the wife of Walter McCray.

She shivered, imagining for the moment,

herself locked in his embrace. The thought brought only horror and disgust.

Angelina Barton was a proud, spoiled, and beautiful young woman of nineteen. It was from her father that she inherited much of her willfulness and stubbornness. He was a strong minded and powerfully built man, who adored his daughter. Although there were times he could make Angelina quake in fear if he bestowed upon her one of his thunderous looks, she had learned to handle him quite nicely. He had been widowed since Angelina was a child of three, and he had given to both his children all the love and affection he possessed. They meant everything in the world to him; he denied them nothing, until now.

Since coming of age, her father had been unrelenting in his insistence to instigate a marriage. He had decided the best choice for her would be Walter McCray, and unbelievably, for the first time in her young life, she could not dissuade him.

The thought of marrying anyone, least of all Walter McCray, was abhorrent to her. In truth, she thought herself to be too good for any mere mortal man. Not that she detested their attentions. On the contrary, she believed it was a natural and correct attitude on their part. It gave her a strange sense of power when they nearly fell at her feet in adoration, lusting after her cool daring beauty, the need to possess her slim young body so obviously mirrored in their eyes. Arrogant and haughty, she silently swore no man would ever gain control over her life, much less her body. To be owned as if she were a horse, to be subjugated to a man's every whim, to obey him without thought of her own, was total degradation. Gladly, she would welcome death before such submission.

If she must marry, her choice would be Andrew Donaldson. She felt not the least aversion toward him, but more important, she knew without a doubt, she would never have the slightest problem in controlling him. It was obvious to her that she would be the strong and dominant party in their relationship.

Andrew was wild for her. Only three nights prior, at a birthday dance given for her best friend Peggy, he had held her in his arms and kissed her in the soft moonlight. His kisses were warm and sweet, but they brought to her none of the trembling she felt sweep through him.

Andrew, being only a year older than herself, was almost as inexperienced as she, but it mattered not; for the music and dancing combined with the starry night, added to the glow of the brief encounter. And brief it had been, for no sooner had she returned his virgin kisses with her own than they suffered the interruption and demise of the romantic interlude. But no matter, the moonlight had done its duty and she knew him to be in love with her.

How could her father allow this? What matter that her husband-to-be was the richest man in the Virginia Colony; he was horrible!

This was the first time in her life that pleading had failed, and she was more than a little amazed that she had lost this battle to her father.

She shuddered with disgust as she allowed her mind to slip back to the previous evening. Mr. McCray had been to dinner, after which, he had complained of a headache and asked if Angelina would be kind enough to accompany him outside for a breath of air.

At her father's nod she agreed, and together they had left the company of the others and stepped out onto the balcony just outside the dining room.

As she leaned against the pillars that supported the roof of the terrace, the evening breezes softly caressing her slim shoulders, a peaceful spirit had descended over Angelina. Unbeknown to her, a gentle sigh of contentment escaped her lips as she gazed into the starry night, her thoughts turning to Andrew's love.

Walter McCray had had something other than young love in his mind at that moment, more exactly—lust! Watching her in the moonlight, he felt a need to possess her so strong that his body shook with passion, and if her father had not been within hearing, he would have pulled her to the couch that stood in the shadow of the terrace and relieved himself of his desire. Not a man to want for long, and never one to take no for an answer, he was a formidable opponent to anyone, and a deadly enemy to those who crossed him.

Watching her now, he made up his mind to have her. Tonight he would speak with her father and press him for a near date. Soon, very soon, for he knew without a doubt her father would offer no objection. She would be his forever.

The thought of possessing her became so strong, that without a word spoken between them, he came to stand close by her side.

Lost in thought, Angelina forgot for a moment he was there, much less did she realize that he stood too close, and was astonished to suddenly find herself locked in an unwelcome embrace.

Although Walter McCray was the richest and most powerful man in Virginia, he was by far the ugliest.

Angelina was, for an instant, bewildered to find his arms about her. Looking over the top of his head, for it came only to her ear, she wondered how she could get away from him, without the loss of her dignity. Realizing the ridiculous picture they presented, she nearly laughed aloud. Many were the times during the evening that she had forced back a giggle at the sight of his bald head gleaming with the reflection of the candles on the dinner table.

Indeed, nature had dealt harshly with Walter McCray. Not only was he shorter than the average woman, but sadly, his arms hung to only half their normal length and yet his hands were larger than most.

She was locked up against him, while his hands, although enormous, could not meet behind her slender body. Yet it wasn't his physical deformities that disgusted Angelina, but the constant lecherous way his eyes roamed over her. Most of all, she detested the ever present saliva that formed in the corners of his mouth.

Right now, she could feel that wet slime leave a cold trail about her golden throat. He was making ardent love to her still form, while mumbling something unintelligable, and she shivered with disgust at his unwanted advances.

Walter McCray, unaccustomed to being refused in anything, took her shivers for ladylike tremors of passion, while her objections he put to mere girlish modesty.

"Really, Mr. McCray," she said, trying to release herself from his clutches, "this is most unseemly. And almost under my father's nose, too. Please unhand me, sir."

He was desperate to move her to a place which would afford more privacy. Passionately, he murmured, "Then perhaps a walk in your lovely garden, which I might add, dims in comparison to your delicate beauty, my dear."

Completely unimpressed by his compliments, her regal cool beauty more than ever apparent in the soft moonlight, she answered primly, "Quite out of the question, Mr. McCray." Silently, she groaned, *You ridiculous fat toad, get your hands off me!* Continuing aloud, she asked gently, "Sir, shall we join the others?"

But Walter McCray was not a man to be put off that easily. Holding her tighter to him with one arm, his free hand slid around and cupped her breast, crushing it harshly with his gigantic fingers.

Keeping a clear head, and resisting an urge to smash his face, she whispered softly, "Mr. McCray, quickly, someone is coming."

His hands dropped immediately to his side, and Angelina, in the instant it took for him to look over his shoulder, had slipped past his short fat form, and was gone.

Complaining of a headache, she had retired almost immediately, unable to keep up the part of congenial hostess with McCray's froglike eyes on her.

It was unthinkable that her father should permit this match. Young and spirited, she reasoned with the naivete of the rich that money was the least important commodity in the world.

Would Aunt Madaline ever allow this to happen to her? Certainly not! More often than not, since as far back as she could remember, she would find her father and his sister locked in combat. At times, these encounters proved to be so fierce as to make one shudder as they neared violent proportions.

How could Angelina be anything else but a strong willed woman with her father's blood flowing through her, and her aunt, who was the closest thing to a mother she had ever known, to follow as an example?

It was out of the question that she would be passively obedient to her father's wishes. Slowly her devious mind began to formulate a plan. Andrew would help her; she would make sure of it!

Chapter 2

She dressed carefully the next morning in a gown meant to entice, for it clung to her slim body so tightly that her breasts nearly bulged out over the too low neck line. She wore it with a short cape, for modesty. It would not do for everyone to see how much she allowed to be exposed.

Now standing in Andrew's library, she waited for the servants to let him know she was here. Her heart beat nervously. This would probably be the most important few moments in her life, for it could decide her whole future.

Thank God, he was home on leave; the first he had taken in nearly a year. What she was about to do was heartless and mean—but necessary. She felt not a moment of pity toward the unsuspecting Andrew.

At last Andrew entered looking very handsome in his new uniform. When she saw his young trusting face, a flicker of pity flashed through her mind for what she was about to do, but she dismissed it as insignificant. She flung herself into his arms, taking him much by surprise.

"Andrew, darling," she sighed seductively, "father insists that I become the wife of Mr. McCray. We must do something right away, before it is too late."

She raised her head to look sweetly into his eyes while she stepped back just enough to allow the cape to fall away and give him full view of what could soon be his. She smiled with satisfaction as she watched his eyes almost leave their sockets when they took in her nearly exposed breasts.

Andrew had had some sexual experience, but none with girls of Angelina's class, believing, falsely, that young ladies of quality did not enjoy sex and a wife performed it as her duty. Now he was at a loss to know what to do.

Finally, with much effort, he tore his eyes from her shocking attire. His face flushed pink as his eyes reached her own, realizing full well the promise she offered him. Still he stood, as if rooted in one spot, unable to say or do anything, his belly so tight with longing that he feared movement, for his hands ached to touch her. All he could do was swallow, again and again.

She stood waiting, watching while he tried to compose himself before her. Desperate, because the last thing she wanted from him was composure, she grabbed his hand. "Andrew, please say something, I am so frightened. Here, feel my heart how it beats." Without a moment's hesitation or the slightest sense of guilt, she placed his hand full on her breast.

Delighted, she watched as his hand remained where she placed it. His eyes devoured her while he moaned in agony and then finally, his fingers began to move gently over her silken flesh.

"Angelina," he croaked brokenly.

She was in his arms and he was kissing her sweetly and reservedly as he expected she wished to be kissed.

Angelina enjoyed his kisses, but in the light of day, his lovemaking brought back none of the sweet pleasure they had shared only a few nights ago. As she returned his ardent kisses, she felt none of the passion that flowed through Andrew. Calculating and cool, she pulled away, "Perhaps we should talk, Andrew," she sighed, while smiling shyly.

It took some time before Andrew could allow her to leave his arms, for her nearness and daring dress caused him some pain and embarrassment, and he knew she could easily see proof of his passion should they part at that moment. At last gaining some control, he spoke, while his voice broke slightly with intense emotion, "You need have no fear, my darling. I shall speak to your father today. It will be you and I who will marry, and I feel it cannot be too soon."

Again she flung herself in his arms, purposely pressing herself tightly against him.

"Nay, Andrew, you do not understand. Father has already made his decision. You cannot change his mind. Darling," she sighed seductively, while pulling back to look into his eyes, "if we love each other, we must take matters into our own hands. We must do something, something desperate."

Angelina was determined, never would she marry Mr. McCray. She knew she was being unfair, and yet not the smallest amount of shame entered her obstinate mind at her disgraceful actions.

She raised her arms to circle his neck, and with a sigh of satisfaction, she felt her breasts slip from the confines of her dress. She hid her face in his shoulder unable to keep a victorious smile from her lips. Her callous mind reasoned, now he would be unable to resist her.

He heard her sigh and took it for one of despair, "Do not be saddened, my love. I will take care of your father's objections. All will be well. I promise you, my sweet Angelina."

She was about to lose her temper. How could he be so dimwitted. Did she not just tell him her father would not change his mind? Was he truly so dense?

With determined effort, she controlled her annoyance. Feeling her breasts pressed against him, she realized he did not know the condition of her dress.

With a pleading voice, she whispered, "Andrew, please listen to me," then she stepped back one step.

She really was a most unusual girl. Her beauty was beyond compare, and for being so very thin, her breasts were most outrageously large. Now, because of the tightness of her dress, they stood out, jutting towards him as if supported by nothing.

Andrew swallowed hard. She looked so sweet and adorable with that little girl expression in her eyes, while being so distraught. He thought she didn't notice that her breasts were exposed to him.

He groaned, while his hands longed to come to rest on her. He would lose control soon. The door was unlocked, his mother or any one of the servants could enter at any moment. God, he could not take much more!

Uncaring of his torment, she continued, "Andrew, will you take me away with you?"

Even in the midst of his extreme suffering, taunted by the delicious sweet promise of her young body so close to him, the thought of elopement shocked him back to near normal. It was out of the question. It meant disgrace. He would never subject her to that. She would be unable to hold her head up in polite society. He was stronger in his love than his passion; he would refuse her gently but firmly.

Chapter 3

The night air, heavily scented with wet grass and wild flowers, brushed cool and silky against her warm skin. After three days of dreary rain it was a relief to finally put her plan into action.

Earlier that evening, she had sent off a note to her friend and comrade, Joseph Crockett, explaining she would be gone for a short time and promising to return as soon as possible. After that she had waited. Hours passed before the house quieted for the night, and still she waited.

Her heart thumped wildly with excitement and she lustily gulped the still moist air deep into her lungs, trying to calm herself. The night, black and soundless, was perfect for her plans. Even the gentle clumping of Buttercup's hooves were muffled against the soft damp earth as the horse was led quietly from the dark pungent barn and away from the mansion.

The house she was born in loomed behind her—white, majestic, and ghostlike against the black sky. Without a backward glance, she walked determinedly from it. Nothing stirred but the leaves and branches of the heavy oaks which bordered the long drive and circled the house. Gently, they performed their own graceful ballet as they swayed to and fro over her head in the sweet spring breezes of an April Virginia night.

She felt a twinge of regret at leaving her beautiful luxurious home, but the time for action could no longer be delayed. It was either leave or be forced to marry.

Now, alone in the dark, her heart palpitated with excitement. She was breathless. Her blood pounded in her ears with anxiety. It was imperative she reach the posting house and be gone before she was reported missing.

During the day, the ride would have been relatively simple, yet impossible. Never was she permitted to ride from her father's estates unescorted.

Aunt Madaline, newly married, had moved with her frontiersman husband to Elizabethton, Tennessee, which Angelina thought to be approximately two weeks of travel by coach, from her home in Alexandria. As far as she knew, the coaches ran regularly, despite the fighting in this area. The last days of travel might involve some degree of danger, for the town bordered upon Cherokee territory, yet Angelina felt only slight concern.

She was proud to relate to nearly anyone who might listen, that the crack Virginia militia, two-thousand strong, under the command of Col. William Christian, had marched against and swept through the Cherokee towns.

Allies of the British, the Cherokee nation had, she thought mistakenly, been brought to their knees. The majority had fled west and south, while those who remained were forced to sign treaties of peace.

With the exception of Dragging Canoe and his followers who still fought savagely, notorious in the havoc they wrought among the people who lived in South Carolina and Georgia, she had little to fear.

Since the capture of Savannah the previous year, the British had won a series of smashing victories due to their increased efforts throughout the South. It was a well known fact the settlements which stretched along the Piedmont from Virginia to Georgia were Tory. Within a year, British authority would be firmly established in the South.

Naively, Angelina reasoned, being a woman she would come to no harm. It was true that normally a lady could travel about without fear of assault. Even the most villianous of criminals were known to treat ladies with respect. She knew well the numerous stories of British atrocities toward the defenseless, still she was not deterred in her action. In truth, she was being extremely foolish and had every reason to be frightened.

Yet even had she enough sense to be fearful of such a trip, Angelina would not have hesitated to travel, so desperate did she consider her circumstances.

She knew once she had a chance to tell her father's only sister of her plight, mixed liberally, of course, with vivid descriptions of Mr. McCray, her aunt would do everything in her power to protect her from this forced marriage and her father's wrath.

Motherless at an early age, she could remember only Aunt Madaline as her mother, and their closeness had not lessened during the years that followed.

She was quite a distance from her home before she judged it safe to mount her mare. Here no one would hear the thunder of hooves as she galloped into the night. The aromas of leather, horse, and freedom, mingled with the freshly washed earth, were ambrosia to her senses and acted as a calmative to her nervous heart.

Never did she feel more alive, for every sense seemed to awaken with pleasure during her forbidden night ride. For her, animal and rider seemed to fuse, to become one object speeding over the gently sloping countryside.

Happily, days of seemingly unending rain had at last come to a conclusion. Her horse's hooves kicked up huge amounts of heavy mud. Still, with all her speed, almost no sound was made. Exhilaration unequaled swept over her as the damp wind tore at her face, flipping the mare's silky mane into her eyes and whistling through a few strands of her waist-length golden hair which fell from under the cap she wore.

Unable to control her happiness, she laughed out loud as she thought of the disgraceful picture she made, dressed in her brother Jim's old clothes, and riding astride her horse as if she were a man.

If her father had even suspected her of such outrageous behavior, she would have been correct in assuming dire consequences. But, like most of the young, she ignored the flicker of fear that threatened to assail her.

Somehow, like the forbidden fruit, this only added to the thrill of enjoyment. Although tonight was far from the first time she had ventured out alone, tonight was different in that she would not be returning a few hours later, with no one the worse for her excursion and herself much the better.

She had been riding for a short time, when she came upon the encampment of a regiment of soldiers. Suddenly, she was overcome with intense patriotism. She gazed out over the hundreds of glowing campfires that dotted the fields on each side of the dirt road. Slowing her horse to an easy trot, her heart soared with pride as she watched Colonel Bowman's Eighth Regiment of Virginia sit congenially about their fires. Softly sung songs of freedom filled the night and washed away the last remnants of her fear.

Colonel Bowman and one of his company

commanders, Capt. Joseph Crockett, whom she knew as a fellow conspirator to the cause, had been to dinner the night before. Her brother Jim had begged to be allowed to join the Virginia regiment, but her father was insistent that he wait at least two more months, until his seventeenth year.

Not far from the glowing camp fires, two men met in the dark shadows of a large tree. The taller of the two could see over his comrade's shoulder and watched as the young boy trotted his horse past the regiment's camp, while he listened to the shorter man speak.

Suddenly, they were interrupted by a sentry on patrol. As the two men heard the sounds of the approaching soldier, they separated and slipped further into the shadows, but not before they were sighted.

The young soldier was more afraid than either of the two older men. Barely were the words, "Who goes there," yelled out, when he raised his rifle and shot into the blackness. There was no time to answer or explain. The soldier began shooting wildly. The taller man was unable to reach his horse, for the sentry stood directly between himself and his animal. Bullets whistled shrilly past him, another exploded into a tree nearby sending a shower of bark flying over his head. He ran towards the young boy who had only now rode past him.

She was nearly at the end of the encampment. Her thoughts still on these courageous men, some of whom she had grown up with who were now in Washington's army, ready to face death for the promise of freedom. Suddenly her proud reverie was broken by the startling pop-pop of gun fire, and the terrifying sounds of running footsteps coming her way.

She was about to turn around to see the cause of the commotion when she was pushed painfully forward, pressed tightly against the horn of her saddle by someone who had jumped on behind her.

Somewhat breathlessly, a deep voice spoke in her ear, "Have no fear, I shall not hurt you."

Helpless, she allowed the owner of the deep voice to rip the reins from her stiff fingers and, kicking the horse's flanks, they went galloping out of sight, with gunshots echoing in the night.

This was unbelievable, absolutely impossible; it could not be happening to her. Lights flashed before her eyes, her breathing became almost non-existent. She was sliding into a faint. Suddenly, another series of pop-pop sounds came from behind. A whistling sound came dangerously close, so close in fact, that Angelina was sure she felt the heat of it as it sped past her arm.

She wanted to scream, yet she was so panic stricken, no sound came from her petrified lips. In her mind, however, she was screaming, begging God for help as her horse galloped into the night, farther and farther away from home, help, and most beloved right now, safety.

Her mind was wild with unasked questions. *Who was he? What was he going to do? Why was he running away and from whom? My God! How was she going to get away from him?*

After some time, to her it seemed an eternity, her panic began to recede and her mind began to clear. She was desperate, but what could she do? Finally, she reasoned that the longer she sat, passive and obediently still, the less chance she had of escaping. Without thought of the consequences, she lunged to her right, while bringing her left leg up and over her horse, forcing her body to fall.

But the man behind her was too quick and strong. Instantly, his weight counteracted her, his arms around her pulling her back, his voice growled deep and menacing in her ear, "Were I you, son, I would not do that again."

Her heart was pounding with such terror, she found she was barely able to breathe. Again, before her eyes, lights flashed and she once more felt the black breathless symptoms of a faint. Now she dared not utter a sound. She hoped beyond reason he would let her off or get off himself when he felt safe, and never know it was a woman he had been riding with.

On and on they raced into the black night. It seemed hours passed before he slowed and rode her horse more gently. They wormed their way through a maze of trees and brush, moving ever deeper into the dark forest.

He was pressed up tightly against her and she shivered with a feeling of approaching doom.

Feeling her trembling movement, he asked if she were cold.

Her answer was a silent shake of her head.

At last, as the first glimmer of dawn broke behind them, she was overcome by sheer exhaustion. Even her terror had to take second place to her weariness and she slumped against his hard body, in a deep sleep.

Jolting her awake, the man spoke, "It appears the horse is tiring. Perhaps we should rest her."

He stopped the horse and dismounted. She was paralyzed with fear. Surely, he would realize he was not traveling with a boy. She dared not think what he might do to her. She must escape! *Now . . . now,* she thought, *do not hesitate!*

Her heels dug deeply into the side of her horse, while her body crouched low over the animal's head, and her soul prayed for success.

The horse had taken but one step in its attempted flight, when Angelina felt herself being propelled through the air and down. She landed with a body shattering thud on her face and belly, while the impact caused a choking mound of dust to rise about her.

The man, holding her arm painfully above and behind her, was laughing at her attempted escape and subsequent fall. "Indeed I am sorry, son," he said between hardy gusts of laughter, "but it seems that I too am in need of your horse. Come, let me help you," he continued as he pulled the back of her shirt and lifted her to stand before him. "You have no need to fear me. I have told you, have I not, that I will not harm you?"

Angelina was never one to permit anyone to laugh at her, especially when she was in some discomfort. Even though her arm ached miserably, she lashed out, swinging her fists and, happily for her, connecting with every movement of her tiny hands. In a few seconds, realizing she was having no results on his muscled arms and shoulders, she lunged in, butting his chest with her head. To her imminent satisfaction, she heard him grunt at the force of impact.

He grabbed her arms and pulled her tightly against him to prevent further struggling. The moment their bodies touched, he knew it was not a young boy fighting him.

"What is this?" he gasped in amazement, as he looked down into the bluest eyes he had ever seen, thickly fringed with long dark brown lashes. Her mouth was pink, wide, and full, while between smudges of dirt, glowed creamy golden skin. She was clearly not a boy. Even if her body had not been pressed so close to his, he would have known it. His hand pulled her hat from her head allowing hair, that was the color of dark gold, to cascade in soft curls down her back and reach past her waist.

He swore an oath as he realized the predicament he was in. "Good Lord, madam, what am I to do with you? What the hell are you about, dressed thus and riding unprotected? Do you not realize we are in the midst of a war? Has no one informed you what soldiers are capable of? And worst of all to ride at night, are you demented?"

She said nothing. Acting very much the part of a simpleton, she could only stare, eyes huge with surprise, unable to contain her astonishment. Her mouth parted with shock.

During the night, her mind had conjured up the most villianous of outlaws, and she was momentarily stunned into silence. Before her stood an incredibly handsome man, tall and muscular, he wore a full black beard which hid his jaw. His eyes, a deep brown, shone gentle and kind from a deeply bronzed face.

Unable and unwilling to resist the temptation of her mouth so close to his, he lowered his head, and before she realized what was happening, his mouth held hers in a deep searching kiss. His mouth was warm, his lips firm, and his beard soft and furry against her skin. Unbelievably, she was not fighting, so stunned was she by his outrageous behavior. His arms were pressing her closer while his hand slid up from her waist to cup a full heavy breast.

The touch of his hand on her shocked her into movement and she tried in vain to push away from him. She was so surprised by the audacity of his actions that it was more reflex than thought when her hand shot out to slap his face.

The kiss ended, he continued to hold her close as he easily caught her hand before it made contact with its intended target. Holding it in his own, he brought it to his lips.

Naively, Angelina thought he was about to kiss her hand and extend an apology, but suddenly he turned it palm up and pressed it to his mouth. It wasn't his lips she felt, but his tongue, moving over her skin. She gasped at the sensation it caused. And all the while, he was holding her close, moving his hips subtly against hers.

No one had ever held her like this before. No one had ever dared.

"Just what is it you are doing, sir?" she spat out in amazement, as yet too shocked to show her building fury.

For a long moment, he looked at her, studying her face. Finally, he grinned wickedly, his eyes twinkling with merriment, "If you truly do not know what I am about, perhaps I could show you again."

Realizing he was teasing her, she reddened and snapped in a haughty tone, "Remove your hands from me this instant. How dare you touch me so? You should be horse whipped for this incredible conduct."

At that remark, he laughed aloud, apparently enjoying her building rage. Releasing her, he stepped back, arms folded across his chest, while his voice trembled with laughter, "Excuse me, madam. If it would not cause you too much inconvenience, would you be so kind as to tell me who you are?"

She resisted the temptation to slap his face, fearing a repeat of his actions. She glared at him with murderous rage, while her upper lip curled slightly with contempt. It was obvious, she had no intention of telling him her name.

After a moment of silence, he continued, "Shall I then think of a name that would seem appropriate?" With a teasing grin, he lightly ran his finger over her lips, which were set in a grim line of anger. She swung her hand and knocked his fingers away.

"Have I not just now told you, sir," she asked icily, "to keep your vile hands off me?"

With an exaggerated bow, while smiling at her fury and superior attitude, he remarked maddeningly, "So you have, my lady, a thousand pardons. Truly, I had no idea I was traveling in such royal company." With his eyes lazily sliding from her face to her toes, he took in her tight pants and tighter shirt, and found it impossible to keep from laughing out loud.

Angelina knew, dressed as she was, she represented not the slightest illusion of the lady she truly was. For now she could do nothing about the condition of her present dress, but what she could do was to set this arrogant beast down.

Again he asked, "Well, my lady, will you tell me your name?"

She gazed up at his grinning face and raising her chin higher still, gave him a look of utter scorn, "You, sir, have no reason to address me. Therefore, obviously no need to know my name."

Confidently, he responded, "And you, madam, are either blind or a fool. Perhaps you have not noticed, we are alone and at least a day's ride from civilization. Are you so dimwitted to believe we may be a week in reaching the nearest settlement, yet I shall have no need to address you?"

After a moment, she answered with a resigned and elaborate sigh, "Very well, since what you say is probably true," she lied without the slightest qualm; reasoning there was no need for him to know who she was, she gave him the name of an old lady who did some of her dressmaking, "My name is Jane . . . Jane Winfield. You may call me Mistress Winfield."

He gave her a short mocking bow again and, with a sly grin, belying any intentions of decorum, announced, "Steven Spencer at your service, Mistress Winfield."

Determined to ignore his very existence, at least as much as humanly possible, she turned from his grinning face. Looking about her, and then glancing back at him, her face flamed a purple red when he next spoke.

Suggesting simply, but with much humor, "Mistress Winfield, may I be so bold as to presume you have a need to relieve yourself? If that be the case, you would be wise to take my advice. Go into the woods, do what you must, but return to me immediately, for to do otherwise would certainly be courting disaster. Indeed, the forest is lively with wild animals and snakes . . . not to mention an occasional human animal who, I am confident, would love to have you for a traveling companion." With a further warning, he added, "You fool yourself, Mistress, if you think all men would behave as gentlemanly as I have thus."

She shuddered as a fresh wave of fear washed over her and, after only a moment's hesitation, walked to the thickest bushes she could find. Her face flamed painfully, mortified that he should discuss so blatantly so personal and private a matter.

His words worked like magic on her overactive imagination. And although she had ample privacy, she thought she felt eyes peering out from every bush, and from all directions. So fast was she in her necessary body functions, that her pants were barely rebuttoned, when she was back at his side.

Chapter 4

Some hours later, with the tip of his boot on her hip, she was roughly shaken awake. She didn't realize, for a second, where she was and looked up in surprise to see this stranger standing over her.

While laughing at her apparent confusion, he said, "Do accept my apology for disturbing you, Mistress Winfield, but it is past the time for us to leave."

Haughtily she asked, "Where are you taking me, sir?"

Her answer was the sound of his deep laughter.

Fixing him with a determined fearless look, she stated, "Sir, I have not the least intention of accompanying you unless I know our destination."

Again deep laughter, "I am afraid, Mistress, you have not the option of refusal," and with that he lifted her into the saddle and mounted behind her. His arms, a steely vise, held her in place as he continued, and from the merry tone of his voice, she could tell he was smiling. "Due to the early arrival of an extremely jealous husband, I have a need to vacate myself from this vicinity for a time. Since civilization is at least a day's ride behind us, and being unable at the present time to retrace my steps, there is no help for it, I am forced to keep you with me."

She tried to squirm as far away from him as possible, and heard him chuckling at her futile attempts. Frustrated, she decided she would be uncomfortable enough, so why make it easier for him? Finally, she settled back where she belonged and felt his hard body pressed up against hers. Again, she heard him laugh and his deep voice sounded close to her ear, "Is that not more comfortable, love?" And still chuckling delightedly, he corrected himself, "Excuse me, I mean Mistress Winfield."

She vowed silently, if she could manage to get home, she would never again take such foolish risks. She promised herself she would be a dutiful daughter from that day on.

"Where are you taking me?" she repeated as the horse began to move slowly through the dense forest once again.

"Do not worry yourself unduly, mistress. You will be safe with me."

"Do you delude yourself into believing that was an answer?"

She received only a deep chuckle in return

and sighed with disgust knowing she would get no answer from him, and gave a silent prayer that he was speaking the truth when he said she would be safe with him.

She racked her brain, trying to come up with a plan of escape. Without her horse, there was little she could do. The only thing possible was to wait until he was asleep and, in the middle of the night, steal away. She knew, once alone, she chanced death any number of ways; yet she had to take that chance, and the sooner the better. She realized as the sun began to set, he was taking her west instead of south. If she got too far from home, she feared she would never find her way back. She wondered if even now it might be too late.

After hours of riding, they reached a small stream where he dismounted. This time, offering her no opportunity to escape, he dragged her off her horse. Slowly and purposely he slid her against his body, until her feet touched the ground.

Wide eyed, she stared up to his face, her heart pounding hard in her chest at their close contact, when slowly his lips descended to meet hers. His warm breath caressed her face. The strength of his arms around her was a daring new sensation and, she was hard put to shake off the mesmerizing effect his nearness had on her.

Trembling, she pulled away before he could kiss her. The scent and feel of him was an experience that left her strangely shaken.

"Mr. Spencer, sir," she pleaded in an unsteady voice, "this cannot go on. We must come to some sort of an agreement. It is not at all the proper thing for you to handle me so." Weakly, she continued, ignoring his apparent enjoyment of her shaken state, "Can we not agree upon this? If I give you my word not to escape, would you then promise to treat me with more circumspection?"

His only answer was the same maddening twisted grin.

Refusing to beg, she stalked off to the stream, washing her grimy face and hands as best she could.

A few moments later, the sounds of gunfire startled her. Quickly she turned about and saw Steven coming towards her, holding a dead rabbit in each hand.

She was famished for she had not eaten since dinner the night before.

While Steven skinned and gutted the two rabbits, Angelina gathered wood for a fire. When he finished, he started a fire in a clearing and spit the rabbits through a long branch, placing it over the flames. Slowly, he turned them so they would cook evenly.

It wasn't long before the aroma of cooking meat made Angelina's stomach growl embarrassingly. It seemed an eternity before it was finally ready. She ate with ravenous hunger, burning her fingers and tongue in her haste.

It wasn't until they had finished eating that he finally asked, "Will you tell me why you were riding unescorted, and at night, about the countryside? Who is it you were running from?"

For a long moment, she looked at him while her quick mind thought of a story. Feeling no need to tell him anything that she considered none of his business, she finally began, using just the right amount of reluctance. "I have been an orphan since birth. The only home I have ever known was with the good sisters at St. Joseph's orphanage near Alexandria.

"Since I was fifteen, I have been put out to work as a maid for some of the rich plantation owners." Her voice quivered beautifully as she continued, "One day, a man came to the orphanage, looking for a maid and companion to his ailing wife. 'An older girl, someone of quality,' he insisted. The sisters believed his story and I was sent to work for him. When I arrived, I found to my dismay, all he had said of himself was a lie. Indeed, he had no wife, but lived alone without even one house servant.

"Naturally, I was adamant that I should return to the orphanage immediately, but this was not to be the case. Instead, he locked me in a room and kept me there for three days. I think he had an idea of starving me into submission.

"As it turned out, the night you jumped upon my horse, he had decided to wait no longer. Well after dark, the door to my room opened. The man came in and locked it again. Without a word addressed to me, he began to disrobe. Finally, he came closer. I . . . I was desperate . . . terrified! I grabbed a lamp off the table that stood near me and hit him over the head. I killed him and took his clothes and horse."

She allowed her voice to tremble slightly with obvious fear as she finished, "When you came upon me, I had no idea where I was going. I just had to get away." She lowered her head to hide her smile.

If he harbored any unsavory thoughts as to their possible relationship, she trusted she had given him cause to fear what consequences his actions might bring. She hoped he believed her.

He did not. He grinned at her obvious fabrication and lifted her hands in his, as if consoling her. His eyes confirmed his doubts. No one who had worked as a maid would have hands such as these. His eyes took in the softness of her skin. There was not a mark to be found on them. Even the nails were perfect. These were the hands of a lady who had maids of her own.

Forcing the smile from his lips, he asked, "How do you know you killed him?"

For a moment, she looked bewildered, "He . . . His head was bleeding," and then finishing as if an afterthought, "He was not breathing."

He looked at her clothes. They were obviously those belonging to a young boy; no man could wear anything that small. Deciding it was useless to question her further, he took a flask from his pocket and offered it to her.

"Here, take a drink of this."

She shook her head, but he insisted, explaining she would need the whiskey's warmth against the coming cold night.

When the fiery liquid passed over her burnt tongue and down her throat, she gasped for air. He laughed as he watched her eyes fill with tears and her hand fly to her throat.

She glared at him and stubbornly took a second swallow. Amazingly, it did not burn quite so badly this time and she felt a pleasant warmth spread slowly through her belly, and a calmness close over her.

She laid back and gazed at the twinkling stars glowing above them in the inky black sky. Purposely, she ignored him as Steven leaned on one arm and looked down at her.

He marveled to himself at her outstanding beauty. At first he had been astounded and angry to find she was a woman. Had she been a boy, he could have put her down and let her find her own way back. Certainly, he couldn't abandon a defenseless woman in the midst of a wilderness. Nay, he had been forced to keep her with him.

Now watching her golden face in the flickering light of the campfire, he mused silently, perhaps some good could come of it after all. Surely he could travel faster alone, but she was marvelous to look at, and almost laughing out loud at his thoughts, with any luck, he might find her marvelous at other things.

For a long moment he inspected her

closely. Her skin glowed a deep shade of gold. It was much darker than what was currently fashionable for ladies, and yet, her manner and speech was that of the upper class.

Finally, he moved somewhat closer and grinned slyly, "I promise you, I find the idea as disagreeable as I know you must, but I fear it shall be necessary for you and I to sleep within contact of each other. The nights have been known to become extremely cold, and we shall surely need the warmth of each other for comfort."

Her clear dark blue eyes flew to his face. Genuine fear showed in their depths. Her words, when she spoke, were forceful even though her voice trembled, "Sir, it is true that I would be unable to prevent you from touching me, should you take such a notion, but if in fact you do as you hint, I swear by all I hold sacred, I shall kill you. Were I you, sir, I would believe what I say. You can not stay awake forever and my chance will come." Her mouth turned grim with determination, as she continued, "No man shall have me till I wed and I have no mind to ever do so. The thought that I should become another's possession is, to say the least, disagreeable."

With a shrug aimed in her direction, he turned away, too weary at the moment for arguments, yet quite confident of the eventuality of their relationship. Taking the one blanket that was rolled behind her saddle, he covered himself comfortably and dozed with a delicious thought of promised future satisfaction.

Later that night, she lay beside him listening to the steady rhythm of his deep breathing. She relaxed some knowing he was asleep. The crackle of the campfire, mixed with a chorus of chirping crickets were the only sounds in the black still night. Her heart thudded wildly with anticipation at her imminent actions.

She waited, it was impossible to know how long, but guessed approximately an hour had passed. Silently, she got to her feet. Standing over him for a moment, the idea of taking his gun crossed her mind. No, too risky, she finally decided.

Carefully, silently, she backed away and walked to her horse. It seemed to take forever to reach the animal. She prayed he wouldn't awaken until she was gone. She was shaking with tension when she finally reached Buttercup's side. Being an accomplished equestrian, it mattered little to her that Steven used her saddle for a pillow. Holding the reins, she guided the mare away from camp.

She was barely twenty feet away, when a voice startled her. "Where might you be going, Mistress Winfield?"

She gave a small scream of fright and in a reflex action, guided by sheer terror, she lunged at him. Taking him off guard, she smashed her small body into his, causing him to fall to the ground, but not before he grabbed her and pulled her down with him. Furiously, she swung her fists to his face and body, hammering him over and over with all her strength.

Calmly, he rolled her over and laid his body full length upon her. As he grabbed her hands and held them tightly in one of his above her head, she stared defiantly into his dark angry eyes.

They were too far from the fire for warmth, but close enough for her to see the dangerous expression in his eyes flicker and grow to life. Her chest heaved, partly from fear and partly from exertion. She watched helplessly as his face came closer to hers.

Forcing herself, she managed to laugh, a sound cold with contempt, "Obviously, sir, you are one of those vile creatures who must resort to taking a woman by force."

Her words worked like a dose of cold water. She almost sighed with relief as she watched his desire ebb and die. Still he held her in place for a long time, gazing deep into her eyes as though he were reading her thoughts.

Finally, a slow lazy grin spread across his mouth, exposing large even white teeth. Arrogantly, he drawled, "Mistress Winfield, in truth, the opposite has been my experience. I have yet to meet a woman I must take by force."

Her voice shook with fear as she answered, trying to sound calm and slightly bored, "Well sir, it appears you have now. Would you be so kind as to remove yourself from me and help me up?"

His eyes crinkled at the corners as he

chuckled, "Mistress Winfield, you have given me cause to wonder, are you truly as brave as you would like me to believe?" He let a moment pass before he continued, "I feel it my duty to remind you of our bargain. It appears you have broken it."

She felt a moment of panic as his mouth came purposely down and covered hers. Wildly, she twisted her head, desperate to free herself from this forced embrace. But with the weight of his body and a hand on her chin, he easily held her still. His lips began to caress her mouth. Gently, he teased her into a response. Feathery light, spine tingling kisses titillated her mouth.

She steeled herself against him, against the novel yet warm tautness that began to spread through the pit of her stomach, and against her blood pounding in her fevered brain.

Finally, with a groan of despair, she began to move her mouth in response, abandoning any further attempt at resistance.

His mouth began the slow sensual exploration of the virginal recesses of her own. At first she responded willingly but timidly, not quite sure what was expected of her. After a long breathless time, his kisses grew possessive and demanding, until she answered the pressure of his mouth with a gentle moan of submission and the sweet searching movement of her own tongue.

His hand released her arms and she slid them around his neck pulling him closer, matching his desire with her own newly born passion. She thought of nothing but what his mouth was doing to her; felt nothing but the pressure of his body on hers; and heard nothing but the ragged breathing and the throbbing of their hearts.

His lips left her hungry mouth and she moaned at the sweet torment as his hot moist breath tingled against her skin and seared her golden throat, sending shivers of delight down her back.

Gently, his voice murmured near her ear, "I told you, I have yet to meet a woman I must take by force."

Her eyes soft and bewildered, stared up to the merry twinkle his dark gaze returned. If he had slapped her face, she couldn't have become more clear headed at that moment. She glared at him in fury, while her lips curled over her teeth with hatred and she spat out, "Bastard!"

He laughed at her rage, helping her to her feet. With his arm about her waist, he walked to the horse, and brought the two of them back to camp. "Now I really must insist we sleep together," he teased playfully. Feeling her stiffen at his side, he looked down and giving her a knowing grin, murmured, "Relax, I am not the one you should fear."

When she lay down, she felt herself tense up as he calmly made himself comfortable beside her, with his arm thrown casually over her middle to keep her in place.

Tears of frustration and fury swelled in her eyes, and she fought valiantly to control the rising panic and fear in her heavy chest. Finally exhaustion won out and she slept.

Sometime during the night, she woke up shivering. The fire was almost out. She added more wood. Cold to the bone, she realized he was right. Swallowing her pride, she curled up close to him, covering herself with half the blanket and hoping his body heat might help warm her.

When she awoke the next morning she was mortified to find herself snuggled up to him, his arms about her, while her head rested on his chest and her leg was thrown comfortably over his.

He laughed but said nothing as he watched her nervously jump away from him and raise herself to a sitting position.

Chapter 5

Her body had never known such exhaustion. Weariness slowly engulfed her brain, causing her once alert and intelligent mind to become dreary and dull. Every inch of her was sore. Mounting her horse was torture and when she was able to rest, after a long day's ride, she found herself powerless to dismount her mare. If it were not for Steven's strong arms carrying her a safe distance away, she would have collapsed at the horse's feet.

She had always thought of herself as being particularly strong and capable of enduring much. Now that she was put to the test, she knew she was failing miserably.

Oddly enough, when she thought she could go on no longer, when she had passed the point of dreamless death-like sleep, to awaken still senseless, she slowly and vaguely became conscious of a toughening of both spirit and body. Somehow, at what point she was unaware, her aches began to lessen, her almost druglike mind began to clear, and although she was still totally worn out after each day's ride, her tired body no longer held her mind in a stupor of exhaustion.

On the contrary, her senses were never so alive nor her heart so ladened with guilt. Over and over, she berated her foolishness. She was determined not to give up and swore she would take the chance to escape when it came.

Each day they stopped well before dusk. She would gather wood for a fire, while Steven hunted for the evening's meal. Their diet was sparse but adequate. The meals they ate each night were hungrily devoured and thoroughly enjoyed as though they were a banquet.

Steven was proficient in his ability to live off the land. Many were the times he would gather delicious sweet berries to add to their meals. Later, she was to be sorry she had not noticed from which type of plants they were taken.

The constant pressure of his body pressed close to hers began to cause her some unexplainable nervousness. She wondered at the odd sensations stirring in her each time his hand carelessly brushed against her breast as he sometimes pulled the reins to the left or right. She thought he didn't notice, but there was little that passed him unnoticed.

He hadn't touched her since the night of her attempted escape, but she was in constant fear that he might demand further payment for her broken promise. In truth, because she was always pressed up against him, he was hard put to keep his hands off her and the wish to reach out and touch her was never far from his thoughts.

Close to dusk, on the sixth day of riding, she dozed. Her hat slipped from her head and hung on her back by a string of cowhide tied at her throat. Unknowingly, she snuggled her head comfortably to Steven's chest. Vaguely, she could feel his warm breath caress her cheek and the gentle rhythmic movement of the horse beneath them.

Comfortably encircled in his arms, listening to the muffled sound of his heart, she sank deeper into a heavy sleep. She was dreaming delicious romantic dreams. She was dancing with Andrew on the darkened terrace of her home, while the sounds of heavenly music drifted over them. Andrew was dancing her towards the shadows where he began kissing her.

It was so dark, she couldn't see his face, only feel the warm sweet pressure of his mouth against hers. She wondered how Andrew had learned to kiss like this, for the last time he had kissed her it was not nearly so wonderful. But soon she dismissed it as unimportant. Only the feel of his lips touching her mattered. His face nuzzled against her neck and ear.

Sleepily, she murmured, "More," and was slightly surprised to hear a deep chuckle in response.

With his lips once again on hers, she moaned approvingly as his hand began to move slowly from her waist to fondle softly, gently, her heavy breast. Her buttons came undone. His hand was like fire against her skin. Her nipples rose taut, straining against the palm of his hand. Finally his fingers brushed softly, expertly, against the pink tips, sending wave after wave of delightful sensations through her.

Her mind was dazed to all but the touch and feel of his hands on her. His lips moved against her own, his mouth growing possessive and demanding. She moaned with pleasure as his welcomed tongue slipped between her teeth.

Now fully awake, she knew it was Steven who was kissing her, touching her, but it mattered not at all, for she wanted him so badly her body shook with longing. She was too far along in her need to care that she called out for him to touch her again.

Without effort, she turned bringing her right leg over the horse so she sat side saddle. Her arms circled his neck and pulled him closer. Both her breasts were exposed to his view, and he brought his face to them, while his hands undid her belt and slid down her stomach.

No man had ever touched her like this and she was stunned at the sensations he imposed on her body. Yet she wasn't satisfied, she wanted more, more.

She was whimpering undeniable sounds of fervid desire, when he raised his head and their eyes, veiled with passion, met for just a moment before his mouth crashed possessively over hers again.

She couldn't breathe; dizzily she clung to him. Her head swam, she was wild for his touch. Her mind knew nothing, cared for nothing but more of the feel of his hands on her body, and his lips on her own.

She was oblivious of the consequences, only needing him, wanting more of the new sensations he was inflicting on her. Lost in a dreamy state of breathless desire, she was falling, loosing all her equilibrium.

With a shock, they found themselves sprawled upon the ground. Through horror filled eyes, she realized Buttercup had stumbled into a hole and was snorting and grunting in agony from an obvious broken leg.

She ran the few steps to the injured animal, lovingly petting her silky smooth hide, while comforting in a soothing voice, all the while looking pleadingly at Steven for help.

Steven only shook his head, his mouth grim.

"No Steven, please," she begged, in a choked voice, while tears blinded her. But Angelina knew the inevitable. Stunned, she watched as Steven put the animal out of its misery.

She blamed Buttercup's accident on Steven, and rightly so she convinced herself.

If he hadn't kidnapped her in the first place, her horse wouldn't have gotten hurt. She glared at him, uncontrolled hatred flashing in her eyes. At that moment, she would have gladly killed him given the opportunity.

That night, after Steven dozed peacefully, she lay next to him studying his strong face in the soft light of the campfire. Thinking of Buttercup, her fury mounted, and she decided tonight she would escape. In her anger, she cared nothing for the dangers surrounding her. This time, she waited, regulating her breathing so he thought her asleep. Finally, after what seemed hours, she knew he was deeply asleep.

Her heart thudded loudly with fear as she slipped silently out of his arms. Forcing herself to remain calm, she reached for a rock the size of a large man's fist. With determinaton, she swung the small boulder high above her and brought it crashing down on Steven's head, hearing a soft groan escape his lips as she did so. Oddly, a flashing thought of pity slipped into her mind, but she quickly squelched it by purposely remembering the death of her horse.

Quickly now, her mind approaching panic, she grabbed for the knife he kept tucked in his belt and, in an instant, she was on her feet and running.

She ran as if the devil himself were pursuing. On and on she fled, never lessening her pace until she thought her lungs would surely burst. It was dawn before she finally gave in to her exhausted body and collapsed in a heap at the base of a tree and slept.

When she awoke, it was well into the next day. She was stiff and sore, and a nagging fear of being lost kept creeping into her mind. She tried desperately not to panic. *Think! Think!* Steven had said six days back, they were a week from a settlement, but which way should she go? He never mentioned in what direction the settlement lay.

At last the sun began to disappear over the giant tree tops. Finally, she reasoned, she might as well continue on the same course west. Surely, she must be close. She prayed, *please God let me find help!*

In reality she had little choice but to continue on, for to retrace her steps would mean certain death, for she had no food or water and she knew it was impossible for her to get home on foot.

She had been walking for two days and her belly rumbled constantly from hunger. What a stupid thing to do, she berated herself for the millionth time. Now she realized she should have stayed with Steven. Anything was better than starving to death.

Last night at dusk she had come upon an old cabin. She prayed as she approached she would find help. But her hopes and prayers proved to be of no avail, for the cabin was deserted of people and empty of food.

At least she was able to sleep, if not in a comfortable bed, at least protected from the damp night air and wild animals. The next morning she left the cabin with some degree of reluctance, but leave it she must, for although the cabin offered her some comfort, she would never survive if she didn't find food.

Suddenly, she stepped out of the thick forest and nearly fell into a large fast flowing river. Had it not been for the sounds of the many birds chirping cheerfully overhead and the wind rustling through the thick tree branches, she would have heard it long before she saw it.

At the first sight of the white capped water, she felt happy relief surge through her. She laughed excitedly, knowing any settlement in the area would most certainly be located on the shore of a river, and fervently thanked God, she had found that river.

Her heart pounded with expectation. She was close, so close. Soon she would find help and food.

Laughing giddily through a tight parched throat, she happily knelt down to drink her fill, nearly drowning herself in her attempt to relieve her thirst. Finally, her thirst satisfied, her thoughts turned to how she could find food. She knew there were edible berries and roots in the forest, for she had eaten them many times with Steven, but she dared not take any, for she had no idea which were poisonous and which were not.

Right now, she was hot and dusty, the scent of her own body disgusting her so completely that a moment later her clothes were off and she was in the water. It was sometime later, after scrubbing herself pink with fine sand, before she emerged glowing and sweetly clean.

Feeling somewhat secure with the knife she had taken from Steven strapped to her waist, she sat on a fallen tree waiting for the sun to dry her. She dreaded putting on the same dirty clothes she had worn for more than a week, but there was no help for it.

A smile touched the corners of her mouth as she imagined Steven's fury when he woke up and found her gone. Her disappearance, added to the lump on his head, surely gave him cause to rage.

Her stomach growled and again she cursed her panic and stupidity for taking his knife and leaving him his gun.

With a sigh of disgust, she got to her feet and dressed herself, thinking again her bath did little good if she must once again wear these stiff and dirty clothes.

Turning from the water's edge, she nearly slammed into a tall Indian. He was regarding her with an odd smirk on his lips and laughter in his eyes. She knew instinctively he had been spying on her. In an instant, she was filled with rage. She felt none of the fear or embarrassment she knew she should feel, only a blinding fury. Mindless with rage, her lips curled with hatred that he should spy on her in her private moments.

Apparently, he had expected her to cower in terror and whimper for mercy and, certainly, she would have done just that if she had not been so angry. Instead, to his surprise, she bent low, pulling out her knife and flinging herself at his arrogant face.

The knife flashed in the sunlight and, even though she managed to inflict on him only the barest of injuries, she was satisfied to hear him grunt as the blade slid easily into his forearm, and she drew blood.

A moment later, he had twisted her arm so violently that the knife slipped with a thud to the ground, leaving her hand numb and useless.

Although she fought him with all her strength, he calmly lifted her with one bronzed arm while clamping his free hand over her mouth. With no effort, he placed her struggling body across his horse which stood some ten feet away. When he released her mouth, she screamed, the sound of her voice echoing loudly about them. Her screaming stopped when his hand pressed firmly down on her neck, and she slipped off into unconsciousness.

Slowly she became aware of the ground passing before her eyes. She was still across the horse. His knees were pressed against her ribs as he trotted through the deep forest.

She lay still, waiting for her head to clear and trying to gather the strength and courage she needed to escape. In a sudden motion, she slipped from the horse. She landed on her back with a thud that left her momentarily breathless. In an instant, she was up and running. But her efforts were useless. Strong brown arms circled her and nimbly lifted her off the ground, before she had covered two yards.

"Let me go, let me go, you stupid savage!" she screamed as she struggled to free herself.

Suddenly a deep voice threatened close to her ear, "You will not try to escape again. It is not an accident I have come upon you. I have been tracking you for two days and I will thank you to keep a civil tongue in your head, Janey, or face the consequences."

She stopped struggling and her mouth fell open in astonishment. His arms released her and she turned to gape in amazement at his smiling face.

She couldn't believe her ears. This Indian called her Janey and spoke perfect English. Only Steven would have known her by that name. For a long moment, she studied the dark face before her and as the dawning overcame puzzelment, she finally croaked out, "Steven?" The eyes were the same as always, twinkling with laughter, but the rest of his face was so different without a beard, she couldn't be positive.

Grinning devilishly down at her, he nodded slightly, "At your service, Mistress Winfield."

"Steven, my God! How . . .?" she started, wanting to ask a million questions.

"Not now," he interrupted, while grabbing her arm and sitting her upon the horse once more.

"Where are we going? How is it you are

dressed this way?"

"Later," was all she got for an answer.

His direction had changed, the sun was to their right. Slowly, in no apparent hurry, he trotted the horse south through a maze of forest so thick as to make daylight appear dusk.

They rode for about an hour when to Angelina's surprise, they came to a clearing and directly in front of her stood the buildings of an Indian village.

She stiffened with terror and turned to face Steven in amazement. She had naturally expected him to flee, thinking he had come upon the village by accident. Yet he did nothing but continue to trot his horse on, bringing them closer to certain death.

"What kind of Indians are these?" she asked fearfully.

"Cherokee."

Aghast, she cried, "Steven! My God! Are you insane? These people are animals. Do you not know how they, in the pay of the British, have been killing and mutilating Patriots since the beginning of the revolution? Turn this horse about this instant."

Calmly, he continued to trot his horse, ignoring her terrified and urgent plea.

Her eyes wide with fear, she was amazed how the people just stood about. Why was no one attacking them? Finally, calming some, she looked around.

Obviously, Steven was not a stranger here. Who was he? What was to become of her? He answered none of her questions, always leaving her to form her own conclusions.

In the center of the village stood a large oblong shaped building, made with circular log walls, held together by what appeared to be dried mud and covered by a conical roof.

The building was surrounded by dozens of small round huts, built in a similar design and with the same materials.

The people who watched as Steven's horse approached, seemed to smile in a friendly manner.

Angelina was shocked at the sight of the women who were dressed so scantily as to be nearly naked. They wore soft fabric, obviously made of animal skins, shaped into vests and tied with a string of cowhide at the center, leaving their arms and middle exposed. Almost all wore short above the knee length skirts of the same material. Both articles were heavily trimmed with long fringe.

Their hair was tied neatly in a knot on the nape of their necks, much the same as was the fashion among white women.

The women stood tall, slender and delicate boned, their skin only slightly darker than her own.

Steven stopped his horse at one particular hut and dismounted, dragging Angelina off. Two men came and stood by Steven. They spoke in a strange language, which sounded pleasant, almost musical to her.

She looked up sharply as Steven took her arm and answered in the same tongue. After some discussion, the two men nodded, smiled and finally walked away.

Angelina was amazed as she stood listening to the men speak. The men were just as outstanding as the women with olive skin, nearly the same shade as Steven's and black shining straight hair, plaited at each side of their head. All had high cheek bones and dark piercing eyes, together with a nose that was definitely aquiline in shape.

Most of the men stood close to Steven in height. No matter their savagery, these people were the most stunning creatures she had ever seen!

Steven pulled her along and, bending, he entered the hut. Inside it was dark. Angelina could see the only light came from a small fire burning in the center. The smoke ascended straight up and out the small opening in the roof.

Steven stood with his back to her, taking off his gun. He was so quiet, she began to feel the sensation of fear prickling down her spine, and goose flesh formed on her arms.

"Are you going to tell me what is happening?"

His continued silence made her more nervous. Calmly, he sat ignoring her presence and began cleaning his rifle.

Finally, she spoke again, "What were you talking about with those two men?"

Nonchalantly, his shoulders shrugged in her direction, "They wanted to know who you were. So I told them."

"You told them what?" she asked, feeling

her anger begin to rise and glad of it, for her nervousness was evaporating fast.

"I told them you are my woman," he stated simply.

"What?" She couldn't believe it. Even with all his arrogance and superiority, she couldn't believe he'd go that far. "How dare you? What right do . . .?"

"Actually, it is quite simple, Janey," he interrupted quietly, "I told them you belong to me," and with a knowing grin, continued, "and you will shortly."

"You are out of your mind," she groaned in a voice that was strangely calm, "I am getting out of here."

With that she turned and started toward the opening. Before she took her second step, Steven was upon her. She felt herself lifted and thrown upon a pile of furs that was, she supposed, the bed.

Steven towered menacingly over her, his voice sharp when he spoke, "You will behave yourself, Janey. I have found you and I shall not let you escape me again." Now his voice softened and with a sly grin he continued, "I will wager after tonight, you will have no wish to leave my bed, least of all my company."

She sputtered in haughty rage, "Why you pompous ass. Before that day comes, I will slit my throat. I would die before I would allow you to touch me. My body is my own. Do you think so much of yourself that you believe I would allow you possession of it?"

"For now, you have no choice in the matter.

I have decided, you will be mine. Dissuade yourself of the notion that you will bring harm to yourself. Do you think I would allow anyone to mar what belongs to me?"

"Belongs to you? I belong to no man!" she snarled.

He stood gazing down at her for some time, while she returned his amused look with a defiant and hate-filled one of her own, when a timid knock was heard at the door.

Steven called out, and a young beautiful girl entered with bowls of hot food.

He spoke to the girl. She put down the bowls and glanced up at him with admiration and adoration clearly showing in her velvety black eyes.

When she left, Angelina nodded in the general direction of the departing girl, "There is a willing subject for your bed; why pick on me?"

He laughed aloud, "Perhaps I wish my women to be less willing, Janey sweet," and chuckled as he watched the involuntary shudder spread through her at his words.

He reached down, picking up the two bowls and handed her one.

For a moment, she was tempted to take it and throw it in his face, but she had not eaten since she had escaped him two days ago, and she was starving.

The smell of roasted deer seeping past its cover, made her stomach growl. She snatched the bowl from his hand and began to eat, greedily.

He sat on the floor before her, cross leg Indian style. They ate in silence.

It wasn't until he finished that he spoke again, "Lie down and rest. I will be back later and do not try to escape again. These people do not take kindly to strangers. If one of the braves should find you wandering about—" he hesitated while fear mounted in her eyes. "Well, let me just say, you may not be quite so pretty when he finishes with you."

She sat still until he left. Her heart pounded with terror. After a few moments she stood up and, with great trepidation, walked toward the doorway. Someone stood outside. Apparently, she was being guarded.

She was scared. Frantically, she began to search for a weapon. If these savages meant to kill her, they would not find an easy job of it.

Taking Steven's gun from his holster and his rifle from the wall, she began to pace the floor, not really knowing what she might do. She tried to think, but could formulate no plan. Surely, no one here would help her. Finally, exhausted, she sat on the pile of furs.

Steven smiled when he returned to find her fast asleep with a rifle across her chest and his pistol carelessly dropped to the floor, obviously fallen from her relaxed hand.

Gently, he removed the weapons.

Chapter 6

She slept soundly, and he had to shake her more than once before she finally awoke.

He pulled her unresisting body to its feet.

She was soft and pliant in his arms. The scent of her, warm and sweet, nearly made him forget his plans of waiting until tonight. His arms tightened for a moment. Still she did not resist. Her head rested sleepily against his chest. A moment later, his face was buried in her neck, his hands pulling her hair, bending her head back.

Realizing his intent, she was suddenly and sharply awake. Pushing herself away from him, she shot him a silent look of intense hatred.

"Come with me," he growled. Grabbing her hand and picking up a bundle that was lying on the floor, he yanked her out of the hut, pulling her along after him.

They walked out of the village and stopped

at the fast flowing river that wormed itself past.

He let go of her hand.

She shot him a puzzled look, wondering what he would do next.

Aware of her confusion, he stated simply, "The river is used for many things. Each morning the women come here to wash their clothes. Many of the men come to fish. But most of all it is considered to have healing powers. When someone is sick, the medicine man brings the person here to cleanse them of evil spirits. For now we will simply use the water to cleanse the body, we shall worry about the spirit later."

Her eyes gazed up at his laughing face, incredulously she gasped, "Sir, it is not possible that you believe I would bathe here, before your eyes?"

"That is exactly what I believe," he answered cooly.

"You are not serious," she laughed.

"I am very serious, Janey. Take your clothes off."

"Never!" she nearly shouted. With that she turned to run, but was halted after only a few steps.

"You shall learn that a dutiful wife is subservient to her husband, and you will obey me in all things." As he spoke, he reached for the buttons of her shirt.

"What wife; what in God's name are you talking about? Stop it, damn it. I said stop!" Hysterically she fought, her small fists contacting more than once against his dark face. But in the end, she stood panting and naked before him.

Her ankle twisted on a rock and sent her to the ground. He dared not help her up. He dared not touch her. His sudden and almost overwhelming desire twisted his stomach into a giant painful knot. His hands clenched tightly into fists. In a moment, he'd lose control. His blood pounded deafeningly in his ears, his breathing grew harsh and shallow. He couldn't tear his eyes from her. She was easily the most beautiful woman he had ever seen. Slim and small, her waist measured no larger than the span of his two hands, yet her breasts were large and heavy, her hips rounded and womanly-soft above long silken legs.

His voice cold, hid a multitude of emotions, as he watched her trembling and crying with frustration at his feet. "Go into the water, Janey. I shall not hurt you."

She got to her feet and stood calmly before him. In a flash she had turned and dove smoothly into the gentle flowing river. He marveled at the regality of her stance. Even nakedness did not take away from her natural confidence.

Sitting on a fallen tree, he watched her graceful movements as she swam about. Nearing the opposite shore, she stopped and glanced back at him. He folded his arms lazily across his chest, confident she would make no attempt to reach the shore and escape naked into the bordering forest.

He was right. Although the idea did cross her mind, she quickly dismissed it. If she managed to escape him, and surely she could with the distance that now separated them, what would she do then? She'd die of exposure if she wandered through the forest naked. The two nights she had spent alone in the woods assured her it was cold enough with clothes. Without them, her chances would be less than none.

It was peaceful and private here. Some distance and much foliage protected her from the view of the village, and she swam for a long time before her limbs tired and she reluctantly left the water.

When she came to stand defiantly before him, he merely pushed the package he had brought with him into her hands. He dared not trust the sound of his voice as his eyes raked her body in its taunting stance and his breathing increased to almost a gasping degree.

Never before had she stood naked before a man and yet, strangely enough, she felt no trace of shame. Only anger and hate filled her mind and she thought there had to be a way to bring about retaliation to this man who had humiliated her so. Revenge was her only hope, her only thought, her only desire.

She gasped with pleasure as she opened the parcel and spied the white material within. Touching it, she realized it was as soft as silk, and the workmanship was astonishingly beautiful. Sewn into the front and back of the vest were hundreds of small turquoise stones. The stones formed designs of circles within circles. Both the skirt and vest were trimmed in long white fringe.

She dressed in the scanty clothes he had given her, her face flushing hotly at his bold look as his eyes focused on her nearly exposed breasts. The vest was too small and barely covered them.

She pulled at the tie, straining the strings to close the vest. But the material would stretch just so far and no more, which left her with a gaping space and almost nothing to the imagination.

Arms and legs naked, embarrassment suddenly replaced anger. Only at night, in the privacy of her bed chamber, did she dress so scantily. How often had Lizzy, her nanny since childhood, shaken her head in disapproval, saying a lady never dressed in that fashion no matter that no one saw her. She almost laughed, imagining Lizzy's puritanical reaction if she could see her now.

Silently, Steven took her hand and led her back to camp. No one gave her a second look, and she knew her clothes were much like the other women's.

He pushed her to the ground, forcing her to sit Indian style near a campfire. Soon she became aware of a large circle of people forming around her. Steven came to sit facing her.

Since first approaching the camp this morning, she had been nagged by suspicions that Steven was a Tory. How else could they be allowed here. Only a known Tory would be welcomed among them. Eyeing him carefully, she asked, "Steven, how is it we are allowed here? These people are ferocious and kill whites on sight. The Cherokee are the Patriots' most feared and hated enemy."

"Fear not my love, for a great grandmother of mine came from this village. I am always accepted here and therefore so are you." He looked at her, watching her reaction to his explanation.

Finally, she nodded slightly, her fear and suspicions laid to rest as she reasoned silently, perhaps he was not a Tory after all.

All around her there was much laughing and talking. The entire village took on a party atmosphere. Many whole deer were roasting nearby.

A few of the younger men were off to one side playing some kind of running game while tossing a ball. Small children ran about, laughing and shouting at the many dogs that freely roamed the village.

Holding two earthen mugs in her hand, the same beautiful girl that had brought them food came up to Angelina and Steven. Steven took both mugs from her. Angelina peered into the young girl's face and found her timid but spiteful stare almost ludicrous. She knew the girl wished herself in her place and Angelina fervently wished the same.

Angelina's thoughts were clearly written on her face. Steven watched with a sly smile as she opened her mouth to voice her conclusions. Before she had a chance to vent them, he crushed her hopes with a decisive, "No!"

Undaunted, she began, "Please, Steven, the girl is so willing."

"If it was my wish to have Agigue, you would have nothing to say of the matter. As it is, at least for now, it is you I want."

Fearlessly, she faced him, "Perhaps you think you can force me into doing your bidding and maybe you are partly right. But whatever might happen, remember, it was only so because I was forced. You may want me, as you say at least for now, but I will never be yours. I, alone, shall choose the man I want, and no one will do it for me."

With a sigh, he spoke, "It is the custom among these people for the man to choose his wife, and to take more than one if this is pleasing to both parties."

Angelina blurted out, "Well, it is not pleasing to me. You can take all the wives you want, as long as I am not among them."

His eyebrows lifted in an arrogant gaze, and with a wicked grin, said, "After tonight, I am willing to wager you will change your mind."

Her face reddened, realizing his intent, and she answered haughtily to his merry laughter, "I have not the slightest doubt, Mr. Spencer, that I shall always think the way I do now."

She had no idea what he was planning, and there was nothing she could do about it anyway. He talked of wives and of wanting her, but she would never consent to being this man's wife. She really disliked him, actually most of the time she hated him. If she weren't so frightened of these people, she would have gotten up and run long ago. But her fears held her in place.

Suddenly, the ever present drums became louder. The young men stopped playing their games. The children stood still, even the dogs stopped running about.

Angelina looked at Steven with a puzzled expression. "What is happening?"

He only raised his hand, motioning her to silence.

The drums were louder than ever, pulsating through her entire body, pounding like her heart with fear of the unknown.

"Steven," she again ventured to ask, "what is it?"

Once again, his only answer was his raised hand.

At last the drums stopped. Angelina nearly sighed aloud with relief. Everyone and everything was silent. From the corner of her eye, Angelina spied movement, and she turned to see its source.

Her mouth fell open at the sight of a huge Indian, at least seven-feet tall, wearing a robe of eagle feathers that started at his shoulders and ended at his feet. The feathers were dyed in every color of the rainbow. His face was tinted a ghoulish green as were his hands and feet. Upon his head were the antlers of a deer.

Red stripes ran horizontally across his face.

Angelina was completely speechless; she never dreamed anything as horrible as this existed.

He was staring at her. His black piercing eyes sent chills of fear down her spine and seemed to bore into her soul. Long mintues passed before he spoke while motioning to Steven to come to him.

She felt herself engulfed in a hypnotic stupor and offered no resistance as Steven took her arm, raised her to her feet, and led her to this horrible giant.

Together, in silence, they stood before him. At last he began to speak in the same musical tone she had heard before, stopping now and then for Steven to speak in return.

Finally, the talking over, he began to chant, yelling words at them as he shuffled around them. Sometimes he stopped and shook a rattle or sticks in their faces and again he danced about.

The drums were louder than ever. The giant had to scream to be heard over them. Suddenly, he stopped and raised his arms above his head, then lowered them quickly to his side. Abruptly, the drums ceased. There was total silence. A few seconds passed and he turned and walked quickly away.

Suddenly the whole camp came to their feet and in unison, they became as wild and excited as children at play.

Smiling women grabbed at her, spinning her about, laughing like youngsters as she was tossed here and there. At first she was terrified but soon from all the laughter and gentle pushing, it became apparent that they were playing some sort of game.

She tried to find Steven, but he was lost in a crowd of men, obviously giving him much the same though slightly rougher treatment.

The women spun her about and as she stumbled and reeled dizzily from one to another, each pushed her along until she stood directly in front of a grinning Steven.

His eyes twinkled with merriment as he asked, "Was that not a most unusual wedding?"

Slowly it dawned on her and her voice croaked, "This is ridiculous!"

Gently, almost lovingly, he answered, "I am afraid not, love. You told me once, no man shall have you till you wed and for now this is the best I can do." He laughed at her look of disgust.

"Steven, this is nonsense. Stop this right now."

Slowly with all eyes still on them, he drew her close and engulfed her stunned rigid form within the circle of his arms.

This seemed to set off another roar of laughter and merriment. Angelina was roughly pulled from him and settled once again on the ground, with Steven before her.

A general party atmosphere prevailed and games were played, while drums began again.

Now she wasn't so scared as mad. Did he

think her such a fool? If he thought a few words spoken in a foreign tongue were enough to scare her into accepting him, he was sadly mistaken.

She sneered into his grinning face and refused the food he offered.

Someone thrust a cup of liquid into her hand, and with her eyes on his, she took a giant swallow. Her eyes grew enormous and glistened with tears as she gasped for air.

He was laughing at her.

Hatefully, she raised her cup in a mock salute and obstinately drank it all. She nearly died from the burning as it traveled down her throat and into her stomach.

She shot him a look, daring him to taunt her again. Truly, she thought she would attack him if he did.

Wisely, he turned away from her and spoke to a man sitting near him.

Thereafter, jug upon jug of the vile tasting brew was passed around and her cup was refilled many times. Oddly enough, as she sipped the drink, the taste began to improve, and she felt herself growing warmer and more relaxed, until the hatred she felt for Steven slowly began to dissipate.

Not having eaten since earlier that day, the liquor affected her almost immediately. After only two cups, she was nearly drunk, but never having attained that state before, she didn't know it.

Strangely, Steven didn't seem so bad after all and she was at least able to laugh at the ridiculous ceremony he had involved her in.

The light of the campfire flickered over his handsome face; truly to her mind, he was becoming more handsome by the minute.

The sun slid down behind the trees, causing the horizon to glow a warm pink. The knot of anger and fear had long since left Angelina's stomach, replaced by the unrealistic delusion that she was in command of the present situation.

So as the sky turned a velvety black, Steven led her to his hut, and Angelina only laughed and offered no resistance as his arm circled her waist.

Chapter 7

Completely forgotten for the moment was her hatred and fear of him. She giggled happily as she stood before him in the dark hut. The soft glow from the red embers of a dying fire cast the two of them in gentle flattering light.

Her words slurred together when she tried to speak, and giving up, she giggled again.

Steven realized she was feeling the full effects of the strong liquor and was thoroughly enjoying himself as he watched her try to keep her balance by constantly stepping backwards.

"Oh Steven, I feel so good," she laughed. "I cannot remember feeling this good before. Whatever it was that I was drinking, certainly makes one feel fabulous," and then frowning slightly, "that is, once you get past the first sip."

And then she sighed as she reeled against

him. Quite naturally, her hand slid up his arm to his broad shoulders and then behind his neck where her fingers began to play with his thick black hair.

He laughed at her antics, as he watched her suddenly swing herself away from him and stagger about the tiny hut while humming happily.

She stopped, suddenly dizzy, and exclaimed with a good deal of honest surprise, "Good Lord, it is hot in here! Can you not open a window?"

He laughed again and with a swing of his arm indicated there were none.

A moment later, a mischievous gleam entered her eyes and a sly grin spread across her mouth as she calmly and suggestively began to untie her vest. "Perhaps a swim to cool off?" she asked sweetly.

"Later," he answered, while he watched mesmerized by the movement of her hands.

Noticing the change of expression in his eyes, she asked with apparent innocence, "It will not cause you distress if I take off these hot things, will it, Steven?"

"It will probably do many things to me, love, but I can safely testify, distress will not be among them," he groaned.

It took her some time and yet all she succeeded in accomplishing was to make the tie which held her vest together tangle into a giant knot. Looking up, she said, "I . . . I cannot seem to . . ."

"Perhaps I can give some assistance," and

in one swift movement, his hands yanked the knot and strings from the garment. A moment later, with his help, she was standing spectacularly naked, golden and luscious before him.

"There, is that not better?" she asked sweetly.

A low "Mmmm," was her only answer, as his eyes took in her beautiful form.

"Is that all you can say?" she pouted.

Suddenly gathering her up in his arms, and just before placing her on the bed of soft furs, he murmured into her neck, "Love, I think there has been enough talk for one night."

The next day was warm, sunny and beautifully clear, but Angelina was never to know it. When she awoke, the hut was still bathed in shadows. From the center of the roof was a small opening which allowed only a dim light to enter.

In Angelina's state, that shallow light brought knife-like pain to her throbbing head. Surely someone was hitting her head with a hammer, for never before had she felt such agony.

Finally she managed to turn her head to see who it was that was attacking her so violently. While moaning aloud in torment, she found to her surprise that she was alone.

Just then, Steven walked in with a bowl in his hand. His voice bellowed in her ears. "Good morning, love, slept well did you?"

"Oh God," was her mournful reply. She

hadn't the strength to tell him to stop screaming.

"Take a sip of this and all will be well," he insisted, thrusting the bowl towards her.

The pain in her head was so intense that she didn't notice the furs falling from around her when she sat up. She was, from the waist up, naked and exposed to his admiring eyes.

His hand reached out and nonchalantly began to fondle her breast as he sat by her side, waiting for her to finish.

The bowl empty, she leaned back with a moan, his hand still on her. Slowly and amazingly her mind cleared. The pain diminished to a bearable degree and she noticed, for the first time, what he was doing.

Fixing him with a steely and hate filled stare, she asked calmly, "What do you think you are doing, sir?"

"Nothing," he replied good-naturedly.

"Then do nothing to someone else somewhere else, if you do not mind," she answered disdainfully, while knocking his hand away and pulling the furs up around her neck.

With a sigh, he said, "I see, madam, that your good humor has gone along with the glorious past evening."

She stared at him, confused, her mind racing back to last night. What had happened? What had she done? Why was she lying naked in his bed? Why did her body ache as if she had been riding her horse too long?

"Perhaps you should drink every night. Certainly," he continued slyly, "you are more cooperative with a little fire water in your veins."

She looked at him, her eyes narrowed, trying to understand what he was saying. Slowly her puzzlement vanished, as scene after scene of the preceding evening flashed before her eyes. She sat up abruptly, grabbing her head and moaning with the sudden movement. "You swine, you bloody bastard!" She swung at him. "How could you have done this to me?"

Quickly, he moved out of reach, and standing above her, he chuckled, "According to my recollection, madam, it was you who did it to me; and very satisfactorily, too, I might add. Six times in fact. God, you were insatiable!"

Tears of frustration slid down her cheeks as she wailed, "Oh I hate you. I will kill you for this."

Laughing at her, he left her alone to recuperate from her misery and mortification.

In her isolation, pictures of what happened the previous night kept flashing through her mind and she groaned with the shameful wantonness of her actions. And every so often, she was heard to mutter, "No, oh God, no!"

Lord, there wasn't a name bad enough she could call him! He had done it on purpose, of course. There must have been more to the drink than she had thought for it to have affected her so.

Granted, his kisses were stimulating, probably more than just stimulating if she was completely honest, but did she have to lose all control? Did she have to beg for more before their lips parted? How could she have permitted his kisses on every part of her body? Worse yet, how could she have reciprocated in full?

She remembered clearly now. God, whatever possessed her to behave in that horrible whorish manner?

When he had placed her on the cushiony pile of furs, his face was close, his mouth so temptingly close. She had stared up at him, wanting him to kiss her, to hold her close to him, more than she had ever wanted anything in her life.

"Steven," she had whispered, "show me, hurry, show me."

He had chuckled softly, "Patience, my love, soon you will know all. For now enjoy what I can do for you. Stop thinking and let your body do nothing but feel while I show you pleasure you have never dreamed of."

The pressure of his mouth against her own parted her lips beneath his and his tongue gently began the slow sensual exploration of her mouth.

Kneeling beside her, his hands had moved unhindered from her face and neck to her slim shoulders and large heavy breasts, causing her to moan with pleasure.

Smiling above her, he had whispered, "Love, 'tis only the very beginning."

And his hands and lips had worked upon her body, touching and loving where no one had ever touched her before. She had raised not one objection, but had closed her eyes and sighed with the pure and overwhelming joy of it all. He had been so gentle that more than once she had to look wondering if it was his hands or his mouth on her.

She had prayed for it to never end while a tautness began to grow across her belly and she strained her body, arching her back when his hands came to rest against her naked flesh.

Trembling now, moaning broken meaningless words of passion, she had called out his name again and again, until his mouth silenced hers. Her arms slid around his neck, pulling him closer.

Then he was on her. Naked flesh scorched naked flesh, breaths mingled and hushed words of love were spoken until finally, her body pliant and willing accepted him.

It had taken superhuman restraint on Steven's part to coax and tease her into the state she was in now. Never before had he been so gentle and now, above all, he wanted to take her, take her wildly and with screaming passion.

He watched in amazement as the gentleness to which she had responded and then returned, disappeared. She had moved to meet his thrusts. She had pulled his face to hers, biting at his lips, wildly sucking his mouth.

Suddenly, in a frenzy, nearly out of control, their bodies had moved together until at last he held her twisting head still and whispered,

"Open your eyes, love; look at me now," and at last in the softly lit hut, the two lovers had forgotten the world's existence, as they gazed into each other's passion-dazed eyes.

For one split second of time, all the world stood still and silent while their bodies had throbbed of their own accord, as if the two people to whom they belonged had no possession of them.

Happily, she had a tender masterful teacher and he a most daring and willing pupil. And he was right, for it was only the beginning.

Now in the darkened hut, she remembered. Once he had (her face flamed again with memory) laughingly begged, "No more, love, I cannot. I am in a state of weakness I cannot remember ever before attaining."

And her answer, as her hand came to boldly stroke him, had been, "Surely, sir, you jest, for I feel great powers stirring here," and laughing happily at his groan of acceptance, her mouth joined her hand.

And then later again the two of them laughed and rolled about until she was sitting on him, leaning down seductively allowing her breasts to brush against his face.

His lips sucking; his tongue always moving . . .

Oh God, she thought shamefully, *I cannot bear it! I shall never again be able to face him.* And then another flash of hatred and she moaned, "I shall kill him."

Chapter 8

It was nearly dark before Steven returned. She heard him enter and move about. Lying still, she refused to turn from the wall.

Finally he spoke, and she could tell without looking, from the merriment in his voice, that he was smiling. "I know you are awake, love. Are you not hungry?"

"Leave me!" she growled.

"Come, come Janey, no tantrums now," he chuckled. "Perhaps you would care to bathe before we eat?"

Calmly she spoke, her voice cold with hatred, "Get out of my sight, you snake in the grass. You should be flogged for what you have done. I hate you!"

"That is not what you said last night," he taunted.

With a scream of fury, she was standing on her feet, unmindful of her nakedness, charging at him.

Laughing, he grabbed her flaying arms and held them to her side, while pushing her back until they both fell upon the pile of furs.

He kissed her then, a slow deliberate kiss, lasting well past the time that her anger disappeared.

A long moment passed after his lips left hers and they lay silently facing each other until finally his eyes began straying to her naked body.

She was filled with hatred and then as she watched his eyes begin to glow with a fire all their own, she felt panic. She tried to pull away.

Licking her lips nervously, her voice broke when she tried to speak, "Steven please, we have got to talk."

He smiled gently, "Love, what could be so important that we should use this moment for talking?"

"You must know, I do not want this," she stated bluntly. "Whatever may have happened last night," (her face red again with remembrance) "you know it was because of that awful brew I was drinking. That was not me. Please, Steven, can you not understand what I am saying?"

He breathed a patient sigh and commented while idly playing with her hair that fell across her breast, watching as it curled around his finger. "Love, it matters little what you want at this point, what is done is done. You have willingly lain with me and that cannot be altered."

As he spoke, his fingers began to brush teasingly against her nipples. She felt them harden and was shocked to feel her body respond to him.

"No!" she gasped, while slapping his hand away.

"Madam," he answered sternly, "whether you want it or not, one fact remains, you are my wife."

"I am not!" she answered vehemently.

"You are!" he insisted and began stroking her.

She tried to pull away again, "Steven, please, have you no honor? Must you take me by force?"

"Madam," he answered menacingly, "how does honor enter into this? I am a man who wishes to enjoy his wife. And from past experience I know her to be more than just a willing partner."

"I told you, I am not your wife. Damn it, be sensible! A medicine man or chief, or whatever he was, spoke some ridiculous sounding jibberish I did not understand, and suddenly, I am your wife? What nonsense!"

Sternly he answered, "It is useless to keep up this conversation. You are my wife and you will act it. When it is possible, we shall stand before a priest."

"Steven, please," she begged, as his arms closed around her, pulling her closer to him.

"Madam, I will thank you to give me no further problems in regard to our marital status."

She was in his arms, pressed close up against him, and now his mouth was on hers, working its special magic that caused her mind to slip out of focus and the room to spin about her.

His mouth strayed to her neck, kissing and nuzzling against that pulsating hollow at its base. She closed her eyes tightly, fearfully awaiting the inevitable.

With all her will power, she forced her mind to focus again, and demanded her brain to remain cool and indifferent to the onslaught of his lovemaking, her body remaining stiff and unyielding in his arms.

He laughed confidently, as he pulled his face away, "You are going to give in, you know."

"I am not!"

His eyes bore down into hers and, determinedly, he continued while his fingers gently traced her lips, "Not only are you going to give in to me, but you are going to beg me not to stop, just like last night."

Her eyes flashed up at his as she hissed, "Never! I was drunk last night. I swear that will never happen again. I will see you dead first."

Slowly, he began to undress, "You make promises and swear quite readily, my love. Are you certain you will be able to keep your word?"

"I will kill you for this, I promise you."

Even to her, her words sounded hollow and meaningless as she stared at him, drawn against her will to the sight of his muscular bronzed body as if in a mesmerized state, watching as he carelessly discarded his clothes. A moment later, he was standing naked before her.

Her eyes widened with fascination as she boldly stared, for this was the first time in a clear sober state of mind, she had seen a man naked. Her senses were lulled into a lethargy as she calmly regarded his body. Her eyes slid up and down his massive form.

She heard a soft laugh come from deep within his chest as he watched her eyes travel over him.

At last, he moved toward her. Suddenly she seemed to come to her senses again and realized fully what was happening. She began to fight.

Hysterically she struggled, sobbing with fear, knowing he was right and she wouldn't be able to hold out against him.

Easily he held her still with her hands over her head, while she begged for him to stop. Her begging turned into cursing, wildly she used every name she had ever heard the men who worked for her father use.

He grinned, surprised by her choice of words, and shook his head reproachfully, "Now where did you ever hear language like that?"

Cold as ice, her eyes regarded him as he loomed above her, "What the hell do you care?" she spat out hatefully, as tears of frustration began to roll from her eyes and then added, "Get off, I swear I will kill you. You dirty bas . . ."

His mouth stopped her words. She tried to twist her face to free her mouth from his, but her own arms held tightly above her head held her firmly in place.

When did she stop fighting him and begin fighting herself? She tried desperately to force her body to remain indifferent to him, but unbelievably, her traitorous body began to respond.

She felt herself falling, sliding to unreality, her head spinning while his lips refused to stop.

"Please," she murmured breathlessly as his mouth finally left hers and nuzzled against her neck, sending shock waves down her spine.

He released her hands and instead of hitting at him, she slid them over his back feeling the hardness of his muscles beneath them, even as she continued to plead, but her voice sounded as if she was murmuring words of love to both their ears, until his mouth once again took possession of hers.

Under Steven's expert hands, she was beyond the point of caring. She groaned for him to stop, but didn't mean it. She wanted him to go on, and when his mouth demanded her complete submission, she responded, abandoning any further impulses of restraint.

A low moan escaped her lips when his mouth came to rest on a pink tipped breast.

She lay naked and beautiful beneath his

greedy eyes. For a moment, his passion grew to such an urgency, he nearly took her without further love play.

She felt as if in a dream.

He whispered, "Love, love, your beauty staggers the mind." Using both hands, he explored her. His fingers sild from her neck to her toes as if she were a piece of sculpture.

She moaned with pleasure, her spirits thrilled at the sensations exploding in her. A tightness formed in her belly. Wildly she clung to him, whispering his name amid broken sobs of passion, while he in turn whispered words of love neither heard.

He touched his mouth to every part of her until her yearning for him turned from wild pleasure to pain.

Suddenly, he pulled his face from hers and looked down into her smokey blue eyes and flushed face.

"Tell me, love," he whispered in gasps, "tell me not to stop."

She didn't answer, still unable to admit her need of him, but pulled his mouth to hers, kissing him until he almost lost all control.

Again he pulled away, "Tell me," he groaned.

Again, she tried to pull him back to her, but this time he resisted, smiling, "No, love, I want to hear you say it. Do you want me to stop?"

He was leaving her without a shred of pride or dignity. And she no longer cared. All he said was true. She wanted him, and didn't care that he was forcing her to admit it. Now, without a moment's hesitation, she cried out, "No Steven, for God's sake do not stop now."

With a victorious smile, he entered her, his mouth holding hers as she groaned out her ecstasy.

Sensations so fantastic as to seem unreal engulfed her. She imagined she was drifting and separated from her body. His movements nearly caused her to scream with delight and only his mouth prevented her cries of pleasure from being heard beyond his own ears.

She pulled him closer, tightly she clung to him, incoherently sobbing disjointed words until at last a shudder that seemed to push the two of them wildly out of control, flashed through them.

She was flung out into the universe, she thought she heard explosions all about her, she was dying . . . dying.

It took some time before her mind cleared and her senses returned to normal. When at last she could breathe with some ease, and dared to look up to his grinning face, she whispered between clenched teeth, "Bastard!"

He chuckled, "I think I shall have to do something about your choice of language, love."

He rolled off, standing casually naked before her and asked jovially, "Are you ready to eat now?"

Her eyes avoided his naked body. Her face still soft and flushed from their moments of passion, darkened at his flagrant immodesty while she quickly pulled the furs over her. Forcing her eyes to look only upon his face, she glared, "Must you stand there like that?"

He chuckled, "Sweet love, do I shock your girlish modesty? You did not seem to mind a few moments ago."

She shot him a look of pure venom, "I hate you, you insufferable swine." He began to laugh again, while her fists pounded the furs around her, "And stop calling me love."

Chapter 9

Two weeks had passed since the day they had entered the Indian village. For Angelina it had been two weeks of intense combat, not only against Steven's unwanted lovemaking, but against herself as well.

Steven's need of her had not diminished in the least. Each night he took her with the same masterful and tender skill, until once again, her senses thrilled beyond all reason. Without mercy, he not only demanded her complete submission, but teased her into responding until she was wild for his touch, begging for more, tortured with unfulfilled desire.

Never did she step willingly into his arms, but it was to her extreme disgust that all thoughts of resistance soon disappeared during the onslaught of his passionate kisses. Each time she swore she would not yield, yet there seemed to be nothing she could do. Her traitorous body, with a will of its own, responded again. She begged and pleaded, fought and screamed out her loathing, but all to no avail.

She thought of going to Chief Attacullaculla and asking him for help. Perhaps, if she explained how she was here against her will, he might do something. But this was impossible. Even if she could find someone to interpret for her, she knew he would never understand her dilemma. This was a totally different world than the one from which she came, and the chief might even be angered if he heard her complain. After all, to his eyes, she was only a squaw and she mistakenly believed, to the Cherokee mind, women were of no importance.

Steven had purposely given her this impression, in order to keep her calm and docile. In actuality, the opposite was true. Women were very powerful figures indeed. Often they sat on the council to right a wrong, and it was the older women who picked the future mates of the young girls. Menstrating women were thought to have special power and were looked upon in awe and fear. On the whole, women were respected and held in the highest regard.

She was bored. There was literally nothing to do. How much longer was he going to keep her here? Steven too acted restless, as if he wished to be gone from here, yet for some unexplained reason they continued to stay. No matter how she nagged, she could not get him to give her any information. Actually, if she became too insistent for some answers, he usually dragged her to the bed and silenced her questions with his mouth.

She stepped out of the hut and looked around. If she had been an Indian woman, she'd be working the fields right now. At this moment, she preferred even that to this constant inactivity.

Wandering idly about the camp, she noticed Steven talking with a white man near the corral. It wasn't a common sight to see white men at the camp and she was curious to see who he was. She walked quickly in their direction, but the man mounted his horse and rode off before she reached them.

"Who was that?" she asked the moment she stopped before him.

"An acquaintance," Steven remarked casually as he guided her back to his hut. When they entered the dimly lit building, he continued, "What would you say if I suggested our stay here should be terminated?"

She laughed happily, "Really, Steven? Are we truly going home? I am most anxious to see . . ." she stopped suddenly.

He smiled as he grabbed her around her waist and pulled her against him, "So you finally admit you have a home, and who is it you are anxious to see?"

"Oh, no one in particular," she lied as she smiled up at his merry face, "just civilization in general."

He chuckled at her obvious lies, and pulled

her resisting form towards the bed of furs, while teasing, "Were I a gambling man, I would wager I know certain ways to get you to admit the truth."

Falling on the furs, she landed on top of him. She struggled against him, but his steely arms held her in place.

"Steven, stop."

"Why," he grinned, "have you something better to do?"

His hand was behind her head, forcing her mouth down to meet his.

"Aye, I have much to do."

And now his warm mouth teased hers to respond. Slowly masterfully, he continued the sweet torture. Pulling her higher above him, his fingers released her breasts from the vest she wore. Slowly his tongue moved over her silken flesh, breathing her own special sweet scent, savoring the taste of her skin while she moaned with the exquisite pleasure he was capable of inflicting on her.

As he continued his pleasurable task, he whispered into the hollow between her breasts, "What is it you have to do?"

And then chuckled softly as she groaned out, "Nothing, nothing at all."

The next morning, Angelina realized upon awakening, there was a sharp sense of excitement in the air. During their morning meal, she asked, "What is it, Steven? Why is everyone bustling about?"

Steven explained, "Tomorrow is the annual game of Istaboli between the Cherokee and

Choctow. And there is much to do, for hundreds of people will be here before the day is done."

Soon Choctaw Indians began arriving. While the visiting tribe was being welcomed and the giant quantities of furs and skins each brought for gambling was inspected, a large group of young Cherokee men were leveling a field which ran more than two-hundred feet in length. Goalposts at least twenty-feet high, made of branches, were erected at each end.

The day continued with much partying until dusk. Finally, that evening, two columns of women formed, separated by squatting praying medicine men. Slowly they began to move, shuffling and chanting while stick wielding players danced around the goalposts.

The women prayed for aid from the Great Spirit in deciding the game to their advantage and they repeated their dancing at least a dozen times.

The next morning at least one hundred men from each tribe, including Steven who had been invited to join the game, stood on opposite ends of the field. Each man held in their hands two sticks, each about three-feet long with a pocket of webbed skin on one end. The two groups of men formed their own large circles. The camp was quiet. Softly at first came the chanting sound of "hump-he" from the men until, slowly growing with intensity and volume, the silent forest finally rang out with the sound of men shouting the chant.

Angelina felt the rhythmic sound invade her spirit. Almost hypnotically, the men brought the onlookers to a feverish pitch of excitement, until the chanting was washed out amid the shouts and screaming of the spectators.

From the side lines, Angelina could only catch an occasional glimpse of Steven as he blended in among the Indians. Finally, an old man threw a skin-covered ball into play and the game began.

When a man scooped up the ball and held it in the end of his stick, there seemed no rules as to what his opponents were allowed to do. Sticks were swung wildly and it mattered not at all if they bashed in a player's head. A few men fell and their suffering was ignored as they were trampled underfoot.

As each man fell, Angelina's heart nearly stopped with dread. She was terrified! What would become of her should Steven die? Would she be allowed to leave here, or would another Indian claim her? *Oh please God,* she prayed silently, *don't let him die.* At least she knew what her circumstances were with Steven.

She wondered if some of the men were dead for they lay so still and, for the time being, were left unattended on the field. She had never seen anything so vicious and shivered with the savagery of it all. As she watched, some of the men staggered off the field, faces bloody with deep gashes. If they put this much blood thirsty rivalry into a game, she could imagine the ferocity of their battles. Hours passed as the bloody struggle continued and in truth, it did seem more a battle than a game.

In their attempt to get the ball, hundreds of men ran about, leaping over one another while they attacked each other in a most unsportsmanlike way. Sometimes she heard the taunting sounds of a gobbling turkey as they insulted each other.

With a sigh of relief, Angelina spied Steven walking slowly and somewhat stiffly from the dusty crowded field. As he came towards her, she looked up puzzled at his sheepish expression.

He grinned weakly, "Janey, please accompany me to our hut."

Still puzzled, she was about to ask why when she noticed his whitening complexion beneath his tan and the sudden shaking of his legs. When she came to her feet, he leaned heavily against her and her legs trembled beneath his weight.

"Steven, what is it? Are you hurt?"

But he only grunted a response.

Finally reaching the hut, Steven gave a deep groan and collapsed just inside the doorway. For the first time Angelina saw his back and nearly screamed at the sight. He had been hit on the back of his head and a large jagged gash about two-inches long was gushing an enormous amount of blood. Already it had covered his back and soaked his pants, and there seemed to be no end to its source as it continued to flow.

He was unconscious and although she struggled and strained, it was impossible for her to move him. Quickly she gathered the furs together and laid them along the side of him. Before rolling him onto the furs, she got the bucket of drinking water they kept in the corner and her old shirt. Ripping the material, she wet it and cleaned the area around the wound. Ripping another piece, she tied it around his head, hoping it would staunch the blood's flow.

Again she wet the cloth and wiped off his back. Pulling off his pants, she rolled him over and covered him with more furs.

Emptying the bucket, she took his pants and the bloody rags and went to the river to clean them and get fresh water.

Her heart pounded with fear as she worked. If Steven died, it would be a catastrophe. Not that she cared for him personally, she assured herself, but rather she needed him to eventually get her home again. He had promised only last night that they would be leaving here within a few days and she believed he had meant it. He seemed to her to be just as anxious to leave here. She knew once she was close to home, she could escape him and this episode in her life would, thank God, be over for good.

When she returned to the hut, Steven was as she had left him. Applying cold rags to his face soon brought him around and he groaned in discomfort. Trying to sit up, he groaned again, "My head."

Gently she guided him back and crooned softly, "Shhh, be still. You will be all right. Get some sleep now."

For the remainder of the evening, he slept fitfully. In the early hours of the morning, he was burning with fever. An hour later he was delirious, and Angelina was in a panic, lest he should die. What could she do? She had nothing that might bring down his fever. How could she get him help? She knew nothing of the language of these people. *Oh God please, she had to do something, something!*

The medicine man! Surely he would be able to help. Angelina was terrified of him, he was horrible, yet she had no alternative but to go to him.

She left the hut quickly before the fear of him lingered too long in her mind, and walked to his hut. Cautiously, she knocked on the door and entered. Her fears were not laid to rest as her eyes fell upon the gruesome and enormous figure of the man who sat chanting softly before a small smokey fire.

He was alone. Angelina forced her trembling legs to move forward. His black eyes followed her as she entered and came toward him. The look in his eyes did not induce friendly conversation, and she had to swallow a few times before she nervously stuttered, "I . . . I need your help. My . . . my man is sick. Can you help him?"

She waited as he stared silently at her. She didn't know if he understood her or not, for he said nothing.

"Please," she begged.

Without a word to her, he finally stood; his immense form towered above her as he walked out of the hut. She followed him to where Steven lay, and watched him as he spied the feverish man. Three times he walked around him while mumbling some strange words before he suddenly left, to return a moment later with a group of men. The men lifted Steven and carried him towards the river.

Amid much chanting and praying, they submerged him many times. When they once more returned Steven to his hut, she found the building filled with the strong sweet pungent scent of incense. The small fire was built up to a roaring state and upon the glowing coals stood a large pot of steaming water.

During the night, Agigue came often bringing strong scented herbs and fresh cool water to be made into tea. One moment Steven was on fire with fever and the next, shivering with cold. Angelina never slept. Continuously, she bathed his hot skin in cool water.

On the evening of the second day, Angelina sat at Steven's side bathing him in cooling wet rags, when she noticed his skin had lost its hot dry feeling. He was damp. His hair, which she had untied from its cowhide string, hung limp and damp on the fur pillow.

She laughed with relief as her hand rested against his cool damp forehead. His eyes flickered open at the sound of her happy laughter and he muttered, "Water."

She laughed again and poured a cup for

him. Her arm reached beneath his shoulder as she helped him sit up, while holding the cup to his lips. His head rested comfortably against her breast as he drank and when he finished, his arm pulled her close so he could stay in that position.

Determinedly, she disengaged herself from his weak embrace and smiled, "It is apparent, sir, you are much like your old self again."

"Nay, madam," he spoke softly, "had I been myself, you would not have escaped me." Giving her a grin, he continued, "If you were a compassionate woman, you would cater to a sick man's needs. You are more comfortable than this damn bed."

She laughed, "Be good, at least for a time, and go to sleep."

"Aye, madam," he sighed as he drifted off to sleep again, "for a time."

A week after the game, the tribe held a friendship dance, inviting many other Cherokee villages to join them. This was the first night since Steven's injury that he had felt strong enough to leave his hut.

Every man and woman in the village sat themselves in a giant circle around a fire. Two men beat out a rhythm with a drum and gourd rattle until another two men stood up and began to move around the glowing fire, in a slow deliberate shuffle. When they had circled the fire, they picked two women. The four of them then continued to move around the flames. When the two women picked two men, Angelina understood that eventually the whole village would be involved in the dance. One of these men picked her and she found herself caught up with the hypnotic beat of the drumming. Her heart pounded in unison with the rhythm while her blood throbbed in her head and she moved along without effort. When she came full circle, she found herself standing before Steven. Trance-like, she offered her hand to him.

Grinning broadly, he came to his feet and took her hand. He was very aware of her response to the hypnotic drums, but instead of joining the dance, he pulled her away from the crowd.

Without thought, she willingly went with him into the forest. The sound of the drums following them, continued their mesmerizing effect on her. She felt without a mind of her own, devoid of willpower.

Deep into the forest, he stopped and leaned against a heavy tree trunk.

She stepped closer. Standing between his legs, he pulled her closer still. The moonlight filtered down through the tree's heavy branches and bathed the two of them in its silvery glow. Still under the effect of the music, for the first time, she offered no resistance.

He undid her vest and pushed it off her shoulders. His mouth was teasing the flesh of her shoulder and sliding to her neck.

When he lifted his head, she raised her face to look in his eyes, her lips parted expectantly. Her hands slid up his bare muscular arms to his shoulders. She stood before him naked to the waist, watching his eyes as they openly admired her. She could feel the heat of his body even though they barely touched.

For a long moment, they looked at each other, each fascinated by what they saw. It had been a week since he had touched her, and she wanted him. Now, without further delay, she needed him! Needed his mouth on hers, his hands on her flesh, his body naked against her own.

She spoke his name as if a question.

Suddenly, his mouth was holding hers and she was pressed tight against his hard body. The feel of her unresisting form against him was a heady experience. He discarded the idea of taking her back to his hut, fearing she would snap out of the spell she was under. Without further thought and with their mouths sitll joined in a searing kiss, he moved deeper into the shadows, guiding her along with him.

Together, they lay down on the soft underbrush.

The drums stirred her to the point where she was wild for him. She gasped again and again as his hands swept over her, calling for him to never stop.

Later, she lay relaxed and spent in his arms. For the first time without a word of anger forming on her lips, she enjoyed at long last the delicious rewards of the aftermath of lovemaking.

Long into the night, the two of them lay close while the music and sounds of celebrating continued.

Chapter 10

She didn't believe it! Steven had never shown the young Indian woman, Agigue, the slightest interest. This could not have been happening without Angelina having a clue. And yet, she doubted the girl would risk a deliberate lie. Surely she realized she would be found out.

It was obvious the girl loved Steven, one only had to see her softened features when her eyes fell upon him, but was her love reciprocated? Angelina strongly questioned it, but couldn't resist the temptation of finding out for certain.

Only moments before, Agigue had shocked Angelina into silence, for she hadn't known until that moment that the girl could speak English. Snidely, she had taunted, "Come see for yourself if you do not believe. Steven is mine. He is as most men, and only uses you for a time."

Quietly Angelina made her way through the thick forest towards the river. Her heart was hammering in her chest. She didn't care if Steven had another woman as long as she was free to go, for she would never stand being one among the many. Bad enough, he took her nightly, but if she was not sufficient for his needs, her pride could stand no more.

She parted the last of the foliage. The river moved past rapidly, creating a roaring sound as it sped over small rocks, causing white foam to splash about the man who stood naked near the water's edge.

She watched as a slow lazy grin spread across Steven's face at the sound of Agigue splashing naked into the water behind him. The girl swam to him and coming from beneath the water, slid against his naked back, her arms circling his waist, clinging tightly to him.

So, she thought, he was expecting her. The girl had not lied after all. She could not seem to tear her eyes away; she waited breathlessly. Steven turned and engulfed Agigue into the circle of his strong arms. His head descended to meet her upturned face. His lips were barely inches from the girl before him when Angelina turned her face away. Her eyes were blinded by tears of fury. Her brain seethed with hatred. She knew, had she a weapon, she could have killed the two of them at that moment.

True, she did not care for him, neither did she want him, but her pride could not stand this kind of treatment. Now she only wished to be gone from here. Never would she willingly consent to be one of his women. She swore to herself she felt no jealousy, only injured pride and absolute hatred. She felt such violent rage within her that it nearly made her nauseous in its intensity.

How could he take another, hold another, and kiss her? She shivered thinking herself the lowest of animals to have enjoyed so completely their private moments together. She felt nothing but disgust that only last night she had willingly gone with him, lain with him, and had probably enjoyed their lovemaking as much, if not more, than Steven. Painfully, she remembered how she had time and again abandoned all resistance and begged him to take her once more.

Suddenly, his words flashed through her seething brain, *Perhaps I wish my women to be less willing, Janey sweet.* Could it be that he was so heartless and cruel that he had already lost interest simply because she had been a willing partner last night?

She felt nothing but revulsion. There was only one thing to do, escape!

He stood in the cool flowing water. A grin spread across his face when he heard the splashing behind him. He thought she might follow and join him. He hoped this meant she would always come to him willingly. After last night, he hoped her attitude had permanently changed toward him.

His heart pounded with anticipation. Her

small hands touched his hips from beneath the water and traveled up to his waist. Her cool wet body was pressed tightly against his back.

He turned. His blood nearly deafening him as it pounded in his ears. His arms circled her small form and his lips came down to take possession of her willing mouth.

His eyes were almost closed. Suddenly, his senses cleared as his brain registered black hair and deeply tanned skin.

"What the hell are you doing here?" he bellowed to her stunned face.

Agigue trembled at his instant rage. With an angry shove, Steven walked away. She watched through tearfilled eyes as he dressed and left her alone.

Later that night, Steven slept soundly beside Angelina. The camp had been quiet for hours. Soundlessly, she slipped a shift over her head. She took Steven's gun and belt from the wall and stole silently from the sleeping camp. Some men were obviously on guard near the outskirts of the village, but no one gave her a second look.

She almost laughed with relief as she realized how easy it was to take a pony and make good her escape. Vaguely, she wondered why she had never tried to do this sooner.

She decided to follow the river until dawn. In the morning she could change her direction towards the rising sun. She knew with this plan, she could eventually find her way home again. The night seemed endless as she walked the horse swiftly along the water's edge. She wondered at the ache she felt deep in her chest, but shrugged away all nagging doubts. She thought only of reaching home and seeing her family again.

At dawn, she turned towards the sun and finally began to make good time. She estimated she was at least four hours of hard riding from the camp. She prayed if she was followed, she'd be lucky enough to keep well ahead. After all, Steven didn't know her real name and she felt no fear of him ever finding her.

That night she stopped her pony and, in total exhaustion, slipped to the ground. Tonight she'd light no fire nor try to find food. She fell immediately into a deep sleep.

The next morning, although still tired, she was up and riding at dawn. She was moving on nervous energy. Only the fear of being recaptured kept her going. She promised her rumbling belly she would stop before dusk and hunt for food.

Later, just before dark, she stopped and began to make camp. No sooner had she gathered the wood for a fire, than did she hear hearty male laughter some yards away.

Terrified, she stopped all movement. She began to crawl through the thick underbrush. She scratched her exposed arms and legs on the thorny ground, moving quietly, until at last she came within sight of a camp.

She counted eighteen British soldiers sitting around a blazing fire, obviously camped for the night. She knew there must be sentries posted about. She couldn't chance staying here. Neither could she venture too far, fearing she might retrace her steps, thereby giving Steven, if he had followed her, ample opportunity to find her. With a silent sigh, she retreated. There would be no dinner tonight. Finally, moving as far away as she dared, she spent another cold hungry night, waiting for dawn.

At first light, she was on the Indian pony galloping away from very possible danger. At last, on the third night, she made camp. After wasting three bullets before killing a rabbit, she swore once she got home she would become an expert in handling a gun.

Each day was much like the next, up at dawn, riding till dusk, finding food and sleeping till first light and again until they seemed to blend into one. She was into her sixth day of riding when she realized she was close to home. The area was once more rolling hills covered with soft green grass. Mile upon mile of beautiful countryside surrounded her.

At dusk, she realized with a throbbing heart and tear-filled eyes, she was no more than three hours from home. She had ridden all day without stopping. Her body ached as she had never believed possible and yet she couldn't resist the temptation of continuing until she reached her destination. Her excitement built with every mile she left behind. At last, hours after sundown, she approached the long familiar drive she had silently stolen away from only five weeks ago. Through a dull and exhausted mind she thought unbelievably, could it have only been five weeks?

She didn't want to think of it now; she longed for her father's strong arms to hold her safely in his huge hard embrace.

At last she reached the front steps and slid wearily from the pony's back. Too exhausted and relieved now to climb the steps, she crawled on her hands and knees. Pulling herself along, with her last ounce of strength, she reached the massive white door and knocked softly. From within she could hear the sound of voices. Old Henry slowly opened the door. His inky black face peered out fearfully into the dark seemingly empty night.

A familiar voice called from behind him and before he could answer, Angelina moaned, through a tight parched throat, "Henry, please, for the love of God, help me."

"Lordy, masta sa, it's Missy!"

Angelina felt steely arms circle and lift her. From a great distance she heard her father's voice, "Angelina! Thank God you are back. Are you all right?"

All she could say was "Father," before she was asleep, snuggled like a child in her father's arms.

Part Two

Chapter 11

Angelina could not deny, dressed as she was in Indian garb, that she had lived among them. She was not surprised when late the next morning her father entered her room with a black scowl on his face. She knew she was in for a hard time.

Settling himself in a chair at her bedside, he waited in silence as he searched her face for a few moments before he began. "Well young lady, are you going to tell me what you have been about?"

"Father," she stuttered nervously, "I . . . I am so sorry to have caused you concern, but I was helpless to let you know my whereabouts."

"Just where the hell have you been for over a month's time? I was out of my mind with worry."

"It . . . it is simple really," she lied, "what happened was, I went for an early morning ride. Foolishly, I wasn't paying attention to the time and distance, and I went too far. Then Buttercup stumbled and went lame. I wandered on foot for hours trying to find my way back. Suddenly, an Indian stepped out of the underbrush and took me captive."

"An Indian!" James Barton cried out in astonishment. "Where the hell were you for an Indian to find you?"

She shrugged, "I do not know." And then continuing, "He took me to his camp and held me there for some time. Finally, I had a chance to escape. In the middle of the night, I took one of the horses and left."

Mr. Barton looked at his daughter sorrowfully, "You were assaulted then?"

A long moment passed before she spoke again, "Nay father," she answered honestly, her face flushing slightly.

"Nonsense, Angelina. I have knowledge of Indians and their ways. Do not insult my intelligence by lying."

Another long moment passed and she reddened even more as she continued, "Father, this Indian was very old. You can believe me when I tell you I was forced to do nothing against my will."

After a long search of her face, Mr. Barton sighed, "Thank God." And then changing the subject, he berated her for a quarter-of-an-hour on the necessity for caution and extracted a promise that she would never ride unescorted again.

During Angelina's absence, her father, to

quiet any possibilities of rumors, let it be known she had gone to visit her ailing aunt. Upon her eventual return, Mr. McCray, unaware of her recent adventure, was again anxious to resume his marital plans.

Angelina was tired from her travels and more than a little despondent due to the upheaval of her emotions in regard to her time spent with Steven. She offered no further objections to her father's wishes. Quite unlike her normal self, she was quiet and subdued. In truth, she felt she deserved no better than a marriage to the freakish man. In her confused, self-loathing state, she considered this just atonement for her sins.

Tonight, three weeks after her return, her father was giving a ball for her twentieth birthday. It was planned that during the festivities her engagement would be announced.

As Lizzy made the finishing touches to Angelina's hair, she could hear the orchestra tuning in the ballroom. She could not seem to shake herself from the lethargy that had engulfed her since her arrival home. Tonight, she would do all that was possible to forget the past. This would, she vowed, be a new beginning and she hoped her future would not prove to be as unpleasant as she feared.

Angelina hurried now, not wishing to upset her father should she arrive late to her own party. She was a vision of loveliness in pure white, which set her unladylike golden skin to glow in contrast. Her blonde hair was piled high in a mass of golden curls, giving her a queenly appearance. Her dress, straight from Paris and cut most daringly off one shoulder in a Grecian style, clung to her breasts and hips, seeming to emphasize her tiny waist.

As the guests began arriving, it was obvious most of the men couldn't keep their eyes off her and she became more like her old vivacious self under their admiring glances. During the evening, she was never at a loss for an escort and although unaware of it, she blossomed enchantingly and most desirably with the pleasant bantering conversation she held with each dancing partner.

At one point, she was standing in a group of people when Walter McCray came to stand beside her. Possessively, he placed his clammy fingers on her elbow. When she turned to acknowledge his presence, he smiled, his watery green eyes crinkling at the corners, "May I have a word with you, my dear?"

"Of course," Angelina murmured demurely, and excused herself from the group.

Walter McCray guided her towards the terrace beyond the opened French doors. Standing outside in the dark, Angelina breathed in the sweet summer air. It was warm and many of the guests walked about enjoying a moment of cool air. In the garden a few lanterns were placed sporadically about, affording some privacy to those who wanted it.

Angelina leaned comfortably against a thick pillar that supported the terrace's roof and turned to face McCray.

"What is it, sir?" she inquired.

"I have not had a moment alone with you all evening, my dear. I merely hoped we could stroll in the garden and talk for a time."

She shrugged, "As you wish."

Together they moved down the few steps to the darkened garden. Finding an empty bench, he bid her to sit beside him. Almost the exact moment she sat, he pulled her to him, smothering her face with unwanted slimy kisses. Breaking free, she quickly jumped to her feet, "Mr. McCray, really! You presume too much. I am not yet your wife."

From the shadows a match flamed to life as a man lit a pipe. Angelina was distracted as her eyes watched the flame and then stunned into shock as the flame showed Steven's face.

Steven moved closer, his eyes never leaving her face as he took Angelina's hand in his and brought it slowly to his lips. Softly he murmured, "Nor will she ever be, Mr. McCray."

Turning around, he pulled her with him, back to the house, leaving a bewildered Walter McCray to follow.

Her world was crashing around her. He was here! How did he find her?

As they entered the ballroom, Angelina's father came quickly towards them. "Oh, I see you have found her," he addressed Steven. And then turning to Angelina, he added, "We were just looking for you. Let me formally introduce you two. Steven Spencer, my daughter Angelina," and then noticing Walter McCray as he came to stand at Angelina's side, he continued, "and her fiance, Walter McCray. Mr. Spencer is here to buy horses. A mutual friend of ours has suggested we might find room for him, for a time."

Angelina's eyes were wide with shock and disbelief; her face whitened to a deathly pallor. She swayed slightly and clutched her father's arm for support.

Steven presented a dashing and handsome figure in his black coat and tight trousers. A white ruffled shirt and cravat emphasized his dark tanned face and thick black hair.

Arrogantly, his brow lifted a notch and a hint of a smile touched the corners of his mouth as his eyes boldly slid from her face and lingered with frank appraisal at her breasts for some moments before continuing down her body.

His overbearing arrogance vanquished her shock and stirred her to near violence. After a moment of silence, her lips curled over her teeth hatefully and she murmured with venom, "You swine."

A grin split Steven's mouth and merriment lit up his eyes. Quite obviously, he was enjoying her surprise and anger. "Most happy to renew our acquaintance once more," and then hesitated meaningfully before he finished with, "Angelina." And then laughing out loud, he continued, "Imagine the shock poor Miss Jane Winfield endured, when she found me on her doorstep claiming to be her husband. Indeed it has taken me some weeks to find the little orphan girl Janey Winfield."

Mr. Barton, completely taken aback by the reaction of his daughter to this young man, and more than a little puzzled by Steven's odd remarks, asked with surprise, "You . . . you know each other?"

Steven smiled wryly, and turned once more to Mr. Barton, "It is apparent sir, Angelina, although I knew her by a different name, has neglected to enlighten you. I am sorry to be the bearer of startling news, but it is impossible for your daughter to be promised in marriage since she is already married to me. Indeed, we have already lived as man and wife for nearly a month."

In unison, Mr. McCray and Barton bellowed, "What?" loud enough to call attention to all.

Everything began to spin before Angelina's eyes. Shaken by the shock of seeing Steven again, she, at that moment, cared little that he had revealed exactly what she wished her father never to know. Nor did she care that the dancing had stopped and people were gathering about the four of them to see what the problem was. All she could think of was her need to get away from him, from his laughing eyes, his arrogant grin, and from her father's building rage.

She had no wish to watch first-hand the violence her father was capable of. He was a large man with a quick temper. At times she had seen that temper erupt and anything within reach of his mighty hands might fly across the room and smash to the floor.

The room seemed to close in around her.

Barely able to breathe, her mind in a whirl, she turned and stumbled unseeingly through the closing crowd. Finally past the thickest part of the assemblage, she ran blindly through the French doors of the ballroom into the garden. In the ensuing confusion, no one thought to follow her. Alone, she walked numbly to the stables, saddled a horse, and although in a ballgown, mounted and rode off. She had no thoughts of danger nor of decorum as her dress slid up her legs to mid-thigh while she raced heedlessly into the night. Pins flew from her hair and tears stung her eyes as she tried to straighten the turmoil of her mind.

It was hours after the last of the guests departed before Angelina calmly brought her horse back. Her face was smudged from flying dust, her hair was splendorous in wild disarray, reaching to her waist.

Outside the barn, she was about to dismount when a voice from the shadows startled her, "Running away shall not save you. I will only find you again. I do not give up what belongs to me."

She jerked the reins and her horse leaped. If it weren't for Steven's quick strong hands holding at the animal's neck, she would have again raced off into the night.

He stood beside her, gently soothing her horse to remain calm; his eyes were looking straight ahead at the golden exposed thigh. Tensely he remarked, "I do not appreciate my wife riding about with her dress pulled up to here;" as he spoke, he placed his hand on her naked leg.

"Sir!" she snapped while trying to pry his hand from her. The shock of his touch on her flesh seemed to sear through her and her voice began to shake, "You may dissuade yourself of that preposterous notion. I am not your wife and you have nothing to say about what I do. Take your hands off me."

Now she was slapping at his hand, but he ignored her and instead of releasing her, he slid his hand under her dress and up her body to her waist.

She was shocked at the sensations his hands caused her, "Keep your hands off me, damn it!"

"Angelina," he answered huskily, "a man has rights. You are my wife."

Fighting against her building desire, she shouted, "When the hell are you going to understand, I am not your wife!"

"Keep your voice down," he demanded as he yanked her forcibly from her horse.

She stood before him, his hands still at her waist. Both her legs were exposed as her body pressed close to his. She was soft and pliant in his arms, allowing his hands to roam freely beneath her dress. Her breathing came in gasps.

His lips were only inches from hers, his eyes gentle as he whispered softly, "Why did you run away?"

At his question, she froze. All her thoughts of hatred returned. Pushing with all her strength against his shoulders, she broke free and spat out, "I hate you!"

Startled at her sudden change in attitude, he allowed her to break free, but he held tight to her skirt. After a few seconds he began to pull. He was smiling, while she, having no alternative, was drawn back to him. Angelina was never one to accept Steven's superior attitude, nor his greater strength. She could never be docile to any force he might devise. Actually, it took only his sudden appearance to bring back the fight in her. Her despondency and self-loathing disappeared for now she had someone much more deserving of her hatred.

She was swinging her arms wildly, punching him, not stopping until he forced her arms still by holding them at her sides. His lips were on hers, yet she continued to fight him, twisting her face to free her mouth. The moment his hands released her arms, she gave a hard shove against him and pushed herself free.

She managed to run but a few steps before he was by her side. Picking her up, he carried her into the barn. She struggled against him, but was no match as he easily brought her into the dimly lit stable and threw her upon a pile of fresh hay in one of the stalls.

Holding her in place with his own body, he easily slipped her dress from her shoulder. She nearly cried out with the bittersweet sensation of his warm moist mouth on her breast. Her body came instantly alive with desire. Although she denied it to herself, these last three weeks she spent in her lonely bed were filled with many sleepless nights, tossing about, tortured with unfulfilled yearnings, which left her wild for his touch. She was pulling his face to meet hers and kissed him with an uncontrolled starved need. Seductively, she rolled her hips against his and moaned with the exquisite pleasure of his body on hers.

She was wild for him, whimpering his name amid broken sobs, starved for the feel of his naked flesh against her own. She was tearing off her dress with trembling fingers, when a voice sounded from somewhere within the barn.

"Who's there? Speak up or I'll shoot!"

"It's alright, Jones," she choked out, "It's me, Miss Angelina."

The stable boy left, while muttering about being scared out of his wits.

A few moments passed. All that could be heard was the harsh sounds of exerted breathing. Finally, with a twinkle of humor in his eyes, he pulled her to her feet and while she tried to adjust her clothing, he led her to the house.

Her father waiting for her and upon hearing the front door open, came out of the library. Spying Angelina with Steven at her heels, the thunderous look of his dark eyes left her no doubt as to his fury. He was shocked at her appearance, eyeing the condition of her torn dress and the hay in her hair, did little to appease his anger.

"One would think after your last adventure, you would have had your fill of midnight rides. Where the hell have you been?" he bellowed.

Close to tears from emotional upset and sheer exhaustion, she raised her eyes to her father, "Father, please, can we talk in the morning?"

"Now, young lady." His face wore a black scowl as he grabbed her by the elbow and not too gently led her to the library.

After an hour behind the closed library doors, the issue was settled. Angelina would marry Steven Spencer the very next day and that would be the end of the matter.

Although she explained the circumstances of the so-called marriage, her father didn't care. She had lain with him and that was all that mattered. No amount of tears or begging swayed him. He was adamant. To his eyes, she was already married; only the legality was necessary now.

Chapter 12

Her temper was equalled in degree only to her passion, and either emotion could explode into violent intensity in a matter of seconds. He smiled broadly as a picture of her, soft and pliant beneath his hands, hungry for him to continue her pleasure, flashed through his mind. Indeed, his bride fascinated him, for he had known no other that could compare to her spirit.

That evening at dinner, conversation was extremely uneasy, when indeed any was in existence. Afterwards, Angelina took a stroll in the massive gardens at the rear of her home. It was dusk, the moon having not yet completely risen. The sun hung low on the horizon, causing the sky to blaze a fuchsia pink. The gentle breeze that caressed Angelina's face and hair effected a cool and calm influence on her perplexed and disordered mind.

What had happened, she reasoned, she had

brought on herself. Steven considered her his wife and because she had lain with him, her father agreed. If she could have honestly said Steven had taken her by force, she knew her father would have had him shot, and although the idea did cross her mind, she quickly squelched it, knowing she could never live with the thought of causing another's death unjustly. The facts were thus, she had willingly lain with him, and now in everyone's eyes she was his wife. She tried to sort out her thoughts, but came back time and again to one irrefutable point. She was married to a man she hated.

She had fought desperately for the last few years against her father's wishes for her to marry. Granted, her father's hope concerning Mr. McCray had been ridiculous. Deep inside her, she realized now that it was too late; she had wanted to marry no one, least of all Steven with his high handed attitude and his abominable arrogance. She knew she could never dominate this strong man and swore solemnly in return, no one would ever control her.

It disgusted her to think, according to law, she was now her husband's property, to do with what he wished. She had not married him willingly, she did not want him. She'd show him, no man would ever own her.

Despairingly she realized, for the moment, there was nothing she could do about her situation. She had wandered in her reverie to the far corner of the garden and stood under a giant oak tree. Leaning back against the heavy trunk of the tree, she closed her eyes and allowed a morose sigh to escape her lips.

"Oh come now, nothing is as bad as that."

Startled, she looked up to see Steven standing relaxed and confident before her. Eyes snapping, she barely controlled her anger, saying haughtily, "I came out here to be alone. I do not wish to be disturbed."

With a nod, he answered simply, "I know," yet he continued to stand before her.

"Well, since you know, then do me the courtesy of leaving me in peace."

"Listen to me, Angelina. It is time you stopped acting like a spoiled child and grew up. You are married now and we might as well make the best of it."

He stepped closer. Placing his hands against the tree, one on each side of her, he prevented her from moving away. Smiling, he whispered close to her, "Shall we call a truce?"

She felt his breath softly caress her cheek. Her eyes were on his mouth. She knew if he kissed her all her resolve of hatred would be swept away. In an instant, she wanted him desperately, longing for his lips on hers, for his hard body pressed tightly against her, but in that same instant, the picture of Steven, naked in the river with his mouth on the Indian girl's, flashed through her mind. "No!" she nearly yelled, while wrenching herself free of his potent magnetism, his tender looks and softly spoken words.

Spinning her back to face him, he stood towering over her, with his hands on her shoulders, his smile gone. He asked grimly, "What do you mean, no? I cannot believe you mean for us to live as brother and sister. Do you forget the passion we shared?" His voice softened some, and a smile touched the corners of his mouth when he added deliberately, "I never heard a murmur of no during those times. In truth, the murmurs I heard were quite the opposite."

Furious for forcing her to remember, her face colored a deep painful red as she snapped, "You really are a cad. Did you ever offer me a choice? What do you think anyone would have done?"

"Perhaps," he nodded thoughtfully, and then his lips twisted in a grin, "but would anyone have enjoyed it quite as thoroughly?"

Enraged, she sputtered, "You swaggering lout, you overbearing bully, if I were a man I would kill you."

"I know, love, you have told me that often enough, but in truth you are very much a woman," he said softly. His one hand released her shoulder and slid down to her breast, gently cupping it and brushing his thumb across her nipple, feeling it grow hard beneath his finger. After a moment he spoke, "Angelina, tell me you do not want me and I may just leave you alone."

She steeled herself against the insistent movement of his fingers; they brought back the constant craving for his hands on her, so strong now that her belly constricted in pain. She closed her eyes, she couldn't allow him to get close to her again. She'd never allow him to deceive her again. Breathing deeply, she finally spoke, her voice so clear and cool, she couldn't for a moment believe it was coming from her. "You know I was forced into this marriage, I did not want it. What you want from me is wrong and I cannot in good conscience come to you. Without love, what you and I would do together is meaningless, and I refuse to be a part of it. I have to get away from here. Perhaps I could visit my aunt in Elizabethton. You could divorce me after I have gone."

Suddenly furious at her threatened departure, his eyes hardened, his mouth turned grim. "Madam, many successful marriages have begun without love. Some even arranged as far back as the birth of a child. You are being infantile and absurdly romantic. It is time you faced the real world and grew up. You are my wife and while I will not demand your submission, I warn you, I cannot be pushed much further. Dissuade yourself of the notion of leaving here. You will not run from this marriage, neither will you, for any amount of time, deny your desire."

Angry again at his insistence, she sneered, "Aye, Steven, in truth I do not deny my desire. I want you as much as any bitch in heat wants her stud."

Stunned at her crass words, his hand froze on her breast. A cold hard look of angry determination crossed his features. Again for a moment neither spoke. Finally, he whispered menacingly, "Indeed madam, you are a bitch. As for one in heat, that is inconsequential, for I would not touch you now, should you beg me. I promise you, there will be a time when you regret those words."

Actually, this was already so, but stubbornly, she did not retract them.

Finally, with a look of total disgust, he bowed slightly and left her alone.

Chapter 13

During the time Angelina had been away from home, Washington had marched to West Point. It was there, during the months of May and June, that he waited for Sir Henry Clinton to push forward and confront him, but suddenly Clinton pulled his forces back to New York.

In an effort to draw his enemy out of the villainous, rough and rocky country of the Highlands, Clinton ruthless pillaged and burned many communities in Connecticut, yet Washington remained fixed.

Finally, after some humiliation, Washington recalled General Anthony Wayne to active duty.

On the fifteenth of July, Wayne was instructed to march south, skirt Bear Mountain, and take a rough trail over Degaffles Rugh and down the woodland to within a half mile of the enemy. It was there that he made camp. On the same moonlit night of his arrival, he captured Stony Point in only twenty minutes. This victory had the greatest effect of morale on the people and the army.

It was this victory, in fact, that stirred Angelina's brother into action. For many months James Barton had been bombarded with his son's pleas to allow him to enlist. On the first of July, Jim turned seventeen and it was then beyond his father's capabilities to prevent him from joining the army.

Almost every day since Angelina's return brought news of another battle or skirmish and more often than not, this news included the death of an old friend or acquaintance. She was terrified she'd next hear it was her brother that was injured or dead.

It had been a month since Jim had left. Like most everyone they knew, he had been anxious to be gone. All Angelina's pleading was to no avail. Her brother would only repeat there was a job to be done, and it was his duty to do it.

His words left her with an icy cloud of fear around her heart. She knew (praying she was wrong) he would be killed or at the very least injured, and her heart crumbled at the thought.

She remembered clearly the day he left. Jim had stood so proud in his new French-supplied uniform, with that enormous and ridiculous rifle in his hand. The gun stood six feet, which was some two inches taller than Jim himself. He thought he made a handsome and mature picture, but to Angelina the uniform and gun seemed to emphasize his thin youthful form.

The light of anticipation that had glowed from his eyes only caused to remind her of when he was a child and about to open a present at Christmas. She felt none of his exuberance, only a sadness at his going and a horrible fear he would never return.

She felt herself age at that moment. All her own problems seemed to vanish with the heavy loss of his leaving. But being more than a little loyal to the colonies, she knew had she been a man, she would be going with him.

Since her earliest recollection, she had hated the British. Her first memories concerning them were of soldiers harassing the peaceful people of her community. They were belligerent in their actions and obnoxious in their attitudes.

As she grew older, stories, whether true or not she never knew, began to circulate telling of the atrocities committed toward the defenseless. Worse yet, because they were of His Majesty's Royal Service, they were seldom if ever punished for their sins.

But it wasn't until the death of Anna Mayhill that she felt her hatred erupt to near violence. Mrs. Mayhill had been a gentle elderly widow who owned a boarding house in the town of Alexandria. Angelina remembered her with a great deal of tenderness. Since she was a child, Mrs. Mayhill had often invited the young children of the town and surrounding areas for tea. During the holidays it wasn't unknown for her to give the smaller children Christmas parties. All the children loved her.

One early morning, a group of rowdy drunken soldiers had come to her home demanding women. Obviously, they were mistaken as to the type of home she ran. No matter how the old lady had tried to explain, they refused to believe they had the wrong house.

One of the group roughly pushed her aside, apparently intent on seeing for himself. When he did so, she fell back and hit her head. Unconcerned with the lady's condition, they left her unattended on the floor as they searched the house. Angry at finding no women in residence, they ransacked the place.

It was hours later before one of the boarders returned from his day's work and found the lady, lying in a pool of blood, and close to death. Before dying, she told him what had happened.

Although the authorities were notified, nothing was ever done to bring those soldiers to justice. Angelina had spent many hours haunted by the poor old lady's death, imagining her fears and helplessness. It was then she vowed, given the chance, she would do all that was possible to rid her country of this vermin.

She realized full well what her brother felt, for three years earlier she had stood with her father and brother before the steps of Independence Hall, cheering along with hundreds of people, as the wild ecstatic crowd listened to the first reading of the Declaration of Independence.

All had agreed that Mr. Jefferson, whom she was proud to relate was a close family friend, had written an astounding piece—one which fired every man and woman in the crowd with love of country and an intense yearning for freedom.

It was then she decided she would do her share for her country's cause. For two years she had been working for the Patriots. More so as of late, since the south had become a stronghold for the British.

There were Tories everywhere, reporting the movement of colonial troops.

Washington, too, had a good spy network, in which Angelina played a small part. Her job was a simple one of transferring notes. Sometimes they were received from someone she knew, but most often, she would go to a designated spot and there in the base of an old tree, she would retrieve a note signed, 'Primrose,' that had been placed in a bottle. She would then pass these messages on to another who would see to it that Joseph Crockett received it. He in turn, she supposed, saw to it that it reached its final destination.

Her work involved little danger, for the distance covered was small and could be done in daylight. Yet had her father known, she doubted he would take kindly to the news for he had very straight laced ideas on what was proper for a woman. Nevertheless, it left her with a good feeling of accomplishment.

Tonight she sat in the library, in the company of her father and Steven. She was reading when she was interrupted by her father mumbling over his papers about the sad state of affairs of the new government. He was muttering aloud, "If I were only twenty years younger, I would show these British clods some real fighting."

Angelina sat on a couch, pretending to read, while a smile played across her mouth as she listened to her father.

His position was well known in the colonies and more times than not, someone from Washington's staff was with him in the library, on one matter or another.

Usually Steven was asked to sit in on these meetings, being a man of some intelligence and by reputation known to be loyal to the Patriots' cause. It gave Angelina no small amount of annoyance to see her father take to her husband so completely. Without a doubt, he treated Steven as a son and she nearly snarled at their obvious friendship. Many were the times she found them locked in deep conversation which, to her extreme annoyance, always concluded at her appearance.

Last night there had been another meeting, a matter of funds. No army was poorer than the Continental Army. Congress was nearly penniless and it was well known that Washington among others, her father included, were paying out of their own pockets for much of the army's support. Things had been easier since October of '78 when the French had sent shipments of coats, breeches and shoes. At least the army would be warm this winter. As for food and munitions, that was another matter.

As usual, Steven and her father began a friendly argument over the finer points of defense and strategy. Steven continually maintained Washington, who had been nominated as general by the Continental Congress, was not the right man for the job. He insisted the man to be merely a rich plantation owner and not a soldier.

Angelina knew little of Washington's abilities of leadership, but she was not totally ignorant of his background, and her natural antagonism toward her husband forced her to interject. "Forgive me for intruding, but I feel I must beg to differ with you, sir. General Washington has not always been a rich aristocrat. In truth, he was born of a secondary family and has attained to greatness purely on his own merits. It is a well known fact, although I lack the particulars, that in his youth he won fame as an outstanding Indian fighter.

"Father and I met him the year preceding the war's beginning and, I for one, remember him to be dynamic and extremely personable."

"You are quite correct, madam, in your

knowledge, slight though it may be, in General Washington's abilities as an Indian fighter. Still, I do not see how this experience has bestowed on him the estimable quality of leadership."

Snidely, she pointed out, "How is it the most intelligent men of our colonies think him right for the job?" And by saying no more she obviously implied her husband, not being of their opinion, was far from endowed with their superior qualities.

She smiled victoriously at his gentlemanly acknowledgement, "A point well taken, madam."

But the thought of her brother Jim in the crack Virginian regiment brought icy shivers down her spine and she prayed these men were right and General Washington would make the correct decisions, ending the war soon.

The two men continued their conversation. Her husband began abusing the character of a fellow Virginian, the same officer her brother had enlisted under, a Major Lee. Again, she could not resist the urge to interrupt and she began to brag of his successful raids on Powles Hook, on the Hudson river.

"Madam, it is clear you think well of your friend Major Lee, but if you knew him as I do, I seriously doubt you would keep him in such high esteem."

"What is it, sir, that you are hinting?" she asked with a sneer.

He shrugged, apparently unwilling to discuss it.

"Nay sir, that is not good enough. I insist. What are you accusing him of?"

"Very well, madam. Major Lee has suggested that deserters of the army be put to death."

She swallowed hard, but refusing to let him see her disgust, she contemptuously replied, "Perhaps he knows, sir, that such a harsh punishment would discourage the practice."

"Aye madam, but is it necessary to cut off their heads and display them? Surely you would agree this is an extreme and savage act."

He watched her shocked response to his statement, and grinned as she finally replied a bit shakily, "A point well taken, sir."

The knowledge nearly nauseated her and she could find no reason for such barbarity. She shivered noticeably thinking of her brother being under Lee's command.

During the two men's conversation, she watched her husband's tall lean form. Her mouth turned grim as she surveyed his tight pants and form fitting jacket. She hated the way his clothes fit so snugly to his muscled body. God, how he annoyed her. Why did he have to strut so? Why, he barely left anything to the imagination in his dress! True to his word, he had not come near her since that terrible night in the garden. But strangely enough, she noticed his attitude toward her was beginning to change. No longer did he ignore her presence, but smiled teasingly, his eyes lighting up with undisguised pleasure when she walked into a room. Adding the same teasing quality to his voice and manner whenever he addressed her, he kept her in a constant state of weariness and unrest.

Angelina, always so confident and sure of herself, began to find herself stuttering her responses and most of the time she was at a loss for words during his jovial encounters. Something was happening. Something she didn't understand, which left her afraid. What was he up to? Perhaps, she smiled sardonically, he thought his pretty manners could tear down the wall between them. She knew he wanted her. It was obvious in the looks he gave her, but she wanted more than lust from an unfaithful lover.

If Steven was waiting for her to make the first move, to break down the barriers that existed between them, he had a long wait ahead, a long wait indeed. She was startled out of her thoughts when she heard her husband's voice addressing her.

"It is late, Angelina. Shall we retire?"

Careful not to allow her animosity toward Steven to show in her father's presence, lest he give her one of his thunderous disapproving talks on the proper behavior of a young wife, she cooly responded, "I think not, Steven. As yet I do not feel the least tired."

He walked to the couch and stood before her, smiling down at her lovely stubborn face. Reaching down he took her book from her hands and pulled her to her feet, while responding authoriatively, "I am afraid I must insist, my dear. I cannot allow my wife to injure her beautiful eyes with too many hours of strain."

Helpless to do anything in the company of her father but allow Steven to accompany her out of the room, she did just that.

Silently they walked side by side up the long stairway to their rooms. At her door, she expected and was somehow disappointed that he made no overtures, for she was ready to set him down. Instead, after smiling a friendly good night, he turned from her, leaving her feeling as a mouse might with a tomcat on the prowl.

She was totally confused by his attitude toward her, but she'd have none of him. She had been forced into this sham of a marriage and she hoped the day was near that she'd see no more of Steven Spencer.

Chapter 14

Steven had been gone for four days on a business trip. Angelina had enjoyed each glorious day of his absence in peaceful tranquility. Now alone in her room, she was waiting for Lizzy to bring her fresh towels, while she finished her bath. Sitting in her tub, she began to sing a rowdy tune, and as she came to the end of the song, she gave a delightful giggle.

"It is most unseemly for a lady of quality to even know such words, never mind repeat them in song," her husband's voice sounded from the doorway of their adjoining rooms.

Startled, she spun about, splashing great quantities of water on the floor. "Steven," she gasped, "I did not know you had returned!"

"Obviously, my dear," he smiled as his eyes widened approvingly at the naked beauty before him, "or you would have kept your voice lower and that little ditty to yourself. By the way, where did a lady with your strict upbringing learn it?" he questioned, while folding his arms across his chest and leaning against the doorjamb.

She blushed under his scrutiny and stuttered nervously, "More was learned at boarding school than needlepoint and proper flower arrangements."

She frowned deeply noticing his attire. His pants, as always, were too tight and form fitting, while his shirt was opened to his waist. It annoyed her thoroughly and she couldn't fathom why.

With a deep chuckle of amusement, he walked slowly past her and sat on her bed. "I am glad I found you still awake, there is something I wish to discuss with you."

Even nakedness didn't deter from her natural confidence and she replied arrogantly, "If you would leave, allowing me the courtesy of bathing in private, I shall join you in a matter of moments, wherever you wish."

Smiling broadly, he responded while making himself comfortable, lying on her bed with his arm propped under his head, "Do not trouble yourself. I am in no hurry. I have planned nothing at this late hour and indeed I am very content to wait."

Angelina tried in vain to cover herself. She was livid that he could sit so calmly watching her at his leisure. All manners of speech quickly evaporated and she spat out nastily, "Who the hell do you think you are to come into my rooms while I am bathing?"

"Madam," he grinned lazily, "you are my wife. Be happy I am content, for the time being, to merely sit here. I put no demands on you." His eyes slid over her appreciatively as he continued, "I have decided we have enjoyed your father's hospitality long enough. It is time we, as a newly married couple, were living in our own home. Since I have nearly finished my business here, I think after my next trip we will leave for the islands. I have been away for some time and I am anxious to see my home again."

She looked at him for a long moment, unable to speak, so flabbergasted was she at his words. She knew her husband owned a home in the Caribbean and another in France, yet she never realized he would wish to live anywhere but here in the colonies. Only recently she had heard him discussing with her father the price of some properties adjoining theirs. She hadn't realized she'd ever be expected to leave. It never occurred to her she'd join her husband in his home. Unrealistically, she thought they would always live here.

Finally, she spat out, "You cannot be serious! You have decided? Have I nothing to say in the matter? I am not leaving here. Why in the world would I wish to live on some uncivilized island when I have everything I want here? Everything I love is here." She became calmer and her tone changed to disdain as she continued, "Of course if you wish to leave, you may certainly do so, but I promise you I shall never leave my father's house. It matters little what you intend or wish. I shall do as I please." She tossed her head and added with an obvious dismissal, "Good night, Steven."

He grinned at her superior attitude, enjoying their verbal combat and retorted softly but firmly, "You may of course believe whatever pleases you madam, but the facts are thus. You are my wife and as my wife you will do as I wish. And I wish for us to be gone from here within a month."

She was furious and cared little at that moment that Steven sat watching her as she grabbed a towel. Before her husband's admiring eyes, she quickly left the tub and slipped into her robe. After securely tying the garment around her, she faced him, ready to do battle. "This is exactly the reason I never wished to marry anyone! You, like all men, seem to think women in general have no mind or feelings and as such are owned by their husbands and subject to their will." She added sarcastically, "Well, let me inform you, dearest husband, in this case it will not suffice. I do not care about your wants."

She began to turn away from him but he grabbed her arm and pulled her back to face him again. Smiling at her hot temper, he gazed into her flashing eyes and asked, "Do you think your father will allow you to stay if I must leave?"

"Oh," she cried, barely able to control herself while the thought of her father's thunderous face flashed before her eyes.

Steven was enjoying her rage. He smiled as he pulled her closer against him. He could feel the warmth of her through the thin fabric of her robe.

She wished she could strike his face and wipe off the arrogant smirk on his lips.

Suddenly, without warning, his mouth was on hers. She was pushing him, trying to break his hold. But twisting her head to free her mouth from his did little, for his lips were now on her throat, sending shock waves down her spine.

His hand opened her robe and fondled her breast. A moment later his mouth joined his hand, branding her flesh with burning greedy kisses.

Almost instantly, her rage turned into wild desire. All her angry thoughts and hatefilled words disappeared, replaced by a passion more intense and consuming than anything she had ever known before.

His hands roamed freely over her damp warm skin. His mouth was once again on hers. His tongue mingled unhindered and delightfully with hers.

There was a humming in her ears. She never realized continuous whimpering sounds were escaping her throat, matched only by Steven's wild and ragged breathing.

He no longer needed to hold her close to him, for her arms came willingly around his neck as she pressed herself tightly against his hard lean body.

He never stopped caressing her beneath

the silky material of the robe.

She was dizzy, her passion wildly out of control. Starved for his touch, she cared only for the moment and the delicious sensations—wanting only his hands on her, his mouth to work its special magic, his body to possess hers.

Many were the nights she had lain awake tossing in her lonely bed, wanting him, needing him. He had awakened desire in her and had shown her delights she had never before believed possible. Her body shook with the promise of long awaited ecstasy.

Unexpectedly, there was a knock at the door and Lizzy's black face peered in. Spying the two young people caught up in a passion filled moment, she beat a hasty retreat.

But her interruption had broken the spell and they stood gasping, facing one another in silence. Angelina retied her robe and backed away, fearful he might touch her again.

After a moment, Steven mumbled a good night and swiftly walked from the room.

Hours later, she was still restlessly pacing the floor of her room, all passion forgotten. This couldn't be! She couldn't leave permanently. She was needed. She had work to do. Something must be done. Someone had to help her. She had a possible assignment tomorrow night, with perhaps more to follow. To be gone indefinitely was out of the question. What in the world was she going to do?

Chapter 15

Far from the comfort of home, in the black of night, a huddled dark figure bent low while pressing close to the base of a tree.

A large force of men were moving north.

The shadowy figure watched for a long time before edging toward the river. Hidden in the thick foliage that bordered the water, the small boat made only the slightest sound of suction as it slid from the mud and entered the water.

At last reaching the other side, the black shadow rode for hours before finding its destination. In the base of a hollowed out tree was the familiar bottle. The agent's work done for the night, a sigh of relief was uttered and then once again the shadowy figure blended into the forest.

Again the following night the agent waited, cold and shivering as the dampness began to seep through the heavy coat. The figure lay flat and watched from the thick underbrush as many soldiers passed on the dirt road.

Slowly it worked its way back toward the water in order to retrace the same steps of the previous night. Secure in the knowledge that the outcome of the approaching battle was a foregone conclusion, the agent smiled knowing the long hours of discomfort were well worth the information gathered. It was important that this knowledge be passed on, for there was no greater defense than knowing the strength of one's enemy.

When at last reaching the water's edge, the boat was nowhere to be seen. Something serious was afoot.

"Would you be looking for your boat, matey?" came a voice from the forest.

Quickly, the agent stepped the few feet back into the foliage. All about could be heard much movement as a search of the woods was begun.

In the shadows, every tree appeared to be the enemy. Before the possibility arose of being distinguished from the shadows, the black figure was running. Shouts could be clearly heard, some shots were fired and still the agent ran.

It took nearly an hour before reaching the back door of the inn, then silently the shadowy figure made its way up the darkened stairway to a reserved room.

Clothing was quickly discarded. Already the sounds of soldiers could be heard entering the establishment. Too late to throw the clothes out the window as the inn was already surrounded, the discarded clothes were pushed under the feather mattress and the covers smoothed again.

Suddenly the sounds of raised angry voices exploded from the adjoining room.

"Do you realize who you are harassing? I am Colonel Beauchamp of His Majesty's Royal Service. I'll have your hide for this, you cloddish imbeciles. Do you think a cursed rebel could enter this establishment and hide while I'm in residence? Be gone with you! Grant me the courtesy of spending what is left of the night in peace."

The red-faced Captain turned and nearly stumbled over his men in a hasty retreat from the fury of the pompous English Colonel.

In the room just beyond the Colonel's stood the naked figure, listening intently. As the sounds of retreating steps were heard, a brilliant smile spread across the agent's face and a silent sigh of relief was uttered.

It wasn't until the next day that the agent realized his papers of identification were missing. Anyone could have picked them up. It was probable that they were dropped during the evening's excursion. It was obvious to the agent, the days of this particular type of work were over for good.

Chapter 16

Angelina had fallen into the habit during the long summer days of taking a refreshing evening swim. No one but Lizzy knew of her time spent relaxing in the cool ocean waters. She loved this time of the day, for the sun disappearing beyond the horizon mirrored a rosy sheen upon the water, giving everything around her a golden red glow.

Nearly every night she swam until the sun left the sky and the moon glowed silver and cool. Tonight, after leaving the water, she went in search of her clothing. Something was wrong, the night was unusually quiet and still. Her clothes were missing! Could she have swam farther down the shore than she had realized?

Gooseflesh spread across her skin, as an eerie feeling of being watched stole over her. Her heart began to pound sharply in her chest. Father had warned her often enough of smugglers and she prayed she wouldn't find a gang of men coming towards her from the woods.

She stood helpless for a moment, unable to think of what she should do, when a voice from the dark startled her, "Are you looking for these?" Involuntarily, she screamed and an instant later she was running, terrified, down the long stretch of beach.

Her heart pounded so hard, she thought it might burst. So wild was she for escape that she nearly outran her pursuer. But after a few moments, she found herself sprawled upon the soft white sand. Her breath was knocked from her with the heavy weight on her back. She began to scream as never before in her life. So hysterical was her mind that she heard nothing of the man's mumblings.

Finally a hand closed firmly over her mouth and a voice whispered in her ear, "Angelina, it is I. Calm down. Can you hear me?"

It took a moment before Steven's words penetrated her fearfilled mind. At last she nodded her head and he turned her onto her back and pulled her to her feet.

She was wild with fury for the fright he had caused her and tried to strike him with her small hands. Blocking her swinging fists, he laughed at her attempt and pulled her close to him, pinning her struggling body against him and her arms at her side. After a moment she calmed some and he whispered into her wet sandy neck, "What a hot tempered little minx you are. So this is what you have been up to each night. I have wondered where you have been going." Abruptly, he released her.

She was still breathless and gasped for air, but stood facing him, mindless of her nakedness, her arms planted on her hips, her legs spread in defiance.

He smiled taking full advantage of the sight offered him, and his eyes raked her body.

Finally able to speak again, she asked cooly and contemptuously, "Was it necessary for you to scare me like that?"

Now losing much of his humor, he retorted seriously, "In the future, madam, you will refrain from disrobing with the exception of the privacy of your bed chamber."

"Bastard," she sneered, "you have nothing to say in regards to the manner of my dress."

"Angelina," he warned, "the beauty of your body is for my eyes only. I will not permit other men to see what belongs to me."

"Damn you to hell, Steven," she remarked scornfully, "you presume too much. My body is my own, not yours, and I shall disrobe where and when I please—in the center of town if I have a mind to, and I would kill anyone who dares to lay a hand on me."

He chuckled at her outrageous comment, "And how would you manage that, my dear? Have you a secret weapon on you?" His eyes slid down her body and he continued merrily, "I think not. What would you do if a man pulled you into his arms like this, scratch his eyes out? Suppose he held your arms at your side, like this. Would you bite and kick when he covered that lovely mouth of yours with his, like this?"

The pressure of his arms around her was almost more than she could bear. The scent of him weakened her to a point where her knees nearly buckled. His lips, warm and firm against her own, were gentle and tender at first, but almost immediately his mouth became possessive and demanding. She had longed for this for so long, dreamt about it almost nightly. She had watched, as if in a trance, as he had taken her in his arms and kissed her, never once offering the slightest objection as his mouth covered hers.

What was the matter with her? She hated him, hated his arrogance, his confidence, and that ever present knowing grin, and yet she wanted him. Oh God how she wanted him. She couldn't keep a groan of longing from escaping her throat.

Desperately, she pressed closer. Her arms circled his neck. Her fingers played with his dark hair that curled over his high collar.

Suddenly, she found herself flung into the thick woods bordering the beach, with his hand placed firmly over her mouth. Her eyes grew wide with shock as twigs pressed hard into her back and scratched at her legs. His face loomed above hers and he warned menacingly, "Do not move; do not make a sound. Your life could depend on it."

Not far away, she heard masculine voices approaching, and a man's voice trying to no avail to quiet them. Suddenly, Steven was on his feet and walking nonchalantly towards the boisterous group.

"Captain Spencer, there you are, sir," said someone amid the men. Calmly, Steven led the men some distance away, almost out of hearing.

Angelina strained her eyes trying to see who they were, but even though the moon was bright, she couldn't recognize any of them. Slowly, she reached her arm out and gathered her clothing which had fallen at the edge of the woods.

As she began to dress, she heard loud gusts of laughter and looked up to see one of the men holding her lacy hand embroidered panties in the air. She could hear Steven's laughter above all else, and she fumed silently as he spoke, catching a word only now and then. He was obviously relating some disgusting story of a private party between himself and a married woman of his acquaintance.

Angelina was shocked by Steven's obvious friendship with so blatant a group of cut throats. Not one among them could be considered respectable. Could they be pirates or smugglers? To her mind, Steven looked the part of a pirate, and for all she knew about the man, he could be a smuggler.

She was once again disgusted to realize she was married to a man she disliked intensely and of whom she knew next to nothing about. For the past few months, she had been so caught up in her own problems of a forced marriage, and then of her brother leaving, that she had barely noticed Steven's coming and goings.

She knew one thing as fact, if they remained together much longer she would eventually be his wife in every sense of the word. It was apparent she had no control over her emotions when he made any advance towards her. She responded even though she didn't like him or want him as a husband.

After a few moments of thought, she made up her mind. She was leaving him, regardless of the consequences. She didn't know how as yet, but soon the time would come.

Upon entering the house a short time later, Angelina was met at the front door by Henry. "Missy, your father asked for you to join him in the library as soon as you return."

Some time passed before Angelina emerged chalk white and totally stunned from the library. Her eyes stared dry and unseeing at her husband as he came through the front door. She leaned back against the library door, taking huge gulps of air.

Steven, who was about to go upstairs, couldn't help but notice the agitated condition of his wife and stopped before her. "Angelina, what is it?" he asked, concern for her apparent in his deep voice. His hands reached out to support her visibly trembling body.

Her eyes focused at last and took in the worried expression of her husband standing before her. Her eyes searched his as if begging for help and in a broken voice she cried, "It's Jim," and repeated again, "it's Jim, it's Jim," and then finally, "he is dead." Her words rushed from her, then she released a torrent of tears. Most of what she said was incoherent. "Oh Steven, he was so young, only a boy. I remember the day he left, so proud and happy, positive he could beat the world with that ridiculous giant gun."

Angelina came unresisting into his arms as Steven engulfed her in a sympathetic embrace. All her anger and restraint were forgotten for the moment as she clung to him, sobbing out her loss.

He was silent as he listened to her mumbled, heartbreaking crying. He knew nothing he could say would bring her the least comfort, so wisely he said nothing.

A moment later, he had carried her up the large winding stairway to her room and laid her gently on the bed. Quickly, his fingers undid the buttons on her dress and before long, she slid naked between cool crisp sheets. Steven placed a cool cloth over her eyes and rang for Lizzy. He told her when she arrived of her mistress's need for sleep and asked if she would please find something to give to her.

Steven sat beside her, holding her in his strong arms until Angelina's sobs quieted and she drifted off into a drugged sleep, relieving her immediate pain for the time being.

It wasn't until the next day that he learned Jim had been killed in a raid on Powles Hook, led by Major Lee. It was the very same skirmish Angelina had bragged to Steven of, only a few weeks ago.

One of Jim's friends, home on leave, had seen him fall and brought the sad news. Of course, without his body for proof, it was impossible to list him as definitely dead. Captain James Butler had said it was possible that the British had taken him prisoner, but knowing the condition prisoners were forced to endure, even then there would be little hope.

Steven remembered visiting a stinking prison the year before in New York, and kept quiet about the fiendish practice of starving the prisoners for a few days and then giving them poisoned bread to eat. Better she think her brother already dead than to envision the suffering that could be inflicted upon him.

Part Three

Chapter 17

There had been much to do. She was adamant. She was not going to be a wife to a man she knew nearly nothing about. She was not leaving her home to live on some godforsaken island, no matter what he might think. This morning he had left on another business trip. His absence offered her possibly the last opportunity to rid herself of him, and she took it. She was going to her aunt. To hell with Steven and what he wanted. If she was lucky, she'd never have to see him again.

Once again a short note was sent off to Joseph Crockett explaining her necessary absence and her promise to return as soon as possible.

Lastly, she lied to her father about plans to meet Steven at the nearby inn for an extended honeymoon trip. He could offer no objection when she quickly packed and left.

Using the family's carriage, she asked her

driver to bring along two heavily armed men for protection, unwilling to risk another kidnapping or worse in her war torn country. She planned to change coaches and send her drivers home at the first opportunity, thereby leaving no trace of her whereabouts.

Angelina had left soon after Steven. The weather impeded the carriage's movement and they made very bad time. Two previous days of dreary rain reduced the normally dusty rutted roads to black muck. Sucking at the wheels of her carriage, it caused the light vehicle to slip dangerously, throwing her brutally from side to side within.

She was weary after a long day of being bounced about unmercifully. She was covered with flying mud from the wheels of her coach; dirty almost beyond recognition. She wondered when she'd be dry and comfortable again.

Only her thoughts made the most unbelievable traveling conditions bearable. She smiled again thinking how simple it had been; her plans had gone without a hitch. All she had had to do was bide her time and wait for Steven to leave on his last buying trip. She snickered aloud as she remembered the astonishment in Steven's eyes early that morning.

She was thankful her father had been present at their loving farewell. She found herself unable to resist a final tease and had wished Steven a safe trip while promising, seductively with her eyes, complete surrender in the very near future and finishing with a loving kiss and a whispered, "Until you return, darling."

She shuddered as she remembered Steven's mouth on hers and the full advantage he had taken by folding her in his arms and promising with an arrogant whisper, "Wait for me in my room tomorrow night, my sweet, and I shall give you all and more of what your eyes beg for."

When she stiffened and tried to pull away, he simply laughed, pulling her tighter against him, and kissed her thoroughly. If it were not for her father's presence, there was no telling what he might have done after that kiss.

She laughed aloud, thinking of Steven's return. How she wished she could see his face when he found not only his room empty, but hers also; gone without a trace. Knowing how furious he would be made her almost warm with delight.

It was getting dark. Angelina knew they would soon stop. She longed for a hot bath and a soft bed to rest her aching bones.

Just after dark, the carriage rolled to a stop in the cobbled courtyard of an inn. Angelina was impatient to stretch her legs and didn't wait for the drivers to help her out. She opened the door herself and jumped outside. She was relieved to at last escape the confines of the carriage.

Anxious to settle herself for the night, she left her drivers to tend the horses and entered the inn to make her own arrangements for a room.

She entered by the closest door, which brought her into the ale room. Once inside, it took her a few moments to accustom herself to the noise and clatter of the rowdy crowd. The ceiling was very low, beamed and darkened with age and dirt. The room was so crowded, she wondered for a moment if she'd be able to pass.

Two women swayed provocatively past tables, bringing tankards of ale to customers while receiving hearty slaps on their bottoms for their efforts. Before Angelina's astonished eyes, they bent over allowing their off-the-shoulder blouses to fall gapingly loose, giving each customer, in turn, full view of pear-shaped, pink-tipped breasts. And as many of the men reached greedily for a squeeze, neither woman gave the slightest notion all was not well. Rather, they laughed, apparently enjoying each of the men's groping and fondling.

One of the women stood still for a moment while the man at her side had his hand up her full skirt, obviously bringing her some enjoyment. She glanced at Angelina, more than a little surprised to see a lady of breeding standing alone at the door of the room.

Angelina looked about wondering what she should do. Finally, she began to weave through the crowd. Dressed as she was in a flowing blue velvet cape, lined with sable, and a muff of the same fur to match, she drew all eyes as she walked through the room. The crowd grew quieter as nearly all the men stopped talking to watch her.

As she passed one particular table, an arm shot out and grabbed at her waist. In an instant, she was sitting on someone's lap amid shrieks of laughter and much knee slapping. It wasn't until the men quieted down once more that she dared order in a haughty disdainful voice, "Unhand me, sir," which only brought about more laughter.

The merriment came to an abrupt halt when she suddenly heard her name called from across the large room.

Turning slightly, she faced her caller and unbelievably spied Steven coming towards her. His eyes glowed murderously and she wasn't sure if it was she or the man upon whom she was still sitting who was the target.

Her mouth dropped open with surprise and after a moment of surveying the situation, Steven merrily called out again, "Angelina, sweetheart. At last you are here. Our room is ready and waiting for us, my sweet. Think of it," he laughed, "a whole night of love before your husband will even know you are gone."

These last words received hoots and laughter from the suddenly silent watching crowd. The man released her and she stood, unable to believe what she was hearing. Totally bewildered, she stood in place as if she were only watching and not immediately involved. By now Steven was upon her, his mouth on hers, her body lifted nimbly in his arms as he walked calmly to the stairs. Now the crowd fairly roared its approval, nearly deafening her. Even if she had tried to protest against Steven's disgusting behavior, she couldn't have been heard above the noise.

It wasn't until they were in his room that he finally spoke, "You fool! What do you think you are doing traveling alone. God knows what would have happened if I was not here."

Her face flaming with mortification, she swung her small fists furiously at his broad chest as he put her down. "Are you mad? I shall never forgive you for this. I am so embarrassed. I shall never again be able to show my face. My God, how could you treat me like a common slut? I am your wife. Do I not deserve your respect accordingly?"

"So madam, you finally admit you are my wife," he answered with a smile.

Confused, she stuttered, "I . . . I" while shaking her head.

He brushed aside her attempts of denial with a wave of his arm while quickly changing the subject, "I think you could use a hot bath and supper. Do you not agree, my love?"

There was a knock on the door and a servant girl entered bearing a tray of food and two glasses with a bottle of wine. Two boys followed, one dragging a small tub while the other carried steaming pails of water. Obviously, this service had been ordered earlier. It took three more trips before the tub was full and they left.

In the meantime, her luggage was brought

up and the servant girl had laid out her pink satin nightgown and a matching transparent robe. Before the girl left the room, Steven spied the two articles on the bed, picked up the gown and said, "This will find no use tonight. Perhaps you might like it, my dear?" With that he took the gown and tossed it to the girl.

Her face glowed imagining herself clothed in such a luxurious garment and she mumbled thanks many times before she finally closed the door behind her departing figure.

Alone, Angelina turned to face Steven and asked, "How did you manage. . . ?"

He interrupted her questions with a grin, "Quite easily, madam. You were a bit too much the loving wife this morning. I knew something was afoot. All I had to do was wait and when I saw the direction you took, I knew where you must spend the night. So I came here and reserved a room for us."

Angelina sat on the corner of the bed with a sigh. All her running from him and her insistence not to have him had proved to be of no consequence. Suddenly, she was too tired to fight against him any longer. She knew Steven would never be gone from her life and at the moment she wasn't at all sorry.

He was a strong determined man. A man she knew she'd never control and yet all these qualities that had plagued her since their first meeting, and had made him seem so unappealing to her in the past, seemed suddenly not to matter in the least. Suddenly she didn't care anymore that she knew nearly nothing about him.

She watched him as he took off his jacket and cravat. He made a startlingly handsome picture in his full white shirt which opened nearly to his waist, tight black trousers, and dark soft knee high leather boots. Always, she had hated the way he carried himself, so confident and sure. His clothing, always perfect, seemed to add to her annoyance. Particularly his form fitting, slightly too-tight trousers brought her much anger, and she could not find a reasonable explanation as to why. In truth, he dressed no differently than many other men, yet there was something about his dress or stance or perhaps both, that had constantly irritated her. Now as she watched him with undisguised admiration, for the first time his tight clothing failed to annoy her, rather the sight of his trim muscled body brought a flush to her skin and a slight shallowness to her breathing.

Steven poured two glasses of wine and standing before her, offered her one. Gently he pulled her to her feet and without a word spoken between them, directed her toward one of the two chairs on the far side of the room.

A tray of cheese, cold ham and dark bread had been placed on a small table and he put it before her. He made himself comfortable in the other chair, placing his feet on her trunk. Leaning back, sipping at his wine, he watched her eat her meal in silence.

During the dinner, he had refilled her glass; now that she was finished, he again filled it. Still not a word was spoken and neither noticed nor cared about the silence.

The wine and the glowing fire in the grate drove away the dampness that had engulfed her and made her warm and comfortable. Angelina felt not the slightest trepidation as Steven's blazing eyes openly admired her, caressing her face and body, while she matched his tender gaze with a gentle one of her own.

A moment later the small table was moved away and Steven was on his knees before her, untying her boots. When he finished she took her brushes from her case and stood before the full length mirror, loosening her waist-length hair.

As she brushed her hair, she watched Steven through the glass. He locked the door and pulled the covers down on the bed. Coming to stand behind her, she watched as he removed his shirt and threw it on the chair.

Their eyes met and held. She dropped her brush beside his shirt when, after a long moment, his arms slipped around her small waist and drew her tightly to him. Burying his dark head in her sweetly scented hair, he breathed deeply of its fragrance while she leaned back against him, delighted by the overwhelming sensual sensations his nearness and touch brought her.

His hand slid to her throat and began to unbutton her pale blue silk blouse. She offered not the slightest resistance as her clothing slipped from her small frame and fell unnoticed to the floor. At last, she stood proudly naked before his admiring eyes, with her hair offering her only cover.

He turned her to face him. His mouth tenderly teased her own. Finding her mouth joined willingly beneath his made his mind reel and his body trembled with longing as he picked her up in his arms and whispered, "Come my love, the bath water is cooling." Gently he placed her in the tub. Once his arms were around her, it was impossible for him to relinquish his hold and it was his hands, not hers, that washed her while he knelt beside the tub.

His lips were on hers again, her mouth soft and pliant beneath the pressure of his as his hands, under the pretext of washing her, began to make love, for over and over did they come to rest on her breasts and again and again did the soapy cloth move between her legs. Finally, the cloth discarded, it was his hands alone that touched her.

Dizzy with passion, he pulled her from the tub to stand before him. Grabbing a towel, he wrapped it gently about her sweetly scented body. Now he began to dry her; brushing the linen towel gently against her skin, until it glowed. At last the towel dropped to the floor and she kicked it away.

His mouth caught her once again, and she whimpered with delight as his tongue began the slow leisurely exploration of her mouth. She was pressed close, swaying in his hard embrace. Her arms slid up his chest and circled his neck, clinging to him, pulling his mouth down to meet hers. Her breasts pressed against his naked chest, burning his skin at their touch. When her mouth left his and slid to his neck, she asked in a broken whisper, "Steven, must we wait any longer? My God, it's been so long. I've been waiting and wanting you forever."

Her words unleashed his control and, like someone possessed, his pants followed her clothes to the floor. She was in his arms as he walked to the bed. Their hearts pounded in unison as he laid her down and covered her body with his. She felt the hardness of him against her belly and gasped with welcoming pleasure as he entered the warm moistness of her. She was wild with excruciating, delicious sensations as his flesh began to move against hers. She was ablaze in her passion, turbulent in her need, and her nails bit deep into his back as she pulled him closer to her. Her mouth devoured his; her tongue drove him to a frenzy, insatiable for the touch of her.

His lips branded her breasts with burning moist kisses, his tongue moving, moving, scorched her skin. His hands reached under her hips, bringing her sharply to him. Holding her in place while she whimpered weakly and sobbed out broken and incoherent sounds, his body raced breathlessly toward satisfaction. They were lost in the mind-exploding throes of desire about to be sated, wilder still as he felt her own response against him.

Moments later, they lay breathless and spent in each other's arms, her face nuzzled to his chest, listening to the steady beating of his heart. Her hand began to move slowly over him, tracing the bristly hair that grew in abundance on his hard flat stomach and muscled chest. Leaving that, she traveled up to his strong jaw, and then gently her fingertips brushed against his smiling lips.

Abruptly, she pulled away and looked up at his face. Seeing with her eyes what her fingers had told her, she slid her body up to bring her face level with his. Looking down into his laughing dark eyes, her hair falling about them, creating their own tiny private world, she began titilating his mouth with feather light kisses while asking, "What is it you find so amusing?"

He chuckled, "You never cease to amaze me, love. I came to intercept your journey and expected to find you, to say the least, somewhat disagreeable. Instead, you become a most willing wife; as a matter of fact, a veritable tigress, to which my unfortunate and probably bleeding back can well attest."

"Complaining already, eh?" she giggled. "Would you have me be as other women, performing their wifely duties hiding beneath the covers with their eyes tightly shut?"

"Nay, never!" he answered as his hands slid down her back and over her rounded hips, pulling her to lie on top of him and pressing her close. "I may not be the most brilliant of men, but no one could ever call me dimwitted. And that I would be, should I complain. For men the world over have gladly suffered the worst life has to offer to obtain a lesser treasure than you."

She laughed, rolling off him and stretching languidly beside him, "Are you comparing me to a treasure?"

"Madam, in truth, you are the greatest treasure I shall ever possess. I would give all I own to keep you."

She smiled as she looked into his tender gaze, "Sir, your tongue is glib tonight. But I have cause to wonder, how much of what you say is truth?"

He grinned, "Madam, have I ever given you cause to doubt me?"

Smiling, she returned, "Aye sir, my doubts have indeed been great. But tonight that is to no avail."

Together they shared another glass of wine, each drinking in turn from the same spot.

His eyes softened as his voice urged, "What was it you told your father that enabled you to leave his house?"

A slow blush crept over her as she replied, "I . . . I told him . . . I was meeting you for our honeymoon."

He laughed heartily, and then emptying the glass of wine, he placed it on the table at their bedside. He leaned closer to her. His mouth was nibbling at her shoulder and neck when he whispered, "I fear it would not be honorable of me to have forced you into a lie. A honeymoon you have said, and a honeymoon it shall be."

Chapter 18

It was two days before either Angelina or Steven thought of leaving the glory and bliss of their honeymoon bed. In the early hours of the third day, Steven quietly left his bride sleeping deeply; she had not yet recuperated from the strenuous and sleepless previous night. Arrangements had to be made if the coach was to be ready for departure within a few hours.

When he returned to the room, he sat on the bed admiring his sleeping wife's lovely face. Gently, he moved a lock of golden hair aside as he kissed a slim naked shoulder.

With a deep sigh of contentment, she turned on her back allowing him full view of beautiful rose-tipped breasts. Her arms slid lazily around his neck and his head buried itself in a most delightful morsel, while a smile of pleasure played upon her lips.

It wasn't long before he was once more beside her, sampling again all that was offered him. And, like a child greedy for sweets, her hands and mouth never left him.

Later, alone in the room, she was finishing her dressing while Steven made arrangements for their breakfast. A smile of remembered passion and fulfillment spread across her lips and her eyes shone with contentment as she put the final pin in place before the mirror.

Glancing about, she searched for her small bag to replace her brushes. Humming happily, she moved Steven's long black cape aside and found her hat somewhat crushed and bedraggled beneath it. Forgetting her hat for the moment, she picked up a parcel of papers that had fallen from an inside pocket of the cape and put it on the chair.

Her eyes fell on the envelope. Written on its face in Steven's bold handwriting were the words: Colonel Banastre Tarleton.

He was by reputation, the bloodthirstiest villian and most hated of all the British soldiers. Heart thumping wildly, she reached for it and, with horrified eyes, scanned what appeared to be the drawing of a fort some thirty miles from Charleston, called Monack's Corner. The papers included maps of gun placements, possible points of entry, and the number of men at the fort.

The attached letter in its own smaller envelope nearly brought Angelina's breathing to a stop. Addressing the hated British soldier as a compatriot, Steven wrote he hoped this information would be of some use.

She couldn't believe it! How could this be? She, a staunch Patriot, was married to a Britisher, her most hated enemy.

Her heart twisted with such pain that for a moment, if a dagger had been thrust into her chest, she would have felt nothing.

"A spy," she groaned aloud, horrified and shivering at the realization. Spinning about as she heard the door to their room open and close, the papers held limply in her hand, she faced him and in an unsteady voice she croaked accusingly, "You are a spy, a common spy!"

"Hardly common, my sweet," he sighed with a tight smile belying the nonchalant shrug of his massive shoulders, while gently taking the papers from her icy fingers. "I prefer to think of myself as an agent, my dear. Spying depicts certain unpleasant tasks with people of unsavory personalities. If the truth be known, battles are rarely won on the field of honor, but rather with the information procured from either side, probably in the back room of some inn or perhaps even a brothel."

The look in her eyes forced him to add, "Angelina, you have much to learn. Nothing is so clear, nor so right or wrong, as you seem to think it."

"Oh God," she moaned. Unbeknown to her, her thoughts were clearly visible on her face.

Steven felt a moment's sorrow for her suffering, but wisely said nothing. Watching the hurt in her eyes turn to blazing hatred, he shrugged aside his sympathy and ordered, "Madam, you are my wife and you shall mind what you are about and refrain from interfering in matters that do not concern you."

She bared her teeth with disgust, "Why you insufferable, obnoxious, turncoat. The very sight of you is so odious, it actually gives me the shivers. What arrogance! Matters that do not concern me, eh?" she mimicked, while tossing her head and flipping her long hair with her hand in a defiant motion. Her eyes narrowed threateningly, "I shall see you hung from the gallows before I am through. Your name will be spat upon for all generations."

With a dangerous half-smile, he came to stand before her.

Undaunted, she faced him, raising her rage-filled eyes to meet his.

He looked down, only half seeing her. His voice was deadly calm as his mind worked quickly to rectify the situation. "Madam, since you have discovered my line of work and have seen fit to honor me with your opinion of it, I am compelled to secure your silence." His lips tightened as he thought further and added almost to himself, "The problem now is how shall I go about it? I take it you would not consider giving your word of honor to keep our little secret?"

She raised her eyes with a deadly look of hatred.

"I thought not," he sighed almost wearily.

"I should have known," she spat out in disgust, "after all, you thought nothing of betraying me, so why not your country. Of course the comparison is ludicrous, yet it nevertheless reveals the type of vile worm you are." Her voice strengthening, she snarled with loathing, "A man without honor."

"You have forgotten madam, this is not my country. What is it you accuse me of? How have I betrayed you?"

A vicious smile spread across her mouth, "I have been aware of your deceit from the first. Why do you think I left the Indian village? Oh God, Steven," she turned away and groaned out painfully, "why did you not let me be?"

Confused at her train of thought, he turned her around to face him again and growled, "What the hell are you talking about?"

"The Indian girl, Agigue. Did you really think I was unaware of what was happening between the two of you?"

She watched as his eyes remained bewildered and impatiently continued, "Oh Steven, do not play the innocent with me! I know how you take what you want. I saw you both naked in the river. I saw you take her in your arms." Her voice broke as tears came at last, "I saw the way you kissed her."

"Was that the day you left the village?" he asked.

She nodded as a giant tear rolled from her glistening eyes.

Suddenly, and to her absolute amazement, Steven threw back his head and laughed, a deep, rich, and happy sound. "What a jealous wife you are, my love. Perhaps, had you watched a bit longer, your jealousy would have been put to rest."

Slyly, he grinned down to her puzzled face and brushed a tear from her silken cheek, he murmured, "If I did not know better, I would think you cared for me. Could I have been mistaken?" His mouth twisted in a cheerful grin, "Is that the reason for your fury?"

Ignoring his pregnant questions, she slapped his lingering fingers away. "Be serious, Steven, this is not a game of whist we play. Do you believe I can allow this to continue? What do you think me, a puppet with no mind? Why, it is possible it was your treachery that brought about my brother's death. I have no choice, Steven, I must tell the authorities!"

"I believe you mean it, my love." His eyes shone with admiration. "It is too bad, my sweet, we are on opposite sides. I think if the two of us had worked together, these ignorant rebels would have not stood a chance, and this war of independence, as you like to call it, would have been over almost before it began."

Stiffly, he bowed before her, "You will excuse me, will you not? It seems your new knowledge must bring about a change in my plans."

Her eyes narrowed with menace as she warned, "Steven, were I you, I would forego all attempts to keep me with you. I promise I shall not remain willingly and I will cause you nothing but trouble.

"Also," she smiled nastily, "should I remain away from home much longer, my father is sure to set an alarm and all will be looking for me."

He smiled at her reasoning, "Madam, from the first moment I met you, you have caused me nothing but trouble, and since your father already believes you to be on your honeymoon, a simple short note should set his mind at rest concerning your extended absence."

She gasped at his deviousness and as he started for the door, she knew instinctively he was about to dismiss her drivers. "No Steven, wait!" Searching for an answer to her dilemma, she began haltingly, and then more confidently as the idea took hold. "We should be able to come to some sort of an agreement. What if . . . what if I gave you . . . my word not to report your activities at least . . . at least for three days, thereby giving you ample time to get away and out of danger. I think this would be exceedingly fair since I could then warn my father, and all would be safe. In a year or so, sooner if you wish," she added quickly, "you could divorce me and that would be the end of the matter."

He smiled down at her hopeful face, allowing her for the moment to believe he was considering her proposal. "Not good enough, my love," he answered at last, crushing her hopes and then giving her cause to hope again with his next words. "You are not the only

Catholic here, you know divorce is out of the question, for either of us. As for the rest of your suggestion," he paused lengthily, "I am sorry but it seems I am equally loyal to my cause as you are to yours. We seem to find ourselves at an impasse."

Angelina's shoulders slumped with despair and she watched silently as Steven opened the door, but his final comment brought all the fighting spirit back into her slim body. "I am sorry to have to lock you in, but in a manner of speaking, you are my prisoner." He added with a grin, "A prisoner of love, you might say. By the way, my dear, if you are considering calling for help, do not trouble yourself. The inn keeper shall be duly informed that my lovely lady has never been the same since her last indisposition, poor darling."

He laughed as he watched her face contort with rage. Had she tried, she would have been unable to speak coherently, so great was her fury. She watched helplessly as Steven walked out and closed the door quietly but firmly behind him.

Angelina stood still for a moment, her mind forcing her seething rage aside as she tried to think of something she could do. She tried the door, hoping against all reason it would open to her touch. It did not.

Running to the window, she flung open the shutters. Looking outside she thought how efficient Steven had been. Their room was two stories high; it was impossible to jump. Just as she was about to pull her head in, she spied a narrow ledge no more than five-inches wide, beyond which was a straight drop to injury or death.

It would be dangerous, but possible. Knowing her petticoats would hamper her movements, she quickly undid the strings that held them to her waist and stepped out of them.

Outwardly she appeared calm, but her heart pounded as she pulled a chair before the window. Throwing caution to the wind and her fears with it, she climbed on the chair and over the windowjamb, out to the ledge.

She clung, paralyzed for a moment, to the building. She refused to look down as waves of dizziness assaulted her. Without realizing, she began to pray aloud, so terrified was she of falling. She moved as a snail, taking forever as she inched her way to the next window.

Without thought, she flung the window shutters open and fell inside. She was still sputtering wild words of prayer, much to the amazement of the naked man and woman who lay across the bed. Angelina's relief was so great, she was unaware of the startled man's angry cursing or the woman's terrified shriek.

In an instant, she was on her feet, running as if the devil himself was upon her. Like a blur, she breezed out the door, slamming it loudly behind her, leaving the occupants in doubt as to what they had truly witnessed.

She had made it to the hall. Now for the

hardest part. She had to get to her drivers before Steven sent them away. If she avoided meeting Steven and took the front steps, she might miss them. It didn't matter anyway if she and Steven had a confrontation, as long as someone who knew her was present. So, without further thought, she ran towards the back steps which obviously led to the stables and her waiting carriage.

Less than halfway down, her movement came to an abrupt halt. Her heart pounded wildly, her breathing became almost nonexistent. All hope was gone. She heard Steven's jaunty whistle and lively steps coming up to meet her. He had finished dismissing the drivers or he wouldn't as yet have returned.

Luckily for her the stairs turned midway, so he hadn't seen her. Angelina's first impulse was to sit down and cry, but she realized with a little more luck, she could still escape him.

Her beathing coming fast again, she turned and silently fled back up the stairs and into the first room she came to. Shutting the door quietly behind her and leaning against it breathlessly, her chest heaved with exertion and fear.

She heard a low startled sound and then a man's deep laugh. She turned white with shock as her eyes registered a very naked man standing only a few feet from her. He was old and gray hair covered nearly every inch of his aging body. She gasped as he chuckled, "My my, the service is certainly improving in this establishment. You are the prettiest wench ever."

He began moving towards her. Panic flooded her. Her hand reached behind her for the door handle, but in her haste she had some trouble getting the door to open. The man was oblivious to her attempts at retreat, so intent were his eyes on her heaving chest. He was so close now she could smell his masculine scent and feel his breath brush against her cheek. His hand reached out and touched her breast.

Angelina shrieked, catching him completely off guard. She raised her knee hard and quick and found her mark. As the man crumbled in a heap of excruciating pain, moaning at her feet, the door finally opened for her and she dashed into the hall and smashed into Steven.

It took him only a moment to understand the situation. He grabbed Angelina tightly about her waist while twisting her arm slightly behind her back to keep her still. Together they watched the man raise himself from the floor. Steven apologized quickly and berated Angelina, explaining her dimwittedness and tendency for violence, explaining further that he was enroute to an asylum and was very sorry indeed for the trouble his sister had caused.

"See to it you keep her locked up in the future," the angry man shouted at their retreating backs. Steven carted her down the long hall to their room like a sack of laundry thrown over his shoulder.

She was close to tears by the time he unceremoniously threw her on the bed. Throwing a package down with her, he ordered, "Put these on."

"No!"

"Angelina, you will be less than comfortable riding a horse in the clothing you are wearing."

She lifted her chin stubbornly, "You fool yourself sir, if you think I am going anywhere with you."

"Madam, you will come with me, make no mistake about it," he answered authoritatively. "If you fight me it will only add credence to my story of your illness." Grabbing her cape, he pulled her from the bed and propelled her from the room. "No tricks now. You have seen what the alternative to me can be."

Chapter 19

When they reached the courtyard, her carriage was gone and two saddled horses stood awaiting them. Without a word, Steven lifted her and sat her upon one of the horses. Keeping the reins to her horse in his hand, he mounted the other and pulled her along as he trotted the animal away from the inn.

Her mind whirled. She had to tell someone. It was imperative her father be warned. How many times had Steven sat in on meetings with her father and someone from Washington's staff? She was desperate!

After they had ridden more than an hour, she began to notice how the foliage that bordered the rutted dirt road was beginning to thicken. She waited until she could no longer easily see through it before she made her move. In one last desperate attempt to escape, she flung herself from the animal and lunged into the woods, running as fast as the thick foliage allowed.

With strength born of terror, she moved quickly, ignoring the pain as the heavy branches slapped into her face and hands. Behind her, Steven cursed. She could hear his running footsteps above the pounding of her heart.

Without a moment's hesitation, she dove head first into the underbrush and rolled to a stop. Twigs and thorns scratched her but she ignored the pain. Determinedly, she controlled her harsh breathing and took giant silent gulps of air to ease the pain in her chest. Her heart pounded. She dared not move, but prayed she had rolled far enough into the underbrush to avoid detection.

She knew he was furious for she could hear him calling her name amid cursing and threats.

She lay still as death. Obviously, from the sounds Steven made, he was searching the bushes near her. After what seemed forever, there was silence.

He was waiting. She knew he was out there somewhere close by. Now it became a battle of wills. She could not give up. This time she had to win. Everything depended on it.

Perhaps an hour passed. She was stiff from being still so long. Her nose itched from being pressed into damp musty dead leaves. Her face and hands ached from deep scratches. She felt an urge to sneeze. *No! No!* her mind screamed and by sheer willpower, she forced the urge to subside.

Still more time passed, yet she remained there. She was hot. The noon hour came and went. She heard nothing.

She began a silent conversation with herself. *Maybe he is gone. No! Do not let him fool you. He is there, believe it! He is there. If only I had a weapon. Would I use it? Would I have the nerve?* Her mind rejected the thought as irrelevant. *I have nothing, nothing but time. How much longer! Please God help me!*

Even though she dared not move her head to look up, she could tell it was at last approaching darkness. It was beginning to cool. The small area she could see without moving slowly began to grow darker. She had only one chance. Certainly he would hear any movement, but under the cover of darkness, it might be possible to escape. *Please,* she groaned silently, *it must get dark enough.*

Surely this was the longest day of her life. Still she waited. At last night came. It proved to be lighter than she had hoped, for the moonlight seemed to be abnormally bright as she raised her eyes and gradually lifted her head.

Slowly, silently, she rolled to her side, almost groaning out loud with the pain as she eased her sore arms down to her sides and lifted her knees to flex her legs. She was stiff but determined. Soundlessly, she prepared to move away. Now she was up on her hands and knees.

Perhaps she might have made good her escape had fate not intervened and called an end to her flight. Something in the dark slithered across her hand. Although she involuntarily jerked her hand away, she somehow managed not to scream out. But luck was not with her. Suddenly she felt a sharp firelike pain in her hand. It had bitten her! "No! Oh God, nooo!" she screamed out loud.

Instantly, she was on her feet and running, mindless of anything but the burning pain in her hand, all the while crying out with fear.

She wasn't out of the brush ten seconds before Steven's strong arms came around her from behind.

"Steven," she babbled as she jumped up and down, "it bit me. A snake bit me!"

He turned her about to face him. In the moonlight he could see her eyes huge with terror, her face scratched and smeared with dried blood and dirt. "Where?" he bellowed, almost panic stricken himself. He was shaking her by the shoulders and yelling into her face, "Where, show me where?"

She raised her hand and showed him the bloody and discolored area.

A knife appeared in his hand. He gripped her wrist tightly. Holding her hand steady, he cut deep.

She screamed out, surprised by the sudden added pain. Ignoring her discomfort and horror, and the enormous amount of blood that flowed from the cut, his mouth was on the wound sucking, spitting, and then sucking again.

The pain and fear was more than she could

bear. She slid into a faint and collapsed in his arms. A few moments later she awoke and found herself alone. Her hand ached miserably as she raised it to her eyes. It was bleeding less now and a tight piece of cloth was tied about her wrist. She heard footsteps approaching. Steven was by her side, forcing whiskey from a flask down her throat. She coughed and gasped as the burning liquid went down.

"Are you all right?"

After a moment, she answered hesitantly, "I think so."

He sighed with relief, "Of course I cannot be positive but it is unlikely the snake was poisonous." After a few moments of thought, he continued, "We are only an hour or so of hard riding from our destination. I think it is best we start immediately and if you should become sick, at least you will find yourself in a comfortable bed with a doctor close by."

Angelina was riding for only twenty minutes before the symptoms began. Her head pounded; she knew she was already feverish and her muscles felt stiff. She prayed her condition would not worsen, but indeed it did.

An hour passed and she was burning up. Her hands were trembling and weak, barely able to hold the reins. Her body began to jerk uncontrollably.

Steven was watching her as they moved fast through the night. He saw her begin to sway in the saddle and heard a moan escape her. Stopping immediately, he jumped on behind her and tied the reins of his horse to her saddle horn. As they continued to ride, she leaned limply against him.

A short time later, Steven drew the horses up and called out for help. Strong arms lifted her down and carried her away.

She was so hot, burning up. She moaned for water. Her muscles jerked involuntarily. She couldn't stop her legs from jumping. She was so sore, everything ached. Regularly, sulfurous liquid was spooned into her mouth, causing her to gag as she tried to fight it off. Then cooling liquid was brought to her lips. She drank greedily.

"Enough, my love," she heard whispered from somewhere above her.

Cold towels were placed on her head and body. She was burning up, she was shivering with cold. When the cold towels heated upon her they were replaced, causing her much discomfort for they felt like ice against her hot skin. Finally after hours of heat and cold, she slept peacefully.

When she awoke, it was dark again. She found herself in a strange small room, measuring no more than six-feet square. The walls and low ceiling shone a deep rich mahogany. The bed she was in occupied a whole wall. The other walls were lined with shelves of books and another held trunks and a desk.

Steven sat beside her, his chin on his chest as he slept in a chair. He came awake immediately upon hearing her stir.

"Where am . . .?"

Before she could finish, he reached over and felt her skin. "You are on *The Savage,* my ship," he smiled happily. "Thank God your fever is gone. Rest now and I will order you some tea. Soon you will feel your old self again." He added with a sly grin, "Knowing you as I do, I am unsure as to whether that will be good or bad."

He left her for a moment and returned quickly with the tea. Holding the cup for her as she sipped the hot strong liquid, he remarked, "Do you realize when you are feverish, you moan constantly? I must admit you gave me quite a scare. Luckily Dr. Banard, the ship's physician, was with me. With all that moaning, I was terrified, and had not the slightest idea of what to do with you."

It was another full day before Angelina felt strong enough to venture from the bed. Steven's attention confused her. He was a spy, the most villainous of all creatures, and yet when he administered to her, he was as caring and gentle as if she were his child.

Angelina was resolute in her insistence that he should be brought to justice and willed herself not to weaken to his kindness. It changed nothing, she reasoned. He was still a spy.

Chapter 20

They had been at sea for more than a week. Angelina was not the least happy or comfortable in Steven's presence for her feeling toward him remained much the same. When it became necessary for them to converse, her responses were forced and stilted. She felt enormous strain, compelled as she was to share his cabin. The room offered barely enough space for one; for the two of them, it was very tight indeed.

Although they shared the same bed, he made no overtures toward her. Each night, pretending sleep, she felt him slide in beside her, her body tense and rigid until she heard his deep even breathing. Every morning when she awoke, he was gone.

Apparently Steven felt none of the strain Angelina was under, for his attitude was congenial and pleasant. He treated her as if the scene at the inn had never occurred. Many were the times she found him watching her with a glowing look of admiration in his eyes, yet the look was not sexual in the least and it left her totally confused.

Weather permitting, Angelina was most often to be found on deck. The men were jovial and kind while treating her with the respect due to the wife of their captain. Mr. Johnson, the first mate, found a chair for her and when she wasn't reading, and he not on duty, spent many congenial hours by her side, most often talking of his wife and their four children.

Dr. Banard, too, found time to sit with her. She and the elderly gentleman sat many long hours before a chess board, until she considered herself to have gained some mastery of the game.

Steven never attempted to join her in conversation, but watched from afar. Angelina, as always, was annoyed to find his eyes continuously upon her, for they glowed with an unnerving tenderness, while an ever present smile of genuine pleasure played over his lips.

On the evening of their eighth day, after another nearly silent dinner, Steven opened one of the trunks and took out a red satin ball gown. Placing it on the bed, he added a matching pair of satin slippers and a black velvet cape. With a sly grin, he remarked, "We are entertaining tonight, my dear. Please do me the honor of wearing this dress."

Angelina almost laughed out loud. Entertaining indeed, and at sea? In the middle of nowhere? Now what was he up to? She was about to refuse when her curiosity got the better of her. With a shrug of delicate shoulders, she decided she might as well play along and see exactly what he was about.

After dressing, she was applying the finishing touches to her hair when Steven again joined her in the small cabin.

Seemingly unaware of her presence, he stripped off his clothes, washed, and dressed in stunning black satin pants and soft black leather boots. A white ruffled silk shirt emphasized his dark tan and a black brocade waistcoat finished his dress.

Angelina's heart nearly stopped at the handsome sight he made. Brushing aside her feelings, she reminded herself that many men were handsome, and handsomer to be sure. But handsomeness was the least important quality in a man.

Glancing at herself in the mirror, she realized how very low cut her gown was, emphasized more so by the tightness of the garment which forced her breasts up and almost out of the dress. She knew she made an alluring and seductive picture and wondered at Steven's motives in asking her to wear this almost indecent dress.

Steven stood quiet, looking her over for a long moment. Finally he spoke, "Angelina, we have a very important engagement tonight. It is imperative you listen to me and do exactly as I say and only as I say."

She could think of nothing other than spying for their special evening's entertainment and smiled cooly while replying sarcastically, "Dearest husband, if by chance you should imagine I would help you succeed in your dirty work, I feel I must inform you that you are sadly mistaken. You will find nothing but trouble and uncooperation from this woman."

Smiling, he answered, "You have already proven yourself to be nothing but trouble to me and, I might add," he continued with a lecherous grin, "most uncooperative, madam. Nay, what I wish from you is to merely keep a certain man busy while others have a chance to go about their business."

She was about to refuse, when he finished with, "Angelina I swear to you, you will not be sorry, for this has nothing to do with my line of work. As a matter of fact, I can promise you much rejoicing and happiness tonight, if you comply with my wishes."

"Can you not tell me more?" she asked, now really interested.

"Not at the moment, but if all goes as planned, you will have every reason after tonight to hold me in the highest regard."

She grimaced, "That sir, is highly unlikely, either tonight or any other night."

He laughed at her show of distaste and, taking her cape and carefully wrapping it about her shoulders, he led her out the door and on deck. As he helped her down to the small boat that waited alongside the schooner, he whispered, "Remember, do not be frightened. I shall be close by. Keep your wits about you and do not panic. Most importantly, do everything you can," his voice lowered meaningfully with his next words, "within reason, that is, to keep Captain Wakefield occupied, no matter what you might hear. All our lives could depend on it."

She shivered slightly from the excitement of the unknown. Her eyes locked with his in the moonlight. What in the world was going on? She would soon find out. She prayed she wasn't making a mistake by trusting Steven.

Settling herself in the boat, she saw they were not alone. The boat held six others, all women! In the bright moonlight, it was easy to see they were probably the ugliest females she had ever seen. They were of every size and color. Each one wore heavy makeup, and most had bright red hair. What were they? Who were they, and where did they come from?

Questions began to form on her lips, when Steven stated simply, "Angelina, you have met my crew before."

Now eyes wide with wonder, Angelina stared in amazement, for each woman was indeed one of Steven's crew, dressed in the gaudiest clothing she had ever seen. Had Steven not told her, she never would have guessed, for even in the strong moonlight they could easily pass as women. She started to giggle, breaking the mournful silence. It was apparent the men were not in favor of the disguise and were following orders under duress.

Angelina's giggle soon turned into merry laughter and was followed by the men as they, in turn, laughed at themselves.

"Enough!" Steven spoke sharply, and added with a conspiratorial whisper, "if you find your assignments so humorous, have the sense to laugh more in keeping with your costumes of the gentler sex. Have you forgotten your voices carry some distance over the water?"

"Sorry, Capt'n," was whispered in return and the rest of the short ride was made in silence but for the steady slap of the oars against the inky water.

Soon the huge black shape of a ship came within sight. It appeared dark and ominous, resembling a Chinese junk without sails. Angelina shivered at the eerie sounds of moaning that came from within. Three lights were visible in the black hull, one in the forecastle and two more below deck. She could detect no movement.

Finally pulling alongside, the small boat banged against the hull and voices were heard from above. "Who goes there? State your business and be quick about it?"

Steven's voice bellowed in return, "Captain Thompson of his Majesty's Royal Navy, here on personal business with your Captain Wakefield."

Angelina was amazed at the calmness of Steven's voice and manner. How expertly he lied, she mused.

A moment later, the orders to come aboard were called down to them. Steven's last order, "On your best behavior, ladies," brought the sound of instant merriment and feminine laughter from his crew. One by one they made their way up the short flight of steps that hung alongside the ship.

Waiting for them at the top of the steps was a man in his late fifties. Angelina could see he had once been quite handsome, but years of drinking and debauchery had brought his body to a shriveled imitation of his former self, and a horrible almost deathlike quality to his haunted eyes.

Steven saluted the officer smartly, "Captain Thompson at your service, sir."

"Welcome to the *Jersey,* Captain," Captain Wakefield answered. "I see you have brought the merchandise I ordered." He eyed Angelina who stood close to Steven, and added, "And mighty good quality I can see at a glance. Please do me the honor of joining us for a drink before you leave."

"Certainly, sir," Steven answered cordially.

The others of their party disappeared below before Angelina and Steven, accompanied by Captain Wakefield, entered his quarters.

Angelina shivered. So this was the infamous prison ship *Jersey* called "Hell Afloat" by her countrymen, and for good reason. Angelina could easily imagine by the dirty conditions above, the venom and horror of the living conditions below.

The smell of filth and disease penetrated her senses. She breathed in death and despair each time she inhaled. Her skin crawled.

The captain's quarters were dark, having only one lamp to illuminate the interior, and perhaps because of the dimness, appeared to be reasonably clean. Captain Wakefield walked immediately to his desk, took out a bottle of dark liquid and three dirty glasses.

Unceremoniously, he handed Angelina and Steven the glasses and filled all three. Undaunted by the condition of their drinking vessels, Steven downed the drink in one gulp.

Angelina, more wary, hesitantly brought the glass to her lips, but did not drink from it as she watched the Captain down two glassfuls in rapid succession.

After much hinting by Captain Wakefield, Steven finally bid them goodnight and left Angelina and the Captain alone.

Angelina stood in uncomfortable silence, but Wakefield wasted no time. Without a word spoken between them, he began disrobing before her. Now she did take a sip of her drink. Panic began to set in while she thought, *I must have been out of my mind to get involved in this*. Suddenly, Steven's words came back to her, *Keep your wits about you and do not panic. I will be close by.*

Licking her lips nervously and praying her voice would sound calm and alluring, she carefully chose her words, "Captain Wakefield, please correct me if I am wrong, but do we not have all evening?" She lowered her voice seductively, "Surely there is no need for hurry. We would only lose that special satisfaction that prolonged ecstasy can bring." And adding with a promise, "I can do many things for you, sir, and hurrying will bring the merest measure of pleasure that could be in store, I can assure you."

As she spoke, she slipped off her cape, while turning her back for a moment and pulling her dress a notch lower.

Turning back to face him, she was satisfied at the results, for his eyes nearly bulged from their sockets and he gulped audibly, "Lord almighty! It's been a long time since I've had a morsel as lovely as you." Suddenly realizing what she said was probably true, he added with a lecherous grin, "As you wish, my dear."

Forcing herself to finish her drink, she asked coyly, "Shall we have another drink, Captain?"

Hastily and obediently, he refilled their glasses.

Lowering her voice to a whisper, she raised her glass to him, "To the night ahead, Captain, may it hold everything you wish and bring our hearts' desire."

With shaking fingers, Captain Wakefield took the glass from her hand. Placing it on the desk, he roughly pulled her into his arms. Hungrily his lips were on her mouth, forcing her lips to part beneath the pressure of his tongue.

She twisted her head away and whispered shakily, "Easy, Captain," but her words fell on deaf ears.

Captain Wakefield was so long without a woman that he was almost instantly out of control. Her cries of restraint were nonexistent to him. The whole room spun in a haze through his passion-filled eyes.

Tightly, he pressed his body against hers, while leaning her back over the desk. His lips covered her shoulder with short desperate kisses and his hands pulled her dress off one shoulder and began reaching greedily for her breast.

It amazed Angelina that she could remain so calm beneath the onslaught of Wakefield's lovemaking, for his kisses and the touch of his hands stirred her not in the least. Her mind remained clear. Her eyes searched the small room for something, anything she might use as a weapon.

Her hands reached behind her, to prevent his pressing her back all the way, and touched a paper weight. Unnoticed by a mesmerized Wakefield, she grasped it solidly in her hand and as his lips once again found hers, she brought it up high and with all her strength, smashed it into his head. She hit him exactly, but quite accidentally, on the temple above his left ear.

In an instant, he pulled away. His eyes held such confusion and pain that for a moment, she couldn't help feeling a stab of pity for the unsuspecting man. Only a second later, he crumbled in a heap at her feet.

Shaking now, she managed to sit herself in

the only available chair before her knees collapsed. With a sigh of relief, she waited for Steven's return, praying he would come before Captain Wakefield awoke, for she was positive she could never hit him again.

Almost the exact moment she sat, gun shots rang out and loud screams of agony erupted from below deck. A moment later the door to the cabin was smashed open and an enormous marine stood in the doorway, yelling for the Captain. Before the man had a chance to properly take in the situation, he too crumbled before Angelina's eyes and lay unconscious at Steven's feet.

Calmly, Steven leaned against the doorjamb and surveyed the damage. With raised eyebrows and a sly grin, he commented, "I see Captain Wakefield, being no different from all men of your acquaintance, has fallen at your feet. No doubt it was your fatal charm, quite irresistible I can testify."

"No doubt," she replied dryly, but terribly grateful to see him so soon.

"Shall we depart, my dear? Unless of course you find the company of Captain Wakefield preferable to mine."

Smiling, she replied, "Actually sir, the man does possess a certain undeniable charm, but alas, being a lady of breeding, I feel it only correct to allow my companion for the evening to escort me home."

"Before we leave the company of our most hospitable host, perhaps you might be interested in meeting another of his guests."

Angelina had walked toward Steven as they spoke. Now she stood looking silently at his handsome smiling face, with a deep furrow of puzzlement on her brow. Finally she asked, "Steven, what in the world. . . ?" Her sentence remained unfinished when, with Steven's assistance, her brother Jim entered the room.

Her eyes opened wide with shock. Her brother stood beside Steven, ragged clothes, terribly dirty, and so horribly thin, yet he was alive!

"Oh my God, Jim! Jim, my God, you are alive!"

An enormous smile spread across Angelina's mouth as she jumped over the sprawled marine and flung herself upon her brother, crying his name again and again with laughing relief. So anxious was her hugging, and so weak was Jim's condition, that she easily knocked him into Steven and pressed him solidly between the two of them.

"Easy, Angelina," Steven said softly. "Your brother is very weak. Come, help me get him into the boat."

Angelina obeyed for once without a word and together they brought the sick and weakened boy back to *The Savage*.

Chapter 21

Later that night, Angelina was pacing the floor of the cabin. Jim had been seriously injured. Dr. Banard said he would probably never regain the use of his arm.

She had just seen to the cleansing of his wound and had watched as he finally fell into an exhausted but peaceful sleep.

Certainly she felt undying gratitude toward Steven, but the fact remained, he was still a spy. Perhaps he was the man responsible for Jim's horrible imprisonment in the first place. Surely, he would now expect some sort of reward for the release of her brother. Oh, what was she to do? She feared any sign of thankfulness on her part would have him thinking she wanted their relationship to alter, which she definitely did not. She was terribly confused. How should she speak to Steven when she saw him again?

She didn't have long to wait. So intent on

her thoughts was she, that she didn't notice the door open and Steven standing just inside the room.

He grinned when he saw her pacing and the worried frown on her face. He could well guess what she was worried about.

She stopped dead in her tracks and spun about to face him, when she heard, "Is something troubling you, my dear?"

"Steven! I did not hear you enter."

"Obviously," he answered dryly.

He stood watching her, smiling, saying nothing.

His smiling eyes brought her much tribulation, her nerves were stretched taut, and he did nothing to set her mind at rest. Her hands twisted anxiously together while her mind searched for something to say. Finally breaking the long silence between them, she asked, "How did you know where he was?"

He grinned, "The night we boarded *The Savage*, I left you for a time in the care of Dr. Banard and made inquiries." Watching her hands as they continued to move, he purposely misread her uneasiness, "You needn't worry about him so. Dr. Banard reported he is luckier than most. He will keep his arm, although he may not ever regain full use of it. It will take some time, but he will be in good health again. As a matter of fact, in only a few days he will be back with your father."

"You are bringing him home?"

"Not I, my dear, but some members of my crew, along with the other prisoners we took off the *Jersey* tonight. They will leave this ship when we dock two nights hence, somewhere along the Delaware coast."

"Are you letting me go, too?" she asked hopefully.

His lips took on a grim line and he snapped harshly, "You know better than that."

He found himself in an instant rage. So powerful was his fury that it surprised even himself. If he had thought for a moment about the extremity of his emotions, he might have realized he was suffering from rejection.

Secretly, he had hoped the night's work would have brought them close again, but seeing her reaction to him, caused him nothing but pain. He thought angrily, *Good God, she has not even thanked me, and after all I have done!*

"Do I?" she asked nastily, "I am afraid I do not. Why is it I am to be kept a prisoner and yet you let the others go?"

Grimly, he stated, "Madam, you speak as if I were your jailer rather than your husband."

With obvious disgust, she sneered, "You, sir, are no husband of mine! You are a spy. Can I make myself any clearer when I say I do not want you?"

He ignored her question and sarcastically remarked, "Your gratitude for rescuing your brother is quite overpowering."

"Aye, I do not deny, sir, I and my family owe you a debt of gratitude. But I cannot help but wonder, did your evil work place him there in the first place?"

"You, madam, are the most ungrateful and suspicious bitch I have ever had the misfortune to meet."

She flipped her hair and faced him haughtily, "It matters little what you think of me Steven, for you are nothing to me. I only wish to go home."

He bellowed, "Your home is with me!"

"I swear you will be sorry if you force me to stay with you. You will find no solace or peace with me. I promise you the day is not far off when you will wish you had never set eyes on me."

Furiously, he returned, "Madam, I am beginning to fear that the day is already upon us."

In order to visit her brother, Angelina found it necessary to go the length of the ship, down a flight of stairs, and through the men's sleeping quarters. She was always sure to knock loudly on the wall before entering, and the men cheerfully accepted her among them.

On the day her brother left the ship, Angelina spent the whole day with him. After he was taken from the ship, she sadly made her way once again through the men's quarters to the stairs. As she started up the dark passage, she walked into a man. He stood directly before her, barring her way.

She was thinking of her brother and felt no premonition of fear as she excused herself.

There was no reply; the man did not move

aside. Now fear firmly placed its icy grip on her throat. She backed down two steps. Her mind was in a whirl. She was trapped below deck. All the crew were above, dispatching the injured men.

It was so dark, she couldn't see who it was that blocked her way. In a voice that was noticeably shaking, she asked, "Who are you? What do you want?"

An evil snicker was all she received for an answer.

A hand reached out and, before she could scream for help, closed over her mouth. The man spoke not a sound. Even had he, she doubted she would hear him, for her heart pounded hysterically in her ears.

He turned her slightly, pressing her against the wall. His body kept her in place. His lips replaced his hand and held her mouth. She tried to twist her face free, but he pressed her head back until it too was pinned against the wall.

She slapped his face.

He laughed. A hand once again covered her mouth. Buttons popped off her blouse. She felt her chemise tear as his hungry hands groped for her breast.

She clawed his face with her nails.

He only laughed again.

Without thought, she brought her knee up and hit him hard.

He grunted and momentarily released her.

Immediately, she took the opportunity his relaxed hands offered and ran up the stairs.

Quickly, she moved across the deck, ignoring the startled looks of the men and running into the captain's quarters, all the while holding her torn blouse together with shaking fingers.

The door slammed shut behind her. Her face was white with fright, her chest heaved from running, her hair was in wild disarray.

Steven, at his desk, came to his feet immediately upon hearing her enter.

When she saw the surprised look on his face, her fear turned to instant rage. All her sorrow over her brother's leaving and her dislike for her husband erupted into uncontrolled fury.

"You abominable swine. Your crew is much like their master. All here take what they wish, never waiting until an offer is made. I hate you. I never knew what it was to hate, until you came into my life. You whoremonger! Dispoiler of virgins!"

Steven went to her, concern showing clearly in his eyes.

She shoved him away from her, "You bloody bastard. If you treasure your life, you will keep your hands from me!"

"Damnation, woman! Enough of your recriminations." And then finally eyeing her torn blouse, he bellowed, "What happened? Who the hell did this to you?"

She snarled, "I do not know or care. I hate all of you! To me you are all one and the same lecherous animals wanting only one thing, a quick tip of my skirts." Her fury grew wilder with every word she spoke. She faced him with a sneer and remarked sarcastically, as if he were someone she had just met, "And you sir, what do you offer for a quick toss in the sack?" Running her hands over her breasts, she laughed wildly, "Tis quality merchandise you see here. There's only been one other before you. Aye, I know you've heard that one before. I agree, in truth, it does not matter."

She was speaking as if he answered her. Clearly, she was hysterical. "What is that? You wish to see before you pay? Of course, of course, I quite understand. Very well, tell me what you think it's worth to you."

As she spoke, she tore at her ripped blouse, pulled it off and threw it with the rest of her clothes all around the room. Naked now, she stood with her hands on her hips, and asked, "Is it to your liking, sir?"

He swallowed hard, not answering, his voice lost in a sudden flood of desire. Forcibly, he kept his hands at his side.

She didn't miss the passion flaming to life in his eyes, and taunted, "Well, is it?"

Still he said nothing.

"Come now, surely this must be worth something," she sneered, while cupping a breast and lifting it for his view.

He walked to her, his arms reaching to console her. "Angelina, calm yourself. Do not do this."

She leaped away as he reached for her and flung herself upon the bed, sliding quickly beneath the sheet.

Following her, he sat on the bed. Gently he gathered her stiff form into the warm circle of his arms. Rocking her as if she were a child, he spoke softly into her hair, "Angelina, tell me who did this to you."

She tried to pull away. He held her still.

"I will not cry, Steven. Do not be kind to me. I mean to hate you."

He chuckled.

"And do not laugh, damn it," she swung her hand up to strike him.

He grasped her hand and brought it to his lips, kissing it tenderly.

His kindness was her undoing, and suddenly, a flood of tears erupted. It was through choking sobs that she finally managed to tell him what had happened.

Early the next morning, all the crew were assembled on deck. Steven, with Angelina at his side, called for the man responsible for abusing his wife to step forward.

No one moved.

In the gentle Caribbean breezes a rope swung menacingly from the yardarm as Steven called, "Quartermaster, make ready your cat-o-nine. Today the bloody coward will get his just reward."

Still no one moved.

"The one I look for should have marks running down the side of his face."

All the men looked at one another. Each in turn, saw the man with the scratch marks. Slowly, the crowd separated, leaving the man to stand alone.

"Step forward, Briggs," Steven ordered.

The man moved haltingly toward Steven and Angelina. Finally he grinned, "Capt'n sir, I meant her no harm. The lady misunderstood."

"Aye Briggs, but I did not. Bind his hands," he ordered. "After this day, seaman, you will think better of touching another's wife."

Two men tied the burly seaman's hands before him. The rope that hung from the sail's yard was tied through his bindings and he was lifted up until his feet left the deck.

The quartermaster waited only for Steven's signal to begin. Steven called out, "Twenty lashes, Mr. Carson," and it began.

Angelina had never seen a whipping before, and she gasped at the horrible punishment. The leather throngs shrilled through the air and made contact with the man's bare back. The first attack of the whip caused his skin to split. His heart rending scream of agony tore through her and she couldn't prevent a shiver of horror. Today, she felt none of the fury of last night and Steven had to force her to stand at his side. She trembled, grabbing hold of the railing until her knuckles turned white.

After the fourth lash, his back was a bloody pulp and as the whip contacted again and again, his blood and pieces of his flesh left his back and splattered the quartermaster and a few others who stood by.

Angelina gagged, and then moaned, swaying slightly as everything began to spin before her eyes.

Steven, standing close by, reached his arm out to support her and whispered, "Steady."

In a blur, she watched the whip continue its duty. She lost count. It must be twenty by now. She couldn't bear any more. She turned to Steven and groaned, "Stop it, stop it now."

Steven, concerned for her suffering, shouted, "Enough!" Immediately, the unconscious man was cut down and a bucket of sea water thrown on his bleeding back.

Regaining consciousness, he was dragged to stand before Angelina. "Due to my wife's gentle heart, you have received only half your just punishment. In the future, were I you, I would not venture to lay my eyes on her again. For I have not the kindness she possesses, and it is I you shall answer to if there be a next time. Mr. Johnson, dismiss the men."

Steven escorted her back to the cabin. She was badly shaken and lay trembling on the bed. She looked at Steven and wondered at his sensitivities. She had seen him as tender as a woman, yet now he showed not the slightest care for the suffering he had just rendered.

Just as he was about to go back on deck, he spoke, "I fear, madam, it will be necessary in the future for you to remain in your cabin and venture out only when I am free to escort you."

"Why?"

"It seems the startling effect you have on

certain members of my crew has begun to dangerously lower their morale. If I do not wish full-fledged mutiny on my hands, I must take proper precautions. Since I cannot dispose of everyone who has improper intentions toward you, I am afraid I must keep you somewhat secluded."

She sat up, suddenly herself again, "You are mad! You lead a pack of wild animals, and I am made to suffer for it? I cannot remain in this stifling cabin all day. I need . . ."

"I am sorry," he interrupted, "I have decided. It is done."

Depositing a jewel encrusted dagger on the bed, he ordered, "In the future, keep this with you." And then he left the room.

Chapter 22

Nearly a week had passed since Jim left the ship. Angelina sat alone in the cabin feeling extremely sorry for herself. She wondered what was to become of her? What would the future hold for her? Would she always be at her husband's mercy?

She was to the point where she couldn't take this forced confinement any longer; she was getting out of this room, and she cared not at all whether Steven liked it or not.

Suddenly, she found herself thrown to the floor by the force of a gigantic explosion. Before she could rise, she heard another and then another. Finally she managed to pull herself to her feet, but the shuddering and shaking of the ship knocked her to the desk and back again to the bed.

Even before she was able to reach the door, she heard gun shots and the torturous screams of dying men. A moment later, something thumped alongside. Probably another ship, she reasoned. Dozens of footsteps could be heard moving about on deck.

The cabin door flew open and the cabin boy, Jeremy, yelled with a look of terror while throwing her a bundle, "We've been attacked, Miss. Capt'n says stay put and change out of those clothes."

In a panic, she stripped down and changed into a pair of pants and a white shirt as fast as her shaking fingers allowed. Her hands trembled so badly, she could barely secure the buttons of her clothes.

She was terrified. If Steven had asked her to change, it must mean he thought they had no chance of winning this battle and she would probably need something to disguise herself. The pants and shirt did little to hide the fact that she was a woman, and her hair hung to her waist as there was no way to bind it.

Suddenly, in the doorway stood a tall, handsome man. His skin was tanned golden brown, his hair bleached by many hours in the sun to near white. His dark blue eyes held a merry twinkle, as if he had just accomplished something he had enjoyed tremendously. He reminded her of a Viking.

Angelina gasped at the intrusion of the stranger. If this man was a pirate, then she had been sadly mistaken in her impressions of what a pirate should look like.

His hat sat at a jaunty angle. In its brim was a large red plume. He wore a brown leather jerkin and under it a full sleeved white shirt which hung open to his waist, baring his tanned smooth chest.

He looked her over appreciatively. His eyes glowed and his mouth broke into a brilliant smile. "What have we here? A pretty piece of pastry indeed."

Angelina had no opportunity to answer, for behind the blonde man stood Steven, his dark face contorted with murderous rage.

The man noticed Angelina's glance and turned swiftly. Angelina watched in amazement as Steven remained for a long moment in the doorway. The expression of hatred that marred his face did not alter. Yet he did nothing but stand there.

Finally, the blonde giant laughed heartily, "Do come in Captain. No harm shall befall you or your lovely passenger."

Steven moved slowly through the doorway and into the tiny room. Now Angelina could see the reason for his hesitation, for behind him stood a short burly man. The man was the epitome of anyone's idea of what a pirate should look like—thick ugly lips beneath a nose that was many times broken. He was missing an eye and the uncovered socket gleamed pink, moist, and empty. A wide scar ran the length of his face from his temple to his chin and pulled at the skin, distorting his whole face and pulling his features down and to the left. In his hand he held a cutlass which he pressed none too gently into Steven's back.

Steven showed not the slightest trace of

fear as he addressed the pirate. "Have I the honor, sir, of addressing Adam Blake?"

"You have," the blonde man replied.

"Your reputation has preceded you, sir."

"What are you about, Captain? Let me see your log and cargo manifold."

As Steven handed the papers from his desk to the pirate, he replied, "I was enroute to Santa Louisa. My only cargo is rare indeed. The daughter of James Barton, one of the richest men in the Virginia Colony. I estimate her worth at one-hundred-thousand pounds." He added cockily, "And I am positive, because of the man's regard for his only girl child, to get it."

Angelina gasped in astonishment.

Adam Blake eyed her and asked wryly, "Does the wench not know she has been kidnapped?"

"Aye, sir, it was only the amount of the ransom of which she was ignorant."

"There is a rule among us, Captain, that all bounty is shared," Adam Blake remarked as he looked Angelina over with an appraising eye. "She should be brought on deck so all may have a turn."

"Nay, sir. Were it any other bounty, I'd agree, but this is a special case. Her father wants her true, but she is promised to a young rich Lord and she must remain undamaged. If she be touched, we might as well rid ourselves of her now, for her father being peculiar about such things, would not pay a copper penny."

After a long hesitation, Adam Blake relented, "Very well, no one shall touch her," and turning to the other pirate, "Hennings, tell no one she is aboard. We will leave this matter in Captain Jack's hands."

Turning to Steven, he stated, "You, Captain, along with half your crew, shall sail with me. Come along."

Angelina uttered a strangled sound as fear plainly showed in her eyes.

Adam Blake grinned, "Have no fear, Mistress Barton. A guard will be posted at your door. You will remain unharmed, at least for the time being."

Angelina watched as the men left the cabin. The short ugly man leered while Steven ignored her and Adam Blake bowed extravagantly. "Good day, mistress. We dock in two days in Port Royal."

Two long days of forced seclusion passed slowly for Angelina. There was barely a moment during each day that she didn't worry of the outcome of the journey. Could Steven protect her? Would she continue to be safe after they made port? Obviously, they were headed for a pirate's den. What would they find there?

On the morning of the third day, Angelina stood before the large windows of the Captain's quarters, and watched an island form out of the blue horizon. As they approached Port Royal, she could see many small white buildings dotting the dark green hilly landscape. Once *The Savage* had anchored, perhaps a hundred yards from shore, there was a knock at her door.

Jeremy peeked his head in and asked her to come along, while passing her a large brimmed hat saying she might find some use for it.

Angelina, already dressed as a boy, put the hat on and forced her long hair up inside. She peered into the tall mirror in the corner of the room. Instinctively, Angelina knew she should try, at least for the time being, to appear as unattractive as possible.

Hurriedly, she discarded the belt and pulled the white full shirt from the knee length breeches she wore. She was only slightly satisfied at her appearance for she knew if a breeze should move the fabric, there'd be no denying the fact that she was a woman, but there was no help for it.

The moment she came on deck, a small boat banged against the hull and she was handed down into the dinghy. In it rode Adam Blake, Hennings, and Steven, plus a crew of four men at the oars. None of the men, including Steven, paid her the slightest heed as they proceeded about the business of getting the boat to the sandy beach.

Angelina breathed deeply of the sweet warm air. The sun beat down, warming her through, and its rays bounced blindingly off the turquoise water. She had never seen water so brilliantly clear before. Looking over the side of the boat, she was amazed that she could see all the way to the white sandy bottom.

She was helped from the dinghy when it ran aground and made to walk behind Steven and Adam Blake as Hennings and most of the men followed.

The beach was quiet, but not completely empty of people. Yet the few men who worked unloading the small boats never gave them a second look. All along the beach stood large crates and from behind her, Angelina could see more small boats loaded with similar crates being brought to the island.

Even though it was still early, the sand was surprisingly hot beneath her feet to the point of nearly burning. Past the hot sand were sharp rocks. The men in their boots gave not the slighest notice as Angelina stumbled painfully along in her bare feet.

At last, gratefully, came the smooth dampness of grass as they walked beneath large fragrant trees. The air suddenly filled with the heavy scent of sweet flowers. Truly, were it not for the fact that the inhabitants of this island were thieves, and probably murderers, it would have been a perfect place.

Finally, they reached a large house and entered. Angelina realized that once this had been a beautiful home, for the sculptured woodwork and filigree railings to the wide wooden steps were still intact. Yet the house was a shambles. It was dark and smelled of stale whiskey. Paint was peeling from the walls. Obviously, there had been a fight for furniture had been turned over and left in place. Pictures hung askew and a variety of holes dotted the dirty walls.

Carefully, she stepped over empty broken bottles of rum as they made their way to a large room off the center hall.

Immediately upon entering, Adam Blake yelled out, "Jack, you black hearted whore's son, where are you?"

A few men lay on the floor, one or two slumped in their chairs over the table. The sound of Blake's voice brought their heads up and they looked at him with sleep filled eyes.

"Hold your arse, Blake. Jack's in bed enjoying a wench. Bedamned, what the hell is all the noise about?"

Steven glanced sideways at Angelina, surprised that the coarse language bothered her not a bit.

Suddenly, a huge fat man appeared in the doorway and bellowed, "What the blasted hell is all the uproar. Can't a poor man get some sleep in this rat-infested whore house. Damnation, it's you, Blake. What hellish cause 'as brought you back so soon? It's been nigh to a week since I saw your ugly face."

"Jack," Blake laughed good-naturedly, "you scurvy swine, if you should ever show yourself in the morning to be of good humor, I'll know then I've died and gone to heaven."

"Blake, you roguish bloody, beggar, if you find my maggoty black soul in heaven, you'll know I fought St. Peter and won. What have you here?"

Blake walked to the fat man and the two talked for a brief moment. A minute later the two men sat themselves at the table and poured themselves tankards of warm flat beer, leaving Steven and Angelina to stand.

"So," Jack started while glaring at Steven, "you've brought us a prize, have you? Tell me why I should let you live and not put another in your place. Surely anyone could do as well."

"You're mistaken, Captain Jack, if you think anyone could do this particular job. You see, her father knows me and although by now he probably wishes me dead, he knows she will be safe with me, at least for the time being. No other would be trusted not to harm her and I mean what I say, she must remain untouched. Of course, if you've a mind, kill the wench and be done with it, but if you're the man I believe you to be, we shall make a handsome deal, very handsome indeed."

Jack growled, obviously unimpressed, "How much are you asking for her?"

Steven smiled, knowing the man's greed would bring him around, and answered nonchalantly, "One hundred thousand pounds," and then grinning wickedly, and bestowing on Angelina an evil leer, he finished, "and worth every penny I might add, sir."

"Bah! You're daft man. No one is worth that much."

Steven laughed knowingly, "Aye Jack, I quite agree. To us she's worth little more than a farthing, but lucky for us her father believes differently. She is destined to make a great match, which would give her father all the prestige he desires."

"For us you say? Are you thinking then to share the bounty?"

"If I be accepted in your community sir, I would be pleased to share my bounty."

Jack laughed in ridicule, his voice lifting a few degrees as he mocked Steven, "Would you indeed, sir? Take heed Spencer, we take no pantywaists in our lot. A man has to prove himself if he's to be accepted here."

"I quite understand, sir."

"Do you now?" he mocked and called out, "Josh, give gentleman Spencer here a taste of what's meant by belonging. If you pass the test, gent, then we'll see," and finishing with an evil laugh, he repeated, "we'll see."

Angelina watched as the man called Josh brought himself up from a lounging position from one of the many dirty chairs that cluttered the room. He was smaller than Steven, but his movements showed him to be as graceful and lightfooted as a dancer. She felt a moment's panic as she saw the man gingerly draw his cutlass and slash it quickly and precisely into the empty air before him.

Captain Jack chuckled, "Someone throw the gent a blade," as he watched the imposing agile movements of his comrade.

Angelina slipped behind a chair near the wall while the others in the room moved not a muscle out of harm's way. Each man's face glowed cheerfully at the approaching deadly sport.

Steven caught and held the sharp cutlass

as Blake threw his own weapon toward him. Patiently, showing not a sign of anxiety, Steven waited as Josh slowly approached him.

A sheen of nervous perspiration covered Angelina as she realized her life also depended on Steven's winning. She daren't look away. Her heart pounded with terror; her eyes burned as they focused and held on the two men.

Chapter 23

They met in the center of the room. All about them were furniture and men. Anything could trip either of them, and a fall could prove fatal.

Each man raised his weapon in a salute and suddenly, the room rang out with the thunderous sounds of metal striking against metal. Sometimes they were only inches apart as they moved and sparred at one another. The room was silent but for the heavy breathing of the two combatants.

Angelina knew nothing of Steven's capabilities as a swordsman, and was relieved to see he was surprisingly knowledgeable and handled himself well. Yet the smaller man was much quicker and more deft. His skill was obvious as he swiftly struck out and contacted his weapon to Steven's arm. Steven grunted and the watching men cheered. Again they stalked each other.

The men, as if animals scenting blood, yelled for the kill. Neither man seemed to notice as their faces remained motionless and each steadily surveyed the other.

Josh lunged at his injured prey but Steven, far from finished, raised his cutlass to offset the vicious blow. The defective weapon snapped at the force of the blow. All that remained in Steven's hand was the handle, and a blunt blade of no more than six inches.

Angelina felt faint. The room began to spin before her. Shaking her head as if to clear it, she forced herself to continue watching.

Josh, cocky and arrogant, gave a short dance before going for the kill. The men roared their approval. Steven's face was grim and expectant.

Finally, screaming out a war cry, Josh lunged for the last time. His cutlass sliced at the air in front of Steven. Stepping quickly to his left, Steven avoided the heaviest part of the blow and grunted once more as the blade cut deeply into his right arm.

Josh, intent on ending the unequal battle, didn't retreat and stalk again, but continued his pursuit just slightly off balance. He swung once more, intending to finish the job. Steven, in his endeavor to back away from the ferocious swinging, fell over a chair. Josh brought his weapon over his head to gain momentum.

Angelina smothered a scream with her hand and forced her eyes to watch. The force of the blade would split Steven's skull in two.

All was lost.

Just before Josh brought the thirsty blade crashing upon Steven's skull, Steven fell to the floor directly in front of the man, and plunged his broken cutlass up and into Josh's surprised belly.

Still holding his weapon over his head, the pirate stared down in apparent amazement at the hilt of the broken weapon as it protruded grotesquely from his abdomen. Finally, the pirate's cutlass clattered noisily to the floor behind him and he slowly followed.

All remained silent for what seemed like an eternity. Angelina now realized as she gulped for air, she must have been holding her breath almost the entire time.

Steven, with both arms bleeding, reached forward and took the dead man's cutlass. Using it as if it were a cane, he came stiffly to his feet. His face white, his breathing harsh, he asked, "Well Captain, what say you? Do I pass your test?"

He stood for a long moment as two puddles of blood formed on the floor beneath his wounds.

Captain Jack smiled cheerfully, not the least upset that this stranger had just killed one of his better men. "Aye, gent, that you have. It'll be as you say. The wench goes untouched and when we receive the ransom, you become one of us."

The men in the room roared once again, their approval apparent at Captain Jack's justice. He motioned to one of them, "Show the gent and his property one of the rooms upstairs." And to Angelina, he remarked, "Dress his wounds carefully and see to it they do not fester, for in the tropics it be not so easy to heal. If he should yet die, you will become our whore. Believe what I say lassie, there's not a man here that wouldn't like to have you."

Angelina shuddered with disgust and fear while the men laughed at her obvious horror.

At last, in the privacy of their room, she waited only until the door closed behind them before bombarding Steven with a barrage of questions. What were they to do? How could they ever manage to escape? What was he planning?

"Easy, easy, love," Steven sighed with a smile. "I've not thought it through yet. I was merely stalling for time." When he saw her eyes grow huge with fright, he hastened to add, "Do not fear so, Angelina. A plan will form and we will be gone from here soon."

Helping him undress, she began to rip his shirt to make bandages for his arms. After a few minutes, she remarked smartly, "I fear you are indeed brave, but it was with my life I noticed, and I do not take it kindly, sir. 'Kill the wench' you said; suppose he had taken you up on your generous offer?"

"Nay Angelina, his greed is too great."

"Lucky for me, you guessed correctly." As she worked, she continued, "You amaze me, Steven. Caught as we are, in the midst of murderers and thieves, and you appear as if you possess no fear."

"Nay, love, I would be a fool if I possessed no fear, but to display it would make me a far greater one. At the first show of weakness, like a pack of jackals, our friends downstairs would set upon and devour us." Lowering his voice meaningfully, he continued, "We must bide our time and take the first opportunity offered, if there be one. It must be soon, for it's not only you and I that must be contended with, but I fear greatly for my men. Imprisoned on *The Savage*, they will be left as animals to wallow in their own feces. You cannot imagine what a ship's hole can become when the men are left unattended."

While they spoke, she had pushed Steven toward the bed and now sat before him in the room's only chair. Looking around her, she could see the room was tiny and contained only an alarmingly small bed, a chest and a chair.

But being a corner room, it held two windows, and although it was still hours till midday, the sun beat down blindingly and unmercifully. Yet the tiny room remained comfortably cool due to the cross ventilation.

The bed Steven sat upon was covered with grimy gray linens which matched the torn curtains and the dingy floor. The air held the gagging odor of unwashed bodies mixed liberally with the pungent scent of stale whiskey.

Looking around in despair, she realized there was no water or medicine with which to clean and dress his wounds.

Suddenly a knock at the door brought her to her feet. She opened it and was amazed to find Adam Blake standing at the doorway, arms laden with medical supplies and water.

"Oh, Captain Blake," she smiled happily, "how wonderful. I was just now wondering what I should do. You can see for yourself there is nothing here with which to clean and dress his wounds."

"Aye, Mistress Barton, I have brought you salves and fresh linen for bandages. Also some water for cleaning."

"Oh Captain, you should not have troubled yourself to bring these supplies in person."

"Believe me, 'tis no trouble," he returned and added, "be there anything more you need?"

"Aye, Captain, the bed's linen is abominable; also I fear the feather tick beneath it."

"Fear not, I shall send clean linen." And handing her a bottle he took from his jacket pocket, he continued, "Use some of this whiskey in the water. It is useful for cleaning open wounds. I'll be gone now. If you need anything more, just call out."

And then, unbelievably, he took Angelina's hand and brought it to his lips, and bowing formally as if he were a true gentleman, he left her with a kindly smile.

Angelina brought the armful of supplies to the bed and put them down. Once again, seated in the chair opposite Steven, she poured a liberal amount of whiskey into the pitcher of water and, with a clean cloth, began to wash the deep cuts.

Steven was unusually silent. Even while Captain Blake had been in the room, the only conversation had been between the blonde man and Angelina.

At last he stared up inquisitively into Steven's blazing eyes. Surprised at his thundrous raging look, she jumped slightly, "What is it?"

He didn't answer, but continued to give her a muderous gaze.

Finally, she asked, "Whatever is the matter with you, Steven? Your silent rage grates on the nerves. What is wrong?"

"I fear I cannot take to your Captain Blake as easily as you."

"My Captain Blake? What nonsense! Because I spoke kindly to the man and was thankful for his generosity? This causes you anger? Have sense, man, should I have turned him away then?"

"Nay, but you needn't have been so overly courteous. Nor need you have smiled quite so brilliantly. I do not want you to speak with him. I easily read the look in his eyes when he watches you. He wants you, be sure."

Fixing him with a steely look of determination, she answered, "But for you, I would not be here in the first place. Need I remind you, I am my own person and will not abide being told what I may or may not do, nor to whom I may or may not speak. I will, as always, do exactly as I wish."

He was about to answer in like, when another knock sounded on the door. When she answered she was surprised at the supplies that were brought in. Four men holding linens and clothing filed past her, each depositing their load upon the chest. And then lastly, three of them pushed a large brass hip-bath into the room. Angelina's eyes widened with glee. She hadn't bathed for days.

Silently, the men began to fill the tub, while another brought a fresh feather tick. Finally finished, one of the men spoke, "Captain Blake's compliments, miss." Quickly he moved from the room, leaving a raging Steven and a smiling Angelina alone.

Angelina was almost happy and much less fearful, having found a friend. She smiled delightedly as she sorted the bed linen and fresh clothing for Steven and herself.

He sat in the chair as she removed the old tick and replaced it with a new one, and then covered it with fresh linen. Adam Blake had even thought of pillow casings.

Steven pulled on a clean shirt and wearily lay down.

Angelina stood at the foot of the bed, unsure of what to do.

Steven saw the confusion in her eyes and remarked, "Take your bath, Angelina, the water cools."

There was no way she could bathe in privacy unless he left the room, and he showed no sign of stirring from his comfortable bed.

"Would you turn away?" she asked hesitantly.

"Nay, Angelina, you ask too much."

Finally, she shrugged. The water proving too much a temptation to refuse, she unbuttoned her shirt and slipped out of her pants. Turning her back to him, she stepped into the tub and sat.

His eyes hungrily watched her every movement, greedily taking in her silken golden body. He felt himself aroused yet he was too tired at the moment to do anything about it, even had she been willing.

She bathed silently, ignoring his piercing eyes, enjoying the warm soapy water as it brushed against her skin. At last refreshed and clean, she stepped from the tub, dried herself with a linen cloth, and dressed in an off-the-shoulder blouse of pink and a full bright red skirt. Her waist length hair hung loose as she had no way of tying it up.

It was some time after she bathed before a man knocked at the door and brought in a tray of food. Adam Blake followed close behind. When he saw Angelina who was for the first time dressed as a woman, his eyes widened with pleasure and he extended his hand in greeting.

"Mistress Barton," he smiled, while bringing her hand to his lips, "you are splendid."

He held her hand to his mouth just a touch too long and Angelina pulled back shyly, "Thank you, Captain Blake. I am eternally grateful."

Steven stiffened. Even when he had saved her brother's life, she had not extended him such heartfelt thanks. Yet for a bath . . . Bah women, a fickle lot. All it took was a show of pretty manners to turn their heads.

Adam Blake smiled and glanced toward Steven, who was pretending to sleep. "It will not do for him to share your bed."

Primly, she replied, "He shall not, sir. The old tick shall serve him well."

He took Angelina's arm and brought her to the other side of the room. "Although I've done what I could to see to your comfort, I fear I cannot prevent Captain Jack's orders. You are required to help with the cooking and the serving as long as you're here, starting tonight. Please believe I wish it were not so. No one as beautiful and delicate as you should be made to do menial labor."

Softly, she whispered in return, "Captain Blake, you have done much for me; I and my father shall be eternally grateful. Do not distress yourself. I am not totally ignorant of work."

"Perhaps you would care for a stroll along the beach before you must begin."

"I think not, Captain," she smiled, "I believe I shall rest for a mite."

"Very well, I shall see you then at dinner."

Steven appeared to be asleep. She eyed the bed enviously. She was tired. The nervous strain and fear she had felt all morning had left her exhausted. Quietly, she moved to the unused side of the bed, lay down, and was soon asleep.

She awoke sometime later to find Steven's

arms around her, her head nuzzled comfortably on his shoulder, and his fingers tenderly stroking her cheek. His eyes were gentle and warm, his voice soft as he spoke, "Take care, Angelina. He is not your friend."

Chapter 24

Later that afternoon, Angelina was led by a young kitchen maid downstairs and into the large kitchen at the back of the house. The room was a bustle of activity. A woman of gargantuan proportions bellowed out orders to two girls who ran wildly about to do her bidding.

As Angelina entered the cook's domain, the woman looked her over with apparent disgust. "What is this? More of Captain Jack's ideas? He brings me the most useless pieces of fluff and with this," she shrugged a fat shoulder, while including the two girls and Angelina in the same category, "I'm to put out three meals a day."

Angelina smiled kindly at the gruff woman, "Madam, I may look a piece of fluff, but I can do my share and more, believe what I say."

"Huf, a lady yet, lord a'mighty, what's this place coming to? I'll wager you've never been in a kitchen before, never mind getting those lily white hands of yours tarnished with honest labor."

"Forgive me madam, but as yet I've seen nothing on this island remotely resembling honest labor."

The cook laughed heartily, "Right you are, lassie. Move your arse now and be quick about it. There's much to be done."

By the time dinner was ready and served to the dozen or so men in the dining room, Angelina was too tired to eat.

Amazingly, as she helped serve the dinner, no one accosted her, and except for an occasional slap to her bottom, the men gave her no trouble.

Steven sat at the table, eating little as he watched Angelina going about her work. In his lap, rested a cocked pistol.

After dinner, she ran to and fro, quickly depositing tankards of ale and rum before the men. Now, as they sat deep in their drinks, the atmosphere became more rowdy. Two of the pirates called for the young girls to join them and they were pulled to sit on the men's laps. Each of the girls silently endured much handling and dared say not a word of objection as to their treatment.

Hennings spied Angelina as she came from the kitchen bearing a tray loaded with tankards of ale. As she passed him, his hand reached out and grasped her arm, knocking the heavy tray to the floor with much splashing and clanging, as he pulled her to sit upon his lap.

He laughed as his hand grabbed at her breast, "Lassie, you are a mite clumsy, but you more than make up for it in comeliness."

Steven took the gun in hand and aimed it at the unsuspecting pirate's belly beneath the table.

Hennings laughed again as Angelina fought to rid his hands from her. "Look a'here, mateys. We've caught ourselves a feisty beauty. I for one would gladly give my share of the ransom for an hour with the lovely lass. What say you, mates?"

Most of the men sitting around the table nodded their agreement to his proposal. One in particular asked, "Aye Hennings, mayhaps we draw lots to see who has first go with her? I for one would give my next bounty to deflower her."

Hennings, with one steely arm around Angelina's waist, was now trying to put his hand under her blouse while she was wildly pushing away his hands as she attempted to get off his lap.

Steven stood, pistol cocked and aimed at Hennings' chest. But before he was noticed, Blake was up, cutlass drawn, leaning across the table. The heavy shining blade pressed menacingly against Hennings' chest, causing a small red stain to appear on his dirty shirt.

Angelina jumped free as his hands fell to his sides.

"Easy, Blake," Hennings grinned tightly, "I was just having a spot of fun. No need for you to interfere."

Blake growled, "Have it then with another, my friend. This lady is worth more than you'll ever see in your life time and I for one will not lose my share for your sport."

Angelina disappeared into the kitchen and stayed there for the remainder of the evening.

After her work was finished for the night, she walked to the back door for a breath of air. She could hear the sound of rowdy laughter coming from the dining room. The men were still drinking and getting louder by the moment.

She breathed a sigh of relief as she stepped outside. Leaning against the building, she enjoyed the cool island breezes as they caressed her sweaty skin. It had been unbearably hot in the kitchen and she was not anxious to leave the cooling evening air.

Suddenly from out of the shadows, came a huge figure. She jumped, stifling a scream.

Blake's face came within the light of the kitchen doorway. "Fear not, Mistress Barton," he smiled, "no harm shall befall you." He stood companionably near her and, after a few moments, he inquired, "Tis a beautiful night, are you too tired for a walk on the beach?"

She hesitated, about to refuse.

"I assure you, you will be safe with me."

She smiled prettily. He was forever thinking of her comfort and safety. She couldn't help but like him. "Indeed sir, I would enjoy a walk on the beach."

As they strolled on the beach, Steven followed, watching, keeping them always within sight.

Adam Blake spoke, "Forgive me, Mistress Barton, for what I said tonight. Nothing else would have swayed the men to my side."

"I quite understand, Captain Blake. Worry of it no more."

They talked in friendly conversation for some time before he turned and they retraced their steps.

As they returned to the house, a sudden light brought their attention to a figure beneath a tree. Steven lounged against the tree's base, lighting a pipe.

Blake chuckled at her side, "I see your watchdog is still on duty."

She didn't answer him, but instead offered him her hand, "Captain Blake, indeed I am fortunate to have you for a friend. The hour is late so I will bid you good night."

Taking her hand and bringing it to his lips, his mouth lingered over it. It was a long time before he released her and then whispered, "Good night, Mistress, till the morrow."

She walked to Steven and accompanied him to their room. Ignoring his presence as he pushed the bolt in place, she stripped off her clothes and pulled a thin chemise over her head.

Turning to watch, he greedily admired his wife's naked form and frowned as the chemise slipped over her. But the garment offered her little cover for it was of a material so thin as to appear totally transparent.

Steven smiled, "There be no need in this climate to dress for bed."

Angelina faced him and snarled, "Take a good look, you strutting ass, for that is all you will take. I do not relish being spied upon."

Turning her back to him, she began to viciously brush her hair. She hated him, more so each day that she was forced to endure his company. Life had given her one blow on another since she had met him.

He chuckled, "Are you upset?"

"Upset? Me?" and she continued sarcastically, "pray tell sir, what could have upset me? Merely because I was kidnapped by you. Bitten by snakes. Offered for ransom by pirates, and made to serve them. Plus mauled by two men in sight of a week. What a pittance! 'Tis nothing at all. Were it not for the kindness of Captain Blake, I'd not have even the slightest comfort."

Coldly, he warned, "The man is sly and as cunning as a fox. He wants you, make no mistake about it. His plan is to have you trust him."

"And that I do," she sneered. "He does not attempt to touch me, which is more than I can say for you since our first meeting. He does not force himself on me."

"And did I force you, madam?" he growled, in growing anger, "I remember a willing wife."

She ignored his building anger. "He is a gentleman. He protected me from Hennings' maulings tonight, while you lifted nary a finger."

"Enough!" he bellowed, "I grow weary of hearing of the man's sterling qualities."

He stripped off his own clothes, got into bed and turned his back to her.

She too, after a hearty beating of her pillow, turned her back.

Chapter 25

It was after breakfast on the following day that Steven dragged an unwilling Angelina with him as he walked down the hot sandy beach. The sun glared blindingly off the clear water and white beach, and she shaded her face with her hand to relieve the sharp pain it brought to her eyes. Silently, she walked by his side until they approached one of the small boats.

"Get in," he ordered.

She obeyed and together he rowed them to *The Savage*. Work was being done aboard. During the battle, the main mast had been damaged and its sail destroyed. Some of the men worked on the repairs while many armed guards watched over them.

Steven's first mate appeared to be in charge of the workers. Angelina stayed at the railing while Steven walked to the man and spoke for a moment. Pointing to the mast, he was obviously discussing the repairs.

Steven finished with, "Tonight. It matters little if the work be done or not. The longer we wait, the weaker the men and the more dangerous it becomes for my wife."

Johnson nodded.

That night was much the same as the previous evening. Angelina worked until the kitchen closed and her muscles ached. Finishing at last, she went up the back stairs to her room. Steven, watching from outside the kitchen, soon followed.

"Where be your friend tonight?" Steven inquired as she entered.

She ignored his question. Turning her back to him, she began to change for bed.

Purposely, he waited until she was naked, smiling at his deviousness, before he told her, "There is no need for you to wear that chemise tonight, for neither of us will find much rest 'till the morrow."

Misunderstanding him, she stated snidely, "Perhaps you think you can sway me with your charming manners to join you for a few moments of pleasure in bed. Make no mistake, sir, you could not be further from the truth."

As she turned away and pulled the garment over her head, he laughed, "I fear our thoughts are not running in the same direction. Although I'd be most happy to pleasure you tonight, that is not what I have in mind. Nay, it appears we must leave our charming home and I fear it must be tonight."

It was late into the night before the sounds of voices from below ceased, and still he waited. Finally he walked to the window and looked down to the kitchen roof while whispering, "Come, it is time. When I get outside, lower yourself into my arms. Silently now."

Soundlessly, he swung himself through the window and stepped down on the roof. Angelina, with Steven's help, followed. When she joined him, he jumped from the low roof. Angelina sat and turned herself. Hanging from the roof, Steven placed his hands around her waist and lowered her to the ground.

A few men sat on the steps of the house talking low. Steven pulled Angelina back into the shadow of the overhanging roof. Slowly and silently, they edged themselves along the side of the building and around the corner. Suddenly, she was being dragged almost off her feet and into the air as Steven ran pulling her along behind him toward the thick tropical foliage that grew close to the back of the house.

It seemed to take forever for them to move through the dense growth, but finally they emerged well down the beach, almost directly before the small boat they had used that morning.

She was gasping for air as she attempted to get into the boat. He pulled her back, "Not that way, love. Tonight we swim. A boat can be easily seen from *The Savage*."

They slipped quietly into the dark cool

water. With slow gentle strides, they made the short trip to the anchored ship in silence.

When they reached the ship, Steven caught a line that hung over the side and bade Angelina to hold fast, promising to return as soon as all was clear.

Holding the heavy cutlass between his teeth for fear it would clang against the hull as he moved, he shinnied up the rope. Slowly, he brought his head above the deck and peered through the darkness for the guards.

A man stood with his back to him, talking to another who leaned comfortably against the repaired main mast.

Quickly he moved down the rope as one of the men walked toward him. Suddenly a thin stream of water flowed past, missing him by a mere six inches.

Angelina nearly giggled out loud as she watched the reason for Steven's hasty scramble.

Steven waited for the man to finish and leave. When he dared to look again, he saw one of the guards sitting at his right, perhaps ten feet away. The guard leaned back against a pile of tarpaulin, making himself comfortable while the other circled the deck.

Steven waited and watched for the man to circle again. When he was once again on the far side of the ship, Steven moved up the rope and pulled himself over the railing. Crouching behind a large crate, he waited for the guard to pass him. When the man walked past Steven, he reached out and hit him on the head with the handle of his cutlass.

The man groaned softly and sank to his knees. Steven hit him again, and caught his limp body before it fell. Soundlessly, he laid the man down and, taking his hat, continued the man's patrol. When his course took him behind the resting man, he did the same to him.

Coming back to the railing, he quickly pulled the rope and Angelina aboard.

She was shivering from the cold and her teeth chattered as she asked, "Are you all right?"

"Aye, love, go to our cabin and warm yourself. My men are still locked below and I must see to them. I'll join you later."

Quickly she obeyed while Steven went below.

Soon orders were whispered and relayed to cut the forward cable. One of the men lifted an ax and severed the thick rope. The ship began to swing into the moving tide. The gentle Caribbean breezes took hold of the raised main sail and *The Savage* began to move slowly and smoothly out of the harbor.

It was some time before Steven was able to leave the ship in the care of Mr. Johnson. Anxious to change, he was astonished upon entering his cabin to find Angelina in the firm grasp of Adam Blake.

"Blake!"

The pirate lifted his cutlass in mock salute, and sarcastically asked, "What are you about, Spencer? Out for an evening's pleasure?"

Steven ignored his sarcasm, "Unhand her, Blake."

The pirate laughed evilly, "Release a tender morsel such as this? Do you think me daft? Did I win her confidence for naught?" Blake's hand slipped from her waist and cupped her breast, as he remarked, "She feels a lusty handful, Spencer."

Steven drew his blade and Angelina was pulled closer into Blake's arms. Her back was pressed tight against him as the cutlass was brought up and pressed menacingly against her throat.

Steven stiffened, enraged that this man should fondle his wife and he was unable to prevent the pirate from doing his worst. His eyes glared murderously at the grinning man, "If you harm her, Blake, you shall die a most unpleasant death indeed."

He laughed, "I've not the slightest intention of harming this lovely lass. That is unless you force me to. Call your first mate and turn this ship back. Captain Jack will wish a word or two with you, no doubt."

Steven smiled grimly and with a slight nod of his head, he grunted, "No doubt."

"Make haste, man. I've nearly reached the end of my patience."

Steven opened the door and bellowed, "Johnson!" A moment later, the first mate stood at the doorway. "Turn this ship about," he stated simply.

"Captain!," the confused man began and then stopped suddenly, as his eyes came to rest on Angelina being held captive by Blake. Instantly realizing the situation, the first mate replied, "Aye Captain," and, with a quick salute, left the room.

Orders to turn the ship about were shouted from above. Blake momentarily relaxed his hold on Angelina and, although he kept her in the same position, he lowered his cutlass to his side.

Angelina, taking the opportunity offered, slammed her elbow into the unsuspecting man's abdomen and at nearly the same moment, slumped to the floor in a dead weight.

Blake, surprised by the sudden attack to his midsection, allowed her to slip from his grasp.

Blake cursed and his face contorted with rage as he brought his weapon up from his side, but Steven wasted not a second. Cutlass still in hand, his eyes glowed as he almost cheerfully drove the long shiny blade into the pirate's chest.

Angelina was aghast at how Steven seemed to enjoy this particular killing. The gurgling sound that escaped through the open wound made her gag. She turned white, her hand flying to her mouth to stop her retching. Breathing deeply, she forced her stomach to calm.

Angelina watched as Steven, in an apparently heartless gesture, wiped the blood-streaked cutlass against the pirate's linen shirt. This was the last straw and she screamed in disgust and hatred, "You murderer, you bloody bastard! You slaughtered him like an animal." And like a wildcat, she lunged at him, trying to viciously rake his face with her nails.

Steven was astonished at her outburst. Their faces were so close they nearly touched as he growled, "Madam, he clearly meant to kill me if that was at all possible. And if so, he would have taken you for his own. And I've told you before, no man shall take what is mine."

He shoved her backwards; again she flew at him. Hysterical now, knowing Steven was right only managed to make her madder. Her pride refused to allow her to admit she had been wrong about Blake. She didn't want to believe he was evil, even though the truth stared her in the face, for he had been the only one on the island who had been kind and protective towards her. Taking her frustration and fury out on Steven, she slapped his face and screamed words she could never mean, "Well, perhaps it would be preferable to you. Anyone, even a pirate, would be more agreeable to me than a spy and a murderer."

He watched her silently as she continued, "My God, was it necessary for him to die?"

He only stared at her, not answering her last question. Calmly, he stepped to the door of his cabin, and called out. Immediately, two members of his crew appeared and upon Steven's command removed the dead man from the room. Before they left, he said, "Tell Mr. Johnson to disregard that last order."

When at last he spoke again, his voice was

as cold as ice, his mouth tight with controlled fury, "Aye, I'm afraid it was indeed necessary for him to die. You are mistaken if you believe he would not have harmed you. I've told you before, he was not your friend." And watching her eyes fix him with a glare of hatred, he continued in the manner of others who suffer the pains of jealousy, "Madam, accept my apologies for intruding between you and your prospective lover. I find myself in a most unfortunate and difficult situation in that I have a wife who prefers anyone to me. But allow me to inform you, madam, you belong to me. No other man shall have you while I live." He added vehemently, "Upon my honor, I swear it." As he finished, he glared at her, almost daring her to refute his statement.

For just a moment, she was so surprised she didn't say a word. She hadn't meant to have Steven believe she would have welcomed the pirate's advances and didn't realize his thoughts were of that persuasion. Yet in her fury, she said nothing to correct his erroneous thinking. What she did do was to face him fearlessly, her small delicate face raised defiantly, as she sneered, "What is honor to a spy and murderer? Let me inform you, my traitorous opponent, I belong to no man, least of all you. It seems I, too, find myself in an unfortunate and difficult situation, married to a spy and murderer, and while I live he shall never know a moment's peace or safety for I won't rest until I see him swing from the gallows."

The taste of killing was not commonplace nor pleasant to his senses. His whole being suddenly flooded with a wide variety of intense emotions, jealousy not the least withstanding. He needed her kindness, tenderness, gratitude and what he found in their stead was anger and hatred.

Was there nothing he could do to find favor in her eyes? He had saved her brother and herself from certain death and received rage and curses for his troubles. He was angry beyond words. He longed to put his hands around her neck and strangle her. His mouth was grim and his voice low with controlled fury, when he next spoke, "Woman, am I to be forever pricked by your viper tongue? Is it my cursed fate to be eternally plagued with your sneering resentment? I am sick to death of this constant fighting?"

She snarled, "Sir, 'tis but the beginning."

He wished he could punish her, but was at a loss besides beating her as to how. He put his hands on her shoulders, not at all sure at the moment what he intended.

"Take your maggoty vermin ridden hands from me," she demanded.

"Enough!" he growled and pulled her to the bed. Seating himself, he pulled her over his lap.

Angelina was so astonished at his actions that she offered no resistance as he pulled up her skirt and placed two hard crisp slaps to her derriere.

She howled with indignity and fury. Her

hand slipped beneath the pillow and touched the handle of the forgotten dagger Steven had given her more than a week ago.

Without a second thought to the consequences, nor a moment of hesitation, she gripped the handle and plunged the knife into Steven. Due to her present position, she could get no leverage to reach behind her; the knife entered mid-thigh, stopping only when it struck a bone.

Stunned, Steven's hand stopped in mid air as the searing pain was soon acknowledged by his brain.

As his grip relaxed, Angelina tumbled unceremoniously from his lap and landed with a thud on the floor. In a second, she was up. Her body was poised for attack, ready for repercussions.

Steven watched her with a dangerous gleam in his eyes. He grinned menacingly, completely ignoring the pain in his leg.

She wielded the knife before him as if daring him to retaliate. Her feet spread, her chest heaved, her eyes flashed fury, "You bloody bastard, if you ever lay a hand on me again, I'll cut out your black heart."

His grin spread until his teeth showed themselves and had she not been so caught up in her own fury, she'd have realized it was not a grin relating merriment. "So, my love, you want to play rough; so be it." And with his last words, he lunged at her, twisting the knife from her hand and knocking her to the floor, landing with his full weight on top of her.

Momentarily stunned by the force of his attack, she did nothing as his grinning face loomed over hers, but her surprise was short lived. Twisting one hand from beneath him, she struck at his face and moved her legs, trying to strike his groin with her knee.

He laughed as he held both her arms over her head and pressed his legs hard against hers, stilling all movement.

She twisted her head away, refusing to look at his victorious smile.

His eyes slowly softened as he gazed at her beautiful profile and whispered, "My vixen wife, witch, bitch. You never cease to plague me, yet I want no other. I want you."

His face came down to nuzzle her neck, his breath hot against her cool moist skin. His lips worked magic, sending shivers of unwanted pleasure down her spine.

She was desperate to get away, but was locked firmly in place. His mouth wouldn't stop. She couldn't bear it! He had to stop, he had to! "Stop," she groaned as if in pain, "I don't want you."

He ignored her plea. His hand reached under her damp blouse and stroked her breast.

She gasped as his finger moved gently, teasing the nipple. Her mind screamed, *Don't give in! No! No! No! He's a spy! He's a murderer! You hate him!* But he had no mercy. Feeling her resistance about to crumble, she cried out, "Nnnoooo!"

Her faced turned and their mouths instantly joined as if starved for each other, neither wanting to ever let go. She was suddenly alive with long denied desire. She couldn't get enough, nor stop the moans of longing and surrender that escaped her.

She was dazed with the extremity of her passion. Her blouse slipped over her head. Her hands released, she pulled him closer, devouring his mouth as it clung to hers.

The weeks she had spent with him since their time together at the inn had been torture. Nearly every moment had been endured with a hatred almost beyond her control. Yet now, with his lips on hers, his warm hands on her body, all hatred vanished. Her mind registered nothing, nothing but wild hungry need.

Her breathing grew shallow and faint. Her body moved on its own accord, without thought. She brushed seductively against him, tempting him, taunting him. Her cool skin turned hot beneath the onslaught of his masterful hands.

He pulled her to her feet. A quick yank at the strings that held her waistband brought her heavy wet skirt to her feet.

He touched her everywhere; she was on fire.

Reaching greedily for him, she slid her hands beneath his wet shirt while trying to push it away. She was moaning into his warm neck, "Take it off, take the damn thing off," while her teeth slid gently against his skin and her tongue followed warmly and seductively across his chest, titilating his mind and senses to near madness. Gasping at the delicious sensations she inflicted on him, he ripped the shirt from his body.

She was on the bed. Motioning him to come to her, she lay back and pleaded, "Hurry, hurry."

His pants were flung from him. Mindless of his bloody leg, he joined her at last.

Together, lost in the throes of desire, ignorant as yet of their love, they joined in white blinding passion. They were mindless of the world outside their door, content for the moment to forget their anger; wanting only to revel in the delight of their touch, to feel, to breathe in their special tantalizing scents, to whisper soft and low. They were hungry to search, to explore, to discover each other once again.

Afterwards, they lay apart, quiet and still, each looking at the other with some surprise as if seeing for the first time.

Neither of them had experienced before this unrealistic nearly hysterical quality in their lovemaking and both were amazed by the intensity of their emotions.

Propped on his elbow, Steven's eyes turned bold as his gaze swept over her. His hand reached for and held a lock of her hair that lay upon her breast. He brought the curl to his face and breathed in its heady sweet scent.

A hint of a smile touched the corners of Steven's mouth as he gazed tenderly at her softened features. Her full lips were slightly swollen from the insistent pressure of his mouth. Her eyes gentle and shy, lowered themselves from his tender gaze. Her feelings confused, impossible to understand, disturbed her. Her eyes slid appreciatively down his body, openly admiring his lean muscular form. Her hand reached to the tempting sight of his hard lean belly, while finally her gaze rested on his leg. Suddenly, she noticed the blood.

Abruptly, she sat up. "Your leg! You're bleeding!"

Laughing, he lay back, " 'Tis what normally happens when one is stabbed."

Contritely, she looked at his smiling face, her teeth biting at her bottom lip.

"In the trunk, you'll find salves and material for bandaging," and looking at the bed, he remarked casually, "I fear the sheet be ruined."

Quickly, she jumped from the bed, donning one of his shirts and began searching the trunk.

Soon she was at his side once again.

As he watched her work on his leg, he calmly regarded this woman who was his wife. A woman of extreme passions and loyalties, complicated, spoiled, childish, yet at the same time more woman than any he had known. Would he ever truly know her or understand her? In spite of everything or because of everything, he knew he wanted her, only her. Why, he couldn't fathom, for she brought him nothing but trouble and torment.

Her cool fingers worked quickly on his leg. Although she was careful to touch only his wound, it was obvious his passions were building again.

Her hands began to shake as she nervously finished. She glanced warily at his face and was not surprised to see him grinning. His eyes crinkled at the corners with merriment. She tried to turn away, but his hand reached out and held her still, "I'm wondering how you would have explained my lifeless body to my crew?"

She shrugged, "At the time, your crew was the farthest thought from my mind."

After a long silence, he sighed wearily.

She looked up guiltily, fearful his wound was giving him pain.

Reading her thoughts, he shook his head and spoke for the first time, softly and gently, "Nay Angelina, 'tis not this little cut that bothers me," and at her puzzled look, he continued, "it is us, you and I. What is to become of us? Why is it you can provoke me to such raging anger that I become something less than a man? Only a few months ago, I would never have believed myself capable of such violence. I am weary of this combat and long for the peace only marriage can bring."

He was quiet for a long moment, watching her face, "Is it that you find me so repulsive?"

She was so taken back by his tender words of longing and more than a little surprised that he was not as confident as he appeared to be, that at first she could only sit silent, shocked, seeing for the first time the very human side of the man she had married. Gone, at least for the moment, were the dominance and arrogance, replaced by a very appealing soft spoken gentleman.

Still she could not bring herself to accept him, for in her mind to do so was to permit his work to continue. As yet, she could not separate the two, for to her they simply were one and the same.

And yet his plea did not leave her untouched. When she finally answered her voice took on a soft quality, one she rarely used in addressing him. "In truth, I do not find you at all repulsive. If anything, the opposite is true."

Still holding her hands, he tried to pull her closer to him when he heard her speak, but she held back, her body stiff, her eyes holding his, cool and honest.

"But also in truth, I am repelled by the knowledge I have of your—" she hesitated, groping for a less harsh name for spying, "shall we say, line of business. I am sorry Steven, for I cannot see how it is possible for us to ever live as others who have married."

His sigh of disappointment at her rejection was unmistakable. Now with renewed determination entering his voice, he inquired a bit stiffly, "Are you telling me, that were I not a spy, you would not be adverse to this marriage?"

"I am not sure," she shrugged, her eyes unwilling to meet his, her cheeks growing pink from her partial admission.

A long silence followed. Finally he spoke, "I want you, madam, as any husband wants his wife. What is it you want of me?"

Sincerely, she pleaded in her last desperate attempt to forestall the inevitable. "I want to return home. I want things to be as they were."

His eyes hardened with the further rejection of these last words, and he stated gruffly, "Madam, you are home. Anywhere I am is your home. I have told you once before it is time you grew up. Obviously, you have not. You are married to me, regardless of your opinion of your husband. Your childhood is behind you and you can never return to it. I swear madam, you will be my wife until the good Lord sees fit to take one of us, but I shall never again take you as a man takes a woman. You, madam, shall come to me. You shall willingly and purposely say, 'I want you,' and until that day comes, you may consider me your husband in name only. On this I vow."

His words filled her with a wide variety of emotions. She was at once filled with joy at his promise of celibacy, but pitched into depths of despair at the knowledge of spending the rest of her life with him. Good Lord, how was she to bear it? Granted, she did not hate him any longer, but still, she found not even the smallest amount of liking or friendship towards him and the thought of a lifelong relationship with him was repellant.

What would they be to each other? What could they be? Hateful enemies? Cool companions? Close friends? What?

Her eyes registered her confused thoughts and Steven did nothing to put her mind at rest. Instead he stated simply, "When we reach my home, excuse me, our home on Santa Louisa, I would appreciate, whatever your feelings about me, a truce in front of the servants. Perhaps you could even act as though I do not disgust you.

"When I find I must entertain, I expect my wife to be a congenial hostess; someone I would be proud to have stand at my side.

"In return, I will see to it that you want for nothing, and anything within reason I can do for you shall be done."

She stared at him in silence until he was finally forced to ask, "Is it a bargain then?"

His idea of a bargain struck her, at that moment, to be the best solution to a horrible situation. She was terribly confused as to her feelings for him. One moment, he was a refined soft spoken gentleman, giving her tender cajoling smiles, and a moment later, a strong passionate lust-seeking male animal. In her inexperience, she didn't realize there could be these two sides and much more in the makeup of the man she had married.

Silently he waited.

Finally she nodded her consent and whispered, "Agreed," knowing in her heart, try as she would, she could never escape this man nor their marriage. And so a pact was drawn. Only time would tell how it all was to end, or if indeed there would be an end.

Part Four

Chapter 26

The Savage docked in Santa Louisa in the early morning hours of a warm sunny day. Steven hired a carriage for them.

They passed through the town of Portsmith. Bleached white buildings and storefronts lined the narrow cobblestone streets. Women in colorful native dresses carefully balanced baskets of food on their turbaned heads and swayed gracefully about. Black shining faces split into dazzling white grins as they passed by. The men, most often dressed in white, bowed and tipped their hats before their carriage.

The sun, although the hour was early, beat blindingly and hot upon them. Angelina could feel the tickle of perspiration slide down the center of her back. Her face was flushed and damp. The heavy dress she wore, although appropriate for Virginia, was definitely not suitable for this hot damp climate.

Steven couldn't help but notice her discomfort and pulled the carriage to a halt before one of the buildings. She looked at him, puzzled that he had stopped.

A middle-aged lady paused when Steven jumped down from the carriage. "Steven Spencer, my dear, it's been a long time since I've seen you last."

"That it has, Mrs. Harrington. How are you and your family?" As he handed Angelina down, he continued, "May I present my wife Angelina. We have only now arrived and I think she is in need of more comfortable clothing." And then, lying because she had no other clothes with her, he added, "All she has brought with her will not do in this climate."

"My dear, you are lovely. I knew Steven would find someone pretty, but I must say, he has outdone my greatest expectations."

"Thank you, Mrs. Harrington," Angelina smiled shyly.

"You will come to tea next week. I will not delay you further. You look as if you are about to melt in that heavy traveling dress."

They bade each other good-bye until next week, and Steven led Angelina into a small dress shop. Before she left he had ordered enough dresses for her to last months without repeating one of them. She, coming from a wealthy family, had never wanted for anything, but this array of flounces and lace he set before her made her gasp with surprise. Materials of every color and as thin as gossamer were laid out. When she picked one, Steven added five. She was overwhelmed at his generosity and constantly begged him to stop, but he would listen to nothing she had to say.

After the dresses were ordered, he proceeded to pick out lingerie, the most beautiful sheer garments she had ever seen.

She blushed hotly as she noticed his wicked grin as he fingered a piece of midnight lace. His eyes slid over her in a teasing manner as he gave orders for what he wanted it made into.

At last they left the dress shop, bringing ony one small parcel with them. Mrs. Tames promised all would follow as soon as possible.

Slowly the horse pulled the carriage past the town and along a road that bordered the ocean. To her right stretched beautiful sandy beaches washed with water the color of turquoise as far as the eye could see. To the left stood thick lush tropical forests. The scent of flowers that grew in wild abundance followed them.

Angelina thought this to be the most beautiful place she had ever seen and did not hesitate to let Steven know.

When the carriage finally pulled to a stop, Angelina's mouth hung open with surprise. Turning to Steven, she asked, "This is not your home?"

He laughed, "Do you like it?"

Amazement written all over her face, she

breathed, "Steven, it's magnificent. How could you bring yourself to leave it?"

Like most homes in the Caribbean, it was two stories and white with a red tiled roof, but the size of it staggered her. It was at least three times larger than her father's home.

The whole second floor was terraced and bordered with filigree iron railings. At each end, wide steps led to the ground.

The house, though enormous, seemed to her built as an afterthought, so lovely were the grounds. Roses of every possible color flooded the lawn. The forest had been pushed back and everywhere she looked were more flowers. She smiled, "An appropriate name, Rose Manor."

For the first few days Angelina had been shy and ill at ease. Being the new mistress of a gigantic home, filled with strangers, at first left her slightly bewildered. But being naturally friendly and possessing a serene quality in her manner, she quickly became accustomed to and accepted her new surroundings.

Her genuine kindness automatically had the house servants plying to do her will. Her cheery laughter could be heard to ring out throughout the house. And all who came in contact with the new mistress left her company much improved in spirits.

Steven was more than a little amazed at the change in Angelina and her apparent willingness to accept her new role. He was never in her company that she wasn't pleasant, lively, and usually teasing him into joining her banter.

When the servants were about, or company present, she, true to her part of the bargain, became a loving and devoted wife. Uncountable were the times she would lean up against him while talking companionably to someone, perhaps taking his arm and placing it about her waist or sliding her hand across his chest and dallying in a wifely fashion to move a stubborn lock of dark hair from his forehead. And all was done as if it were the most natural and ordinary of occurrences.

If she knew of her effect on Steven at these close encounters, she gave no notice. But the moment they were alone again, she once more became the congenial but slightly proper and distant lady she had become since the bargain was set.

The change in her was astounding and immediate. Suddenly she was a woman who cared about others and their feelings. Steven said nothing, not daring to question her. But in his heart, he never missed the short tempered, spoiled, young lady he had married. Now he gloried in his fabulous luck that Angelina should have become almost overnight a serene, unselfish, genuinely caring young woman.

It wasn't more than a week after her arrival when she came to him one day in his library, knocking softly before she entered.

Glancing up from the papers on his desk, he smiled at seeing her glide smoothly and gracefully across the floor.

"Angelina, what a pleasant surprise." As he spoke, he came around the desk and sat on a corner of it while she stood before him. "Is there something I can do for you?"

"Aye Steven," she smiled hopefully, "there is much you can do. I pray you will listen and concede to my plea."

"Madam," he assured her, "you need only to ask and it shall be done."

"Please believe me, Steven, I do not interfere except out of necessity." After a slight hesitation, she continued. "The quarters for the blacks are abominable. Human beings cannot and should not live thus. I understand you have freed them, but they fare no better for it. And the children, Steven, they wear what one could only refer to as rags. Could not one of the richest landowners in Santa Louisa afford to pay his workers justly? Why their quarters are worse than a stable. They'll soon be disease ridden if not properly cared for."

He looked down into her inquisitive and hopeful face. Taking her two hands in his, he smiled good-naturedly. "I fear I have been remiss in my duties. It seems that in my long absence much has degenerated here. Madam, it is done. It pleases me to see you so interested in the well being of my people."

Noticing the grateful and relieved look in her eyes, he went on to say in a teasing and playful fashion, while bringing her hands to his lips, "Am I to be rewarded for my good deeds?"

"Sir," she bantered in return, while smiling brightly, "I feel certain the good deeds you accomplish bring their own just rewards."

Without Steven's knowledge, she began to teach the younger children about her religion. Although they were schooled in reading and arithmetic, she found their education to be seriously lacking concerning religion. Most of the natives, she discovered, were believers in black magic or voodoo, while many others liberally mixed Christianity with it.

Her teachings were not the case of studying questions and answers, but merely a conversation which informed.

It was usual for Steven to go into the town of Portsmouth, some eight miles away, every Thursday morning for supplies. Angelina reasoned this should be the morning she visited and talked to the children. Arms ladened with goods and sweets, she soon became a welcome sight among them.

Nearly a month passed before Steven was informed of Angelina's classes.

One day he called her into the library to speak to her concerning their first ball, and mentioned casually, "Word has it I am now the husband of a Sunday school teacher," he grinned good-naturedly.

She smiled timidly, not positive of his reaction to this news. "It does not upset you, does it, Steven? In truth I do little more than just talk to them, but my group of listeners seems to grow larger each time."

Laughing, he stood before her, his eyes tenderly sweeping her face as he replied sincerely, "There is little you could do that would upset me, Angelina." His knuckles brushed along the silken skin of her jaw and neck as he continued, "You have all the authority and power to do anything you wish, my love, and you will find me, like all others around here, your willing and adoring slave."

Chapter 27

Angelina soon settled into a routine in her new home. Each morning she would ride one of Steven's spirited horses. After lunch, she would most often write letters to her family and friends, but this and an occasional visit to Mrs. Harrington's for tea was not enough to occupy every afternoon.

One afternoon, much to the gardener's amazement and chagrin, he found her on her knees tending the flowers. Smudges of mud marred her flawless complexion and caked thickly beneath her long nails as she happily planted and transplanted flowers. Quieting the gardener's fears at what the master might think, she continued to work for some time.

At last, near dinner, her back aching, she rose to her feet and surveyed her day's work, extremely satisfied with what she had accomplished.

Unmindful of her mud-caked dress, she

went into the house to prepare herself for dinner. Stopping first in the kitchen, she asked Jenny to have the house boys bring up some hot water for a bath.

Jenny, black as night and of unknown age, was aghast at the sight of her mistress. She bristled about, scolding Angelina as if she were a child, complaining how the young woman would ruin her complexion and hands by doing such needless menial work.

No amount of Angelina's promises of how much she loved it would suffice and Angelina finally left her to her mumblings. Just before the kitchen door closed behind her, she heard her remark some people didn't know their place.

This last remark was too much and Angelina burst out laughing as she left the kitchen and at a run went through the dining room and started up the stairs.

From the center hall, the stairs led to a wide hall on the second floor. Angelina was barely at the top landing when she heard sounds of whimpering and soft crying which seemed to come from the second floor linen closet.

Investigating the sound, Angelina threw open the linen closet door. The room was large enough, in fact, to be a small bedroom. It had shelves lining four walls and tables in the center, all heaped high with linens of every type and color.

Some sheets and blankets had been knocked off the tables and thrown into a messy pile on the floor.

When Angelina's eyes rested upon the struggling young figure of her personal maid being brutally attacked by the white foreman, she gasped at the sight of his naked rear, and screamed, "Mr. Landen! What do you think you are doing? Get up and get out of here now!"

The look of contempt and hatred that marred her face was matched only by Mr. Landen's look of surprise and outrage. The sudden interruption of his lust was by no means a welcome happening. Standing before her, he was so overcome with his power over the blacks that worked the plantation, that he felt no guilt or remorse. Considering as he did the blacks to be something less than human and his right to use them as he pleased, he felt no need to answer for his actions, especially to this lovely little morsel.

Even as he growled, "This ain't none of your business, ma'am," an idea came to him of what fun all three of them could have if perhaps he could tempt this golden beauty into joining them.

He waited in silence, wondering how best to say what he wanted and then realized he had forgotten to raise his pants. Noticing how she couldn't seem to stop her eyes from wandering to his nakedness, he grinned and knew he need say nothing.

But John Landen was sadly mistaken by Angelina's temporary muteness and her straying eyes. She was merely shocked into silence and the pink flush that covered her golden skin had nothing to do with lust, but was rather the results of extreme embarrassment at the man's state of undress.

Since the first moment of the initial meeting, when all the people who worked the plantation were introduced to the new mistress, Angelina felt extreme disgust for this man. His eyes had openly raked her body, making her feel naked and afraid. His eyes shone brightly with lust whenever she saw him. For the last two months she had carefully kept out of his way. He was important to Steven and she wished to cause no trouble.

Now standing proudly, while his enormous organ still hard and throbbing was raised and pointed straight at her, his eyes took on a lecherous quality.

Cicely moaned at his feet. Blood was oozing from her lips and more was trickling from her exposed legs as she stared glassy eyed at her mistress.

The sight of her maid's distress brought Angelina out of her shocked state. Trying to remain cool and calm, and desperate to keep her eyes from his exposed body, she faced him. Her eyes flashed with pure hatred and she ordered in her most authoritative voice, "Mr. Landen, you will leave my house this instant. We have no further need of your services."

Grinning wickedly, he answered, "Perhaps the lady of the house would like to sample some of my wares, ma'am." As he spoke, he fondled himself disgustingly, "I've been known to give great satisfaction, and there's always room for one more. See for yourself. Come on girl, give it a try."

Allowing him to continue no further, Angelina turned and ran from the room and sped with all haste to hers. In a frenzy, she tore apart her closet, searching for her riding crop, something she kept with her when she rode but till now never had occasion to use.

In a flash she was back in the linen closet. Unbelievably, Mr. Landen was again astride Cicely, his bare bottom raising and lowering itself as if the man who owned it had not the least care in the world.

A garbled sound of fury came from deep within Angelina's throat as she raised the riding crop and lowered it. Shrilly, it whistled through the air and finally contacted crisply with its naked mark.

A bellow of mind-shattering pain and rage filled the tiny room, and again another, before the foreman could get to his feet.

Dazed with pain, he stood still naked from the waist down before her, but Angelina gave not a moment's hesitation before she swung the crop with all the force and strength she could muster to snap across his now limp member. She was satisfied to hear a scream of horror and smiled as the man wobbled before her, nearly losing consciousness from the excruciating pain.

His brain was filled with fire. He was unable to see her through the red haze that swam before his eyes. He screamed a blood curdling sound and tried to protect himself with his hands, all the while begging her to stop. And then in a reflex action, he lunged blindly at his attacker.

Undaunted, Angelina calmly stepped to one side as he passed. Her mind registered none of the man's suffering, but only the sight of the pitiful young girl crumpled and bleeding at her feet.

Her disgust and hate were so great, it seemed once she started to strike him, she was unable to stop. His harrowing screams and curses brought Steven from the library at a gallop, followed by most of the servants in the house.

To say that Steven was surprised at the sight that greeted him upon opening the door to the linen closet, would have been an extreme understatement. Here he found his lovely young wife, small and delicate, smeared with dried mud from head to toe, her hair in wild disarray, severely beating his half naked foreman with her riding crop. All the while her maid lay, also half naked, bloody, and unconscious, at Angelina's feet.

It didn't take Steven a second to understand the situation and take control. He grabbed Angelina's arm with one hand and pulled her away in the same motion. An instant later, the foreman's body sagged to the floor after his face made contact with two crisp sharp blows from Steven's fists.

Mr. Landen looked up stupidly at the couple who stood before him. His mind dazed, he was mumbling incoherently, his face and body wracked with pain. Blood spouted freely from an obvious broken nose and already one of his eyes was swelling closed.

Steven quietly warned the bloodied man, "Get out of this house and off my property in an hour, or I'll have you shot on sight."

With his arm now firmly and protectively about Angelina's waist, Steven pulled her from the room, shooting orders over his shoulder to the wide eyed servants for the care of the injured girl.

When at last he got Angelina to her room, she collapsed against him, the reaction to her fury and fear now settling upon her.

Holding her in the safety of his arms, he sat in an armchair as she sobbed into his chest, her whole body shaking uncontrollably while she mumbled brokenly all that had happened.

After she quieted some, except for an occasional hiccuping sob, Steven asked, "Angelina, why did you not call me or one of the servants?"

Looking up into his gently smiling eyes, her own glistened with tears. She looked so delicate and lovely that it took some effort to control his feelings. Finally she answered brokenly, "I'm sorry Steven, I did not think. It was just so shocking and I was so angry, I forgot."

He laughed and kissed her on her muddy forehead while his arms held her slender form closer, rocking her and comforting her, until the water arrived for her bath.

Chapter 28

Angelina smiled as she faced the long line of guests. She and Steven had been standing on their reception line for almost an hour and it seemed to Angelina there was no end to the long line that waited for their introductions. This was the first ball Steven had given since he and Angelina had arrived nearly two months ago.

Almost eveyone who lived on Santa Louisa had come to meet the new mistress of Rose Manor. Angelina was surprised for she hadn't realized so many people lived on the island. She smiled happily as the people passed her. She knew she would be far from lonely in the future when so many people offered what appeared to be genuine friendship. They were willing to accept her simply because she was Steven's wife.

A young woman, perhaps five years older than Angelina, accompanied by a man many years her senior, ignored her outstretched hand and flung herself at Steven. With no more than a mumbled, "Steven, I've missed you so," her arms were around his neck and her red painted mouth planted firmly on his.

Angelina simply stared shocked that the woman could be so openly brazen. Apparently she and Steven were more than slightly acquainted. The older gentleman stood silent before Angelina and gave an obvious embarrassed cough.

Steven laughed at the woman's outrageous actions as she finally allowed his lips to leave her own.

Angelina was infuriated that this woman should snub her so obviously in her own home, and smiled stiffly as Miriam and Jonathan Webb were introduced to her. She was amazed that Jonathan Webb accepted this kind of behavior from his wife in public.

Barely able to hold her temper in check, she acknowledged with false sincerity, "How nice of you to come Mr. Webb, Mrs. Webb. It so does one's heart good, does it not," she addressed Mr. Webb, "to watch as old friends are reunited?" And as Steven strangled a laugh in his throat, nearly choking as he did so, she continued with an apparently innocent smile, "You are indeed fortunate, sir, to have such an obviously friendly wife."

Steven stiffened at the insult, ready to step forward lest Miriam retaliate with force, while his arm slid protectively around his wife's waist, bringing her closer to his side.

Miriam, wise to her insulting remark, muttered, "Why you little . . ." as she was hastily dragged from Angelina's company by her red faced husband.

"Well said, my dear."

Angelina looked into the merry blue eyes of Mrs. Harrington. "That little hussy has been getting away with the most abominable behavior for long enough. If it were not for the fact that her husband is most prominent and powerful, she would be shunned by all polite society." And after scrutinizing Angelina thoroughly and smiling as she noticed Steven's arm still around her, she continued, "I think Steven needs a young lady like you to protect him from the likes of her."

Angelina looked up at her husband's beaming face and smiled with sugary sweetness, "Oh, I am sure, madam, that my husband, when he has a mind to that is, can defend himself quite admirably." And then changing her tone, she continued charmingly, "Let me tell you how happy I am you have come, Mrs. Harrington. I am so pleased to have you for a friend."

Her sarcasm was not lost on Steven as he soon after took her in his arms and led her in the first dance of the evening. "Allow me, madam, to extend to you my deepest apologies. It was indeed unfortunate for that to have happened before your eyes."

She smiled sweetly up to him, her finger at his lip removing the last trace of red lip rouge. "Am I correct then in assuming all would have been well had I not been present?"

"Nay, my love," he smiled tenderly, "It is not my wish to kiss another. I mean only that I would never do anything to embarrass you. I hold you in the highest esteem and in truth, I was somewhat startled and can offer only my surprise as an excuse for the length of that kiss."

She laughed at his sheepish expression.

"Am I forgiven then?"

"Aye Steven," she laughed happily, "when you ask so sweetly, accompanied by that particular look in your eyes, it is in me to refuse you nothing."

She blushed prettily as he gave her a devilish grin, "It may be to my benefit, love, to practice that look you speak of for it may come in handy at a later time."

As they danced and laughed together, they appeared to all present to be a loving couple. It was obvious Steven adored her, while she returned sweet shyness to his passionate looks.

From the side of the room, Mrs. Harrington approached Miriam, who was watching the young couple jealously, her face a mask of hatred. "It would be wise, my dear, to leave him be. He apparently found someone he adores. This time I'm afraid you shall not win."

Miriam smiled slowly and evilly, "Why, my dear Mrs. Harrington, whatever do you mean?"

Later that same night, after the last of their guests had left, Angelina sat alone in her room, brushing her hair. Through her mirror, she saw Steven enter and close the door behind him. Before making himself comfortable in her lounge chair, he began looking around as if searching for someone.

"What is it, Steven? You act as though you expect to find someone other than myself in my chambers."

Grinning, he remarked, "I half expected to find Miriam in here. Tonight I could not move that she wasn't at my side."

She laughed, "More likely than not it would be your chambers, rather than mine, where one might find the lovely Mrs. Webb."

He sighed and grinned good naturedly, "Perhaps I should then share this chamber with you. I have no wish to find our friend lurking in a closet or behind the draperies."

"The way the lady, and I fear I use the term lightly, hovered about you tonight, one might begin to wonder which of us is truly your wife."

"Surely you do not accuse me of enjoying her attentions? I promise you they are unwanted."

"Nay, Steven, her actions are obvious and I consider none of this to be your fault."

"You have done well tonight, my love. I have lost count of the compliments I received on your account. Everyone believes you to be sweet and gentle, and I most fortunate to have you for my wife."

She laughed happily, "And you said nothing to dissuade them of their erroneous opinions, I take it? Very gallant of you, Steven."

Chapter 29

"Angelina, I am sorry to put restrictions on you, but I must insist that you are not to venture out alone. As a matter of fact, I do not care what time of the day it may be, if you find you have an appointment somewhere, you will take Manuel with you. You will be safe in his hands. I must demand your word in this matter."

She sat before him while he paced the green carpet of the library floor. Finally after she remained silent, he looked at her. "Angelina?" he said as if her name were a question.

"Very well, Steven," she responded with a weary sigh, "you have my word on it."

"Good," he said flatly. "Now one more thing. It will not do for the wife of a prominent landowner and loyal subject to the crown to consort with known low-life and riff-raff. From now on the King's Inn is off limits for you. It is much too dangerous for you to visit there."

She started at his last comment. Dozens of thoughts seemed to flash through her mind at almost the same instant. How did he know of the King's Inn? Were Mary and Joe Faver, the proprietors of the establishment, now in danger due to Steven's knowledge? How much and what did he know of her involvement? What would he do about it?

Outwardly calm, her face registered nothing of her inner fears. She smiled lazily up to his agitated face. "Steven really, what nonsense. Mary and Joe are as loyal to the crown as yourself." Now laughing, she continued, "I would venture there is not a single rebel besides myself to be found on the whole island."

Steven watched her carefully, thinking how very good she was. Had he not known differently, he would surely have believed her. Grimly he stated, "Madam, if you believe it is not well known throughout this island that the King's Inn is a den of cutthroats and villians and sympathizers of your rebel friends, you do not know what you are about. May I inquire what would happen if one night during one of your visits, the inn was overrun by British soldiers? Do you think someone will always be there to help you to safety?"

She gasped as she realized it had been Steven who had dragged her into the shadows and finally led her to her horse.

He gave no notice of her surprise as he continued. "Do you think your beautiful face will keep you out of some stinking hole in one of their ships? If you believe that, you are dead wrong. From now on you will send Manuel with a note, giving any and all information you wish. You can decide later on a code or signature that could be yours alone.

"I realize you must do what your heart believes to be right and honorable, and I will not try to prevent you from your patriotic duties. In return, I only ask that you keep yourself above reproach and, most importantly, safe." He looked at her for a long moment before he asked, "Need I worry any longer?"

She shook her head slightly.

"Will you give me your word, Angelina?"

"Steven, first I must . . ."

He interrupted, "Have no fear, Angelina. I will do nothing to bring harm to your friends. The knowledge I have of your—" he grinned while deliberately taunting her with her own words, "shall we say, your line of business, shall lie dormant in my mind and upon my word of honor shall not pass my lips."

"Very well, Steven," she answered after a long thoughtful pause, "you have my word. I shall not visit the King's Inn again."

Steven sighed with relief as the library door closed behind the departing figure of his wife. His mind slipped back again to the previous evening. Never in his life had he received such a shock, nor felt such cold terrifying fear.

From the shadows he had been watching

the delivery of nearly an arsenal of guns and ammunition to be sent at a later date to the colonies, when there came a soft rapping on the inn's back door. It was the code, two sharp sounds, followed by a scratching. It was three in the morning. Steven decided he would stay a bit longer, perhaps something interesting was afoot.

The door to the inn opened and a black shrouded figure of a woman slipped into the establishment.

He was still outside in the shadows of some out-buildings when the door opened again. There stood Angelina, her face bathed in the glow of a lantern's light. It lasted only a moment, but Steven's whole body broke into a cold sweat thinking what might happen to her if she were caught.

From Steven's vantage point, he could clearly see both the back door and the street. Suddenly it seemed his worst fears were about to come true. Angelina began to walk unsuspectingly in the direction of the two patrolling British soldiers. Steven knew the two men would waylay the lone woman whom they would naturally believe to be a prostitute for soldiers would think of no other reason why she should be about at three in the morning but for the plying of her trade.

If Angelina should be recognized, it would bring disaster down on them. In an instant, he left the shadows, grabbed her arm, and with his hand firmly over her mouth, flung her back into the darkness.

The soldiers' voices were the only sound that could be heard.

Angelina's heart thumped wildly in terror. The man held her in a steely vice. His hand was still firmly over her mouth, when she heard the two young soldiers pass in friendly conversation.

Finally the man moved, pulling her along with him. Caring little if she stumbled, he nearly dragged her to her waiting horse. In an instant she was sitting on her saddle while the stranger growled out, "Hurry!" and slapped the horse's hind quarters.

Steven relaxed some, but keeping ever alert for more soldiers, made his way to his own horse and he too returned home. He promised himself on the way this would stop right now before tragedy struck.

Before he retired, he opened his wife's door and looked in her room. Obviously she had heard him coming for she lay in bed pretending to sleep. But he had seen her asleep many times and knew this was not one of them. With a smile, he closed the door and returned to his room.

Tomorrow would be soon enough to speak with her of this. Knowing she was safe so greatly relieved his mind that he felt an intense desire to laugh aloud.

Obviously she had been relaying pieces of information that the young officers they entertained so often had carelessly imparted to her. Although he feared for her, his pride in her courage grew many times. He realized she not only ventured out alone in the dark nights to deliver her messages, but probably in her own way was securing victory to the colonies. Steven, being a reasonable and intelligent man, no matter his political persuasions, knew in the end the rebels would bring about a victory. For no one could dominate a people so united in spirit for love of freedom. And so their relationship took another turn as each began to respect and admire the other and their dedication to a cause.

The island, being part of the British Empire, was nearly overrun with soldiers. Many balls and parties were given in their honor. It pleased Angelina to no end to be able to give charity balls and hand over the entire proceeds, before her husband's amused eyes, to Manuel who would in turn see to it that it reached the King's Inn.

Steven knew full well what his lovely wife was up to but gave her no pressure to dissuade her from her patriotic duties, while she in return never questioned him about his loyalties. Had she done so, it very well might have greatly relieved much of the soul searching and tension she would soon suffer.

Steven had once remarked with a twinkle of merriment in his eyes, "I wonder, my love, what Mrs. Harrington and the rest of the society ladies of our community would say if they knew that dear Mrs. Spencer was a rebel spy. I wonder if they would be happy to know that all the monies collected at her charity balls were handed over to the enemy."

She smiled, her eyes flashing with devilment, "Why, Steven, I have not the slightest notion of what you are about."

Chapter 30

Life at her new home stretched lazy and pleasant, one day much resembling another. Angelina fairly blossomed in her new surroundings. Everything she did, from gardening and long walks to an occasional dip in a private lake she had discovered on one of her daily rides, brought a happy contented glow to her eyes and a vivacious smile to her lips.

It seemed to her that she was discovering everything as though seeing it for the first time, from the simple beauty of a delicate rose to her husband's tender smile.

She wondered about Steven's change of attitude. He treated her so tenderly and lovingly that many times he shocked her into tongue-tied silence. She never realized the drastic change in her own attitude was the cause. Very simply, it was easy for him to be congenial and pleasant to a wife as sweet and kind as she had become.

She knew there was nothing he wouldn't give her, absolutely nothing she could ask for would he refuse. And she very much liked the position of honor that his attitude placed her in.

True to his word, he kept a respectable distance between them. Not that he wasn't known to touch her. On the contrary, on any pretext, his hand reached for hers or his arm would slip companionably about her waist, pulling her body within contact with his. His finger might stroke her cheek as he spoke to her, and all was done as if she were the most treasured and precious of all his possessions, and yet it went no further than that.

Angelina smiled, while leaning back comfortably in her bath, as she realized how much she really enjoyed her new role as the wife of the master of Rose Manor. Their bedrooms were connected by a small room each used for bathing. Angelina was careful to bathe only when Steven was gone from the house. She hadn't seen him since early that morning and thought he was probably on one of his missions.

Surprisingly, in her new home far away from her family and the fury of the war, she seemed to be able, if not to accept, to at least ignore Steven's line of business. She knew it was unpatriotic, but her husband seemed to be wearing down her resistance. It was almost as if she didn't care anymore.

She laughed aloud. That was impossible. But she realized she was beginning to separate the man and his work, appreciating the one while despising the other.

Suddenly she wondered what had happened to her extreme hatred and determination to see her husband destroyed? Her change of opinion confused and upset her. She liked everything to be neat and orderly and yet all her thoughts were a jumble of contradictions.

She sighed wearily; at one time life had seemed so simple. Evil was bad, good was not. Now her maturing mind reasoned her husband's work was bad, but he was far from an evil man. He cared deeply for all people, especially those he came in contact with, which was apparent in his everyday life. He had freed her brother and many others from that horrible floating hell. Was that the work of an evil man? Surely not.

Another matter began to press on her mind as she sat relaxed in the warm water. Angelina was amazed at how much the bargain between herself and Steven was beginning to affect her. She had never thought desire or passion to be a female oriented emotion, yet she was haunted nightly by the most sensuous, passion-filled dreams. And each night to her dismay, the dreams became more intense and soul shaking. It was a common occurrence for her to find herself brutally awakened, saturated with perspiration, after dreaming of his hands gently exploring her body, his flesh pressing close against hers, his mouth possessing her own. And each time it seemed so real that it was only after she was awake for quite a few moments that she realized it had been a dream.

Deep in these thoughts of her newfound emotions, she never noticed the door to Steven's room open.

He grinned, finding the tub occupied by his lovely wife, and lied, for he had heard her laugh only a moment before. "Pardon me, Angelina. I did not know you were using the bath."

Startled at the interruption of her thoughts, she sat up straight, offering him a clear view of silken shiny wet breasts, a sight he gladly accepted.

Not since that night four months ago aboard *The Savage* had he seen her naked, and it brought an instant tightness across his abdomen and a throbbing to his brain. An excitement he couldn't remember ever experiencing before penetrated his entire being. He barely heard her over the pounding in his ears.

"Oh Steven," Angelina said, while blushing under his heated stare, "I did not realize you were home yet. Just a moment and I shall be finished."

"Madam, please do not trouble yourself to hurry on my account," he smiled, while leaning against the doorjamb to his room. Seemingly calm, his eyes belied any attempt at casualness his attitude tried to convey.

She was very hesitant to stand before him. Not so much embarrassed by his leering stare, but afraid that if she stood he would realize her condition. She wasn't sure yet how to tell him, although it would soon be impossible to hide it from him.

Clearly, he had no intentions of leaving. Finally realizing she had no alternative, she grabbed a towel and, while pressing it against her, stood up.

Stepping forward to help her, Steven's eyes never left her. How could it be he marveled, she was even more lovely than he remembered. Only four months ago, almost to the day, and she had changed dramatically. Her body was so sensuous, her breasts enormous, her waist slightly thickened while her arms and legs remained girlishly thin.

Suddenly the light dawned. Angelina saw it mirrored in his eyes, and didn't stop him as he moved the towel aside. Instantly his passion died, replaced by amazement. Slowly his fingers traced her waist and abdomen. Hesitantly, he asked, "Four months?"

She nodded.

"Were you not going to tell me?"

She shrugged, "I did not know how. It did not matter really," she smiled shyly, "you would surely have found out eventually."

She trembled so under his examining touch that she was sure her legs would fail her and she would fall against him. And when his hands rested upon her enlarged breasts and stroked them gently, she nearly swooned. "Steven, please," she groaned, "do not touch me so."

Quickly, his hands fell to his side, and once again she covered herself with the towel.

"Indeed I am sorry. It is just that I was so surprised. Still, I cannot believe it. I am to be a father in what, five months?" His mouth split into a happy grin as he asked, "What has the doctor to say of your condition? Did he find you in excellent health?"

She shook her head, "As yet I have seen no doctor."

His smile faded. Clearly he was annoyed. "Dress yourself immediately, Angelina. You are going now!"

Within an hour Steven's carriage was standing outside Dr. Jenkin's office in Portsmith.

Chapter 31

It had been two weeks since Steven's discovery of her pregnancy, and Angelina was becoming increasingly upset. He saw to her every comfort and need to the point of badgering. With her nerves taut, she wished fervently for peace from his constant ministrations.

While readying herself for an evening's entertainment, Angelina sat relaxed for the moment under the care of Cicely's knowledgeable hands. She was working Angelina's long golden hair into a magnificent halo of soft curls, when Steven entered. As of late, it was becoming a habit for him to enter her room each evening, without knocking, bearing a small tray upon which rested a decanter and two brandy snifters.

Nonchalantly, he dismissed Cicely which added to Angelina's building annoyance.

Glaring at him through her mirror, she remarked, "Sir, how is it you come to my room, enter without knocking, interrupt my dressing, and dismiss my maid, and all without my permission. Really Steven, sometimes you are so annoying. I cannot stand much more of your care. I am near the point where I am about to scream.

"Not a moment has passed since you have discovered your future parenthood that I have not been plagued by your overzealous ministrations and concern. Believe me when I tell you, I have had enough."

Smiling at her reflection, he sat behind her on her lounge chair and while offering her a drink, he answered, "Angelina love, you misunderstand. I have not come because you are to be the mother of my child, but merely because you are a most attractive and delectable woman whose company I enjoy tremendously. I wish only to spend a quiet moment with you before the evening's festivities begin for I know from past experience, I can consider myself lucky indeed if I can claim you for one dance. Since you have come here, you are in such demand that I fear some young blade might turn your head."

Laughing softly, she remarked, "Have no fear Steven, you most of all should know my head does not turn quite so easily."

Her robe separated when she turned in her chair and reached for the brandy, giving Steven a tantalizing view of her long trim shapely leg and partially exposed breast.

His blood hammered in his brain. It only

took the knowledge that she sat before him naked beneath her robe, to set his starved body on fire. Since he had known her, she had never seemed more appealing. She did nothing to close the gaping front of her dressing gown. Smiling, she realized full well the effect she was having on him.

Leaning back silently, she rested her back against the dressing table, crossed her legs, and swung her bare foot toward him, as she spoke. "Truly, I am sorry, Steven," she smiled in her own sweet yet provocative fashion. "It seems I am somewhat nervous today."

He nodded his acceptance of her apology while sitting before her, his eyes greedily enjoying the view. Pouring her another drink, he smiled slyly, "You have been jittery as of late, love. Perhaps there is something I can do for you, something to calm your nerves?"

She smiled seductively, the brandy taking immediate effect on her empty stomach. While sipping at her drink, and noting the sudden warmth of her room, she leaned back further still, resting on her elbows while her dressing gown slipped open even more. Wantonly, she allowed him view of her leg and most of her hip. She watched as his eyes traveled up her body and smiled, "Is that what you call it now, a nerve tonic?"

Steven grinned, his eyes glowing with a dangerous gleam. "I do believe you are teasing me, Angelina."

"Teasing you, Steven? Why on earth would I want to do that?" she asked giving him a look that was wide eyed and innocent.

"Perhaps you wish to remind me, in your own gentle way, that first you are a lovely, seductive and tantalizing woman and in the future I am to think of you as such, and secondly as the mother of my child."

Steven nearly lost all control and had to grip the arms of the chair tightly to keep his hands at his side, as he watched her smile and stretch languidly before him, raising her arms carelessly above her head and enticingly pushing her breasts toward him as she arched her back and sighed sweetly, "Steven, at times you are most astute."

Forcing his passions under control, he grinned lazily as he warned, "Perhaps I should remind you, love, that I am your husband, and more importantly, a man who is not used to unfulfilling his desires. I can promise you, the fruits you so generously display for the picking shall not ripen and die shriveled on the vine, but shall be plucked without hesitation at the first opportunity. Remember, I know the taste of this particular fruit and hunger constantly for another sampling of its ripe honey nectar. After all, you would not have me be remiss in the performance of my husbandly duties."

Slowly, while answering his smile with one of her own, she pulled her gown close around her which only added to his enjoyment for the snugness displayed a voluptuous shape to his admiring eyes. "Aye sir, I perceive your meaning," she laughed, "but unless memory fails, it was you who set the bargain. Could it be that the sight of a mere leg would make you break your word?" With that she stood and placed her foot upon the lounge next to him, baring her leg for his view and taunting him into breaking his promise.

Lazily, he smiled up at her confident face. "Madam, were I to touch you, would you stay so cool? Would you not fall passionately and sobbing into my arms as you have done in the past? Shall I put you to the test?"

"Nay sir," she warned laughing, "it would be no test, for we both know the outcome. If you do, you break the bargain."

"Madam, is it not you who beg for my touch?"

"Nay," she lied, "I do not. This is my room and I shall dress or not as I please while in it."

Standing, he pulled her to him and holding her close against him, he whispered, "Very well madam, I concede you this point." His lips only inches from hers, he continued, "It shall not be long before you seek out my bed. We both know this as fact. I only wonder how much longer I am to wait." He was looking in her eyes, and recognized his own need mirrored in them when he smiled and whispered, "Aye, love, the end is almost here."

His nearness clouded her mind and she could think of no answer to his statement. His lips were so close; it had been so long since he held her, since he had kissed her. She watched his mouth, her own lips parted expectantly, her mind willing his lips to cover hers.

Abruptly, he released her, "Finish dressing love, our guests will arrive shortly."

Weak-kneed, Angelina stumped into her chair and called for Cicely. While she dressed, she wondered at his remarks. She had known great passion under his skillful hands. Remembering brought a tightness across her belly that passed into pain. Could she go to him? Her tortured dreams of longing would end at last if he once again held her in his strong arms and kissed her until she nearly fainted.

Enough! She couldn't think now. She wouldn't think now!

Chapter 32

The next day, Angelina slipped out of bed only moments after the sun rose. She hummed a merry tune while she hurriedly dressed for a dawn meeting with her husband. She laughed aloud as she realized in meeting her husband, for all appearances, she could be meeting her lover, so unusual was the place and time of the rendezvous.

It was necessary to wake up the stable boy for no one was awake anywhere on the plantation. Steven suggested they meet on a grassy knoll, on the far side of the plantation, near an old dilapidated cabin. He was to be gone from the house for the night, and expected to return by first light.

Angelina had not asked Steven where he would be going, knowing full well he attended to business in much the same fashion as herself, except she no longer left the house to do it. When she reached the designated area, she dismounted and tethered her horse to a tree. While she waited for Steven, her mind slipped back to the previous evening.

It seemed half the garrison had been present and Angelina had no lack of dancing partners. At one point she had been dancing with a particularly handsome British officer and laughing at the outrageous compliment he had just given her when, over the Captain's shoulder, she looked into Steven's eyes. His look was filled with such murderous rage and fury that she, for an instant, trembled beneath the intensity of it. And then an instant later he smiled so charmingly, Angelina's heart fluttered as if she were still a very young girl and she felt herself blushing under his regarding tender gaze.

The dance ended. She thanked the officer prettily and made her way to the terrace for a breath of air and a moment's solitude to settle her shaken emotions. Steven had never smiled at her like that before. His look implied more than a mere smile should and it shook her to the core. She wandered from the terrace toward the garden, stopping at one of the arbors and sitting down to relax for a moment.

Steven was following close behind for no sooner did she sit than she heard his voice.

"Madam, I do not intrude if I join you for a moment?"

Smiling, she answered playfully, "You, sir, could never intrude. I find your company most agreeable as of late." She moved slightly, giving him room to sit beside her. Sighing contentedly, she continued, "Is it not pleasant in the garden, Steven? Truly I love your home."

"Angelina," he admonished, "you injure me sorely. Am I to believe you still feel as if this place is only my home? Are you not comfortable and happy here?"

"Oh aye, Steven. You have made me more than comfortable and I very much feel at home here. As for happiness, I believe if one is happy in his heart, he is happy anywhere."

"And are you happy in your heart, love?"

She smiled while saying nothing, a gentle, shy look in her eyes.

He smiled pleasantly, "Would you do me the honor of allowing me this dance?"

She laughed delightedly, "Sir, truly it is most unseemly for us to dance out here, alone in the dark."

"Nonsense," he responded jovially, as he pulled her to her feet and into the circle of his arms, "You are my wife, even if it is for the present in name only. Besides, who will see us?"

The music drifted softly from the open doors of the ballroom as they moved dreamily, locked in each other's arms, lost in each other's eyes, turning in small circles about the garden.

It was a perfect night. The air was warm and sweet with the perfume of flowers. Stars glistened overhead and the moon shone down illuminating the garden in silvery light. And when the music ended, they stayed enclosed in an embrace, neither willing to leave the other's arms.

She stood staring up at him, watching as his head descended to hers, knowing he was about to finally kiss her and wanting him so desperately to do just that.

Inches from her mouth, he groaned, "Angelina, your beauty staggers the mind."

"Steven," she moaned almost the same instant as his mouth closed on hers.

The kiss they shared held all the torment and yearning of the last four months of celibacy. Every sleepless lonely night, every moment of remembered ecstasy, every tortured second of unfulfilled desire.

Tenderly, gently, as if she were a delicate rose, his hands stroked her willing and pliant body. The strength of his arms around her brought her wild excitement, nearly buckling her knees, she wondered fleetingly why she was ever out of them. She was lightheaded with the touch of his muscular lean body as she pressed tighter to him. Dizzy from the scent and feel of him, her hands slid up his broad shoulders and clamped together as they circled his neck.

His mouth left hers, her mind a fiery frenzy of need. She gasped at the tumultuous sensations his lips caused as they brushed featherlight against her cheek and nuzzled her neck.

Softly, he whispered, "Darling, I have business to attend to tonight and I will not be back until early tomorrow. Meet me, please, at dawn on the grassy knoll by the old shack. Please, love. There is something I want to tell you. Something you must know."

Hoping the meeting would bring about the end of her loneliness, she willingly agreed. "Aye Steven," she sighed sweetly, "I will meet you."

Now as she waited, she wondered at the strange feelings stirring within her. Her heart fluttered when he looked at her. His presence brought a smile to her lips. She found herself seeking out his company on almost any pretext. She realized she genuinely liked him. No matter, he was her enemy. Clearly it was possible to separate the man and his business.

Suddenly, an idea entered her head. Could it be possible? Was she in love with her husband? She knew she was attracted to him and had been almost from the first moment they had met. But this was different. There was still an attraction, but much more. Something new and undefined had been added. She giggled out loud. How ridiculous if it were true. Women did not fall in love with their husbands.

Angelina laughed again, overcome with this new sweet delectable knowledge. Only a few months had passed since she had wished him dead and had felt such hatred that she was positive no other emotion could be as strong. But she had been wrong. Perhaps she had loved him all along. Could that have been the reason for her extreme hatred when she thought she had been betrayed?

She shook her head as if to clear it from confusing thoughts. It mattered little; the only thing she was sure of right now was that she loved her husband, and the knowledge brought a smile to her eyes and laughter bubbling from her lips.

An arm suddenly reached out and circled her waist startling Angelina into a shriek. Deep in thought, she had heard no one approach her. In less then a few seconds a number of sensations swept over her. First she was scared and then relaxed, reasoning it was Steven behind her, and then terrified, realizing it was not.

She struggled trying to free herself from a steely vise that circled her. Horrible evil laughter was echoing in her brain and the man's free arm came up and squeezed her breast bringing her excruciating pain, and hysterical fear to her terrified mind.

She screamed again and again while praying Steven was close by. She was flung around and forced to face her attacker.

"Shut up, you dirty whore bitch," John Landen growled in her face.

Angelina was so surprised at seeing Mr. Landen that she was momentarily stunned into silence.

A few seconds passed. Landen enjoyed the look of astonishment in her eyes, and watched cheerfully as that look turned to terror.

"Steven will kill you if you touch me, Mr.

Landen," Angelina warned, her voice trembling even more than her body.

"By the time I've finished with you, my lady," he sneered, "no one will know who touched you, nor will they recognize what's left of you." He laughed evilly as he continued, "Did you think I would simply leave here after what you did? I've been waiting weeks to get my revenge."

She tried to pull away, and screamed again, but was immediately silenced by a fist smashing into her cheek bone and another into her mouth. Flecks of light flashed before her eyes. She grunted each time his fist slammed into her. Pain was shattering her whole being She didn't recognize the guttural sounds that escaped her throat. She would have screamed again had she realized his fists were pommelling her stomach. But although she felt breathless with the force of each blow, her mind was dazed with pain and she never realized the warm stickiness that was sliding down her legs was blood and the searing ripping pain that spread through her back was the death of her baby.

Then as blessed blackness closed over her limp body, she fell to the ground. John Landen gave this hated creature a final kick to her head slipping her mercifully into unconsciousness.

Surely he would have continued his job of vengeance had not the galloping sounds of a horse riding swiftly towards him prevented its completion. Instead, he ran like the coward he was, never stopping until nightfall when at last he reached the town of Portsmith and bought passage on a ship. He was confident he'd never again see nor hear from Angelina or Steven. But that was not to be the case.

Chapter 33

Steven was returning from his business appointment. He hoped the cause appreciated his sacrifice for he knew that he and Angelina could have been reconciled last night had it not been for this damn war. He'd had enough. Too many had died horrifying deaths needlessly, uselessly.

Now he had more immediate and important things on his mind. He hoped his young wife waited for him at their designated meeting place. It was long past the time for her to know about him. Time at last to clear the cloud that constantly hovered over their relationship.

He'd had enough of waiting. He thought it was near impossible to love her more than he already did. He only prayed she was beginning to return those feelings. She had to come to him willingly before he would make love to her again. He prayed the time was now. There was nothing he wouldn't do for her. Nothing he wouldn't give her. Perhaps today they would talk of it. Perhaps tonight they would do more than talk.

Steven approached the grassy knoll and smiled happily as he saw Angelina's horse tethered to a tree. But the smile froze on his lips as he came closer and saw his wife's limp body lying bloody and unconscious some twenty feet away.

His heart pounded wildly with dread. Instantly, he was beside her, his ear pressed against her chest, listening. But he could hear nothing except the hysterical buzzing in his ears and the wild pounding of his own heart.

Taking huge gulps of air, he forced his panic under control. Shaking his head as if to clear it, he bent down and listened again.

She was alive! *Thank God! Please just stay alive,* he prayed. *Please God, please, please, please . . .*

As gently as possible, he lifted her and walked the hundred yards or so to the old cabin. Once inside, he laid her on an old dilapidated bed. His clothing was full of her blood. He was terrified; never before had he seen such blood. Her color was as white as death, except for the discolored bruises all about her face. He had to get help, but was loothe to leave her. If he left her, it would be more than twenty minutes before he could return. But she had to have a doctor.

Tenderly, he kissed her brow and forced

himself to leave.

He rode as if the devil himself pursued him and it was less than ten minutes later that he reined up his horse and bellowed orders to the startled servants. Not bothering to dismount, he turned and sped back the way he had come.

When he reached the cabin, Angelina was as he had left her. Terrified to look, yet unable not to, he raised her skirts and pulled down her lacy panties. There was blood everywhere. Her chemise was soaked with it as were her stockings and shoes. He thought it impossible to lose so much blood and live, and still it was dribbling out of her.

There was a large clot about the size of his fist. He guessed it to be the baby. Quickly, he ripped off his shirt and tore it into strips of cloth. Gently he cleaned her and pressed a wad of material to her body hoping it would help to staunch the blood's flow. Finally he raised her legs and covered her with his coat. Praying he was doing the right thing, he held her close to him and waited for help to arrive.

It seemed as if hours passed before he heard the sound of horses followed by many wagons. It was apparent Cicely had taken nearly half the plantation with her. Even the doctor was surprised that nothing seemed to be forgotten. From brandy and wine to hot soup. From clean bedding to the bed itself. Everything possible for the comfort of the young mistress was thought of and brought along.

After an examination by the doctor, Steven breathed a sigh of relief to hear nothing appeared to be broken. He was sorry for the loss of the baby, but thankful he still had her.

The doctor didn't seem to think that she had lost too much blood. Before he finished examining her she came to, the pain in her face being so intense he quickly gave her something to ease it.

It was hours later. A single candle stood on the table near the bed. Steven sat alone, watching her. She was awake. The effects of the morphine still clouded her mind, and she felt discomfort in her face and stomach.

She looked at him for a long moment before asking tearfully, "The baby?"

"Do not worry of it now, love. It is important only that you are safe and will soon be well." Continuing tenderly, "I promise you, there will be more babies."

Her face was swollen beyond recognition. Her left eye was closed. Both her lips were cut and triple their normal size. A gash on her head, covered now with bandages, was discolored blue and purple.

She was crying softly, "Hold me, Steven. My body aches so."

Gently he gathered her in his arms as he sat on the bed. "Who was it, Angelina?"

She sobbed, "Mr. Landen. Oh Steven, he hurt me."

Her tears of suffering affected him more than he could have imagined. "I know. I have seen. Have no fear for if he is still on the island, he will die for this. And I promise you, his death will not be an easy one. Talk no more of it, love, it is over and no one shall ever hurt you again."

It was three days before Angelina was strong enough to sit up and feed herself.

Steven was adamant. No one was to touch her but the doctor and himself. He was so fearful of her well being that he trusted no one. It was impossible for him to put her in another's hands. Not being able to see her, even for a short time, left him mindless with anxiety.

Once he was positive she would recuperate, he breathed easier and promised the ever nagging Cicely that she could administer to her young mistress beginning tomorrow.

Alone in the cabin at last, he sat in a chair beside her bed and eyed her carefully, considering her delicate beauty and the purple bruises to her lips, eye, and forehead. His heart constricted in pain as he watched her smile at him.

Handing her a cup of strong hot tea, their eyes met and he commented, "You look lovely tonight."

She laughed, "Indeed I must. If you consider my battered face lovely, I shudder to think what you believe is ugly."

Smiling, he continued, "Madam, to me you will always be beautiful. You seem so delicate, I almost fear to touch you."

She smiled pleasantly, "Have no fear, Steven. I am weak—yes, but I will not break."

And then she flushed hotly as she remembered his ministrations of only an hour ago. She was helpless to refuse his insisting that he should bathe her. A blush stained her cheeks a darker shade still when she remembered how his hands had moved over her. Gently he cleaned her bruised skin. She had closed her eyes tightly and turned her face away, unable to face him as his hands went about their duties, necessarily touching her most personal and private parts in a purely clinical manner.

He knew from the pained look in her eyes, and her reddened complexion, just how her thoughts were running. Finally, he asked, "Are you feeling more comfortable now?"

"Aye," she responded, looking about the small room, unable to meet his eyes.

Taking a brush from her bedstand, he sat companionably beside her on the bed and began to brush her waist length golden hair. His voice was pleasant and soothing as he spoke. "I know you are feeling some embarrassment, love, but do not fret so. It is only I your husband who looks upon your body. I wish you to feel perfectly at ease in my care for I doubt you could find another who would treat you with more tenderness and concern, nor love you more."

She turned to face him, their faces very close as he continued. His eyes never left hers as he whispered hoarsely, his voice shaking with emotion, "If it were only possible to take your suffering upon myself, I promise you it would have been done." And then sighing in frustration, "These are the times men such as I wish themselves poets for I cannot find the words to tell you what I feel."

She smiled delightedly. This was the first time he had said he loved her. She reached up and touched her fingertips to his cheek, smiling tenderly, "You need not worry about your lack of fancy words, Steven, for you do very well indeed. And your eyes continue to tell me when your words end."

When it was time to extinguish the candle and sleep, she watched as he settled himself in the chair beside her again. "Steven please, it is not necessary for you to remain uncomfortable and sleep sitting up. Come, share this huge bed."

She saw in his eyes he was about to refuse. "I promise you, your being beside me will cause me not the slightest discomfort."

Thereafter, each night he slept in his wife's bed. Holding her close against him, soothing her when she stirred or moaned in her sleep. And she felt happy and safe, pressed close to him.

As she grew stronger daily, she looked forward to the nights as the best part of each day. They lay beside one another with her head nestled on his shoulder and his arm protectively about her. She wished the morning never to come as they spoke in the darkness, each relaxed and comfortable in the other's company. Here, after being married for close to a year, they truly began to know and understand one another. And each silently dreaded the day when she was well enough to be brought home, where they would return to their separate rooms.

"Please Steven," she begged sweetly, while barely suppressing a giggle, "you really must listen to me. I cannot bear lying about a moment longer. You must allow me, for a time at least, to sit in a chair. It has been over a week now since my injury, and I feel very well."

But she looked anything but well. Her face was somewhat less swollen, but very much discolored. Now the predominant color was green still mixed liberally with many shades of blue and purple.

"If you insist, my love," he smiled, helpless to resist any request of hers. "You know I can refuse you nothing. Come, let me help you."

Carefully, as if she were a china doll, he lifted her from the bed and placed her in a chair. He fussed over her, bringing pillows from the bed for her back, and blankets for cover to prevent a chill.

"Steven," she laughed, "what difference is this? I feel I am still abed." Eyeing him appraisingly, she teased, "Sir, if by chance the day should come when you find yourself in need of employment, I could recommend you highly, for you make an admirable nursemaid."

Laughing at her remarks, he replied, "Have no fear, madam, for my funds have not as yet depreciated to require me to seek employment." And giving her a teasing grin, he continued jovially, "Would it not cause you some disturbance if I should become nursemaid to some other beautiful and desirable young woman?"

She did not answer him.

He waited, watching her, his lips holding the faintest trace of a smile, "Will you not answer me, Angelina? Would it not cause you some disturbance?"

"Aye, Steven, you are correct. I shall not answer you," she laughed.

"Come my love, what harm is there in a simple answer?" he coaxed, as his eyes glowed with humor.

Finally, after a long pause, she raised her eyes to meet his, and uttered a long sigh of resignation, "Very well, if you insist. Aye, I confess it would not sit well with me."

He took her hand and raised it to his lips, kissing her palm and then her wrist so slowly and sensuously, it caused her to gasp.

All the while his eyes glowed with happy satisfaction at her admission and the intensity of his searing look brought a pink flush to her cheeks.

Chapter 34

Angelina, in a hurry, walked swiftly to the barn, anxious for her morning ride. She was meeting Steven and they planned a long ride together. As she neared the door, she slowed her steps and listened, surprised to hear a woman's voice coming from within.

"Do you know how very attractive you are?"

And she heard her husband's answer, "Thank you, Miriam. Is Jonathan not with you today?"

"Oh, he had some business to attend to in Portsmith. I found myself with nothing to do today. Would you care to go riding with me?"

"Nay, Miriam. I hope to ride with Angelina today. Perhaps you would care to join us?"

Now she was at the doorway. She watched as Miriam moved close to him and slipped her arms around Steven's neck, while she purred prettily, "Steven, kiss me please. Make love to me. I want you so badly."

For a moment, Angelina felt sick. She turned and was about to run from them when she suddenly remembered Steven saying once before, "If you had not been so quick to leave, you might have seen . . ." Slowly, she turned herself around and forced her unwilling eyes to watch.

At first Steven felt no need to resist the lovely young woman. His mind in a fog, he felt her full breasts push against his chest. He wanted her. His body and emotions had been starved for six long months. He felt a need to possess her so strong, it shook his soul. But suddenly it wasn't Miriam whose kisses he was returning with sudden wild desire, but Angelina's. Angelina who laughed, teased, and promised nothing, but he wanted no other.

The kiss seemed to Angelina's mind to last forever. Steven's hands were finally behind his neck, trying to free himself of her arms. When he did succeed, it was not to Angelina's satisfaction, for he was much too kind and gentle with the hussy.

Her beautiful face was flushed with desire and her slanted dark eyes were half closed with passion as she pressed herself closer.

"Miriam, I do not wish to appear unkind or ungracious. Indeed, you have given me a great compliment. But in all fairness to you, I must decline your generous offer. It seems my thoughts are elsewhere as of late, and it would not be honorable of me should I take advantage of you at this time, nor any time in the foreseeable future."

"But, Steven, my darling," she pouted beautifully, "surely there is no reason why we cannot continue our long relationship. We are not children. We hurt no one if we indulge in our own private moments of pleasure. You know Jonathan has been incapable of giving me satisfaction for a long time."

Obviously uncomfortable, he answered, "That may be, Miriam, but I too can offer you no satisfaction."

She looked at him for a long moment. Suddenly, she laughed a delightful, tinkling, and slightly mocking sound, "Steven, you are not telling me you are in love with your wife?"

And when he said nothing to deny her words, she laughed again, her eyes wide with astonishment, "Oh Steven, really, how terribly common." And then changing her attitude once more, while her hands caressed his chest, she continued, "Please my darling, for old time's sake, let's go in the back room. Just this one last time?"

If the truth was known, it took a great deal of willpower for Steven to refuse. It seemed forever since he had touched Angelina. For so long now he had wanted his wife. It would be so simple to use Miriam in her place, but to what avail? Angelina's bewitching face would only come between them again and it would, in the end, prove to be of no enjoyment for either of them.

Angelina held her breath, not daring to breathe as she waited for his answer.

After a long pause, he finally spoke, "I am sorry, Miriam, it is not possible for us to have any relationship other than simply being friends."

It was obvious to Angelina that Miriam was not about to take no for an answer. Finally speaking, she remarked coyly, "Were I you, Miriam, I would take the man at his word and find me another playmate. He did, after all, refuse your kind offer."

Startled, they both turned to see Angelina leaning, apparently calm and at ease, against the inside wall of the barn. Her eyes were as icy as her voice, while she slapped her riding crop menacingly against her boot.

Miriam's face tightened with hatred as she passed wordlessly by Angelina. She offered no excuses or apology nor a murmur of good-bye, but fixed her with a look of such intense evil and menace, that Angelina, for a moment, felt her body go rigid with fear.

Steven smiled as he watched his wife's lovely graceful form move slowly towards him. "How long have you been standing there?" he asked as a smile of genuine pleasure played about his mouth.

"Long enough," she answered curtly. "Do you always have this particular problem of unwanted female attention?"

He shrugged, "It happens from time to time. But it is of no consequence."

She glared at him, her anger apparent.

"Did I not pass the test?" he grinned.

"Only just," she answered, still annoyed,

"which barely satisfies. You allowed her kiss to last much too long. It was obvious, sir, that you enjoyed her attentions."

He laughed, "Aye perhaps, but in the end I did not succumb to her charms. Temptation does not count, it is what you do with it that matters."

"Perhaps I should call Miriam back," she teased, "for it appears this temptation was particularly agreeable."

"Nay," he returned, "it is not Miriam I want, I find her a bit too frivolous for my taste. A wife such as she, is no prize to any man. As of late, I find my needs are more in tune with my own wife; for I believe the real worth of a man is how long he can remain faithful to his love, not how many loves he can acquire."

"Aye Steven, I think you are correct in these beliefs. For myself, I could care for no man who would not hold me above all others and forever be true."

He was standing before her, blocking her way to her horse, smiling gently down at her.

For a long moment they looked at each other. Suddenly, she gave him a devilish grin and slid her hands up his chest.

He groaned playfully, "It is my cursed fate to be forever taunted by teasing females?"

Looking sweetly up at him, a trace of a sly grin played about her mouth. With her eyes half closed and her lips parted invitingly, she waited. For weeks now, she had been trying to tempt him into breaking the bargain, but as yet to no avail. She smiled tenderly and almost purred as she lied, "Steven really, why is my every action suspect? Many are the times you touch me in a familiar and affectionate manner, why is it then I may not do the same without ulterior motives?"

"Touché, my love," he grinned, "could I have had a mental lapse of some sort? Have I a fever?" he laughed, while placing the palm of his hand against his head. "Was that me complaining that my lovely wife was touching me?"

The barn rang out with happy laughter as the two young people prepared their horses for a ride.

Chapter 35

She was determined to have an end to this stupid and seemingly everlasting bargain, but equally determined it would not be she who would end it. For long enough now, she had suffered through endless nights of tortured longing and sleep that bombarded her with the most arousing, sensual, passion-filled dreams. She smiled to herself, thinking how inconceivable these feelings would have been only a few short months ago, and realized she had changed a great deal.

Her face flamed with the thought of going to him and telling him she wanted him. And indeed she did. Actually, as of late, it was uppermost in her mind. She knew this was what he waited for, yet she couldn't; she just couldn't do it.

Again and again, she had tried to get Steven to break his word, but he held his desire in tight control. His iron will fought against every temptation she threw at him. And indeed these temptations were purposeful and not of meager consequences.

Twice she had sat silent in a tub of cooling water, feeling as if she were about to freeze to death, while she waited for him to enter the room. She could hear him as he moved about his bed chamber. Finally she had groaned with frustration as the door to his room closed and the sound of his jaunty whistle wound its way out of her range of hearing.

The next time, her long wait brought her only a small amount of pleasure and near pneumonia, for she was chilled and covered with goose flesh when he finally opened the door, and then he only muttered an apology and quickly left her to what he believed was the finish of her bath.

Countless were the times she had purposely brushed seductively against him, perhaps caressing his chest as she spoke softly. She knew by the pained expression in his eyes that these moments stirred him deeply, yet it brought her no satisfaction for he remained true to his word.

Tonight she swore all this nonsense would end. She was positive this would do it and she felt not the least amount of guilt that she would use her recent illness to trick him.

It was very late. She had bathed and liberally used the perfume she knew he preferred. Now she sat before her mirror, brushing her hair. When at last satisfied with its glossy texture, she began to search her closet.

When she found the correct garment, she stripped off her nightgown and slipped into the same robe of midnight lace Steven had had made to order for her. The robe according to his instructions had nothing to secure it. Standing before her mirror, she nodded her final approval and then went to the bath to set her plan in motion.

She wanted to giggle. This was so simple, she berated herself for not thinking of it sooner. Purposely, she placed an empty porcelain pitcher on the edge of a cabinet that held the towels. Carefully, she lay down on the floor between the cabinet and the tub. After adjusting her robe to barely cover herself, knowing it would open when Steven lifted her in his arms, she gave a loud moan, and reached up and smashed the pitcher to the floor.

Only a moment passed before the door from Steven's room was flung open. Steven stood just inside the room. His heart hammered in his ears as he saw what he thought to be the unconscious figure of his wife lying on the floor.

Quickly he went to her side, calling out her name, and received only silence for an answer. Instinctively, he laid his ear to her heart and oddly found it beating wildly.

With a puzzled look, he glanced at her face. He couldn't be sure, but he doubted she had fainted. He whispered her name so close to her mouth that his lips brushed enticingly against hers. She responded by parting her lips and whispering his name groggily in return. But when she firmly slid her arms about his neck, allowing her robe to gape open, he was positive she had planned the whole thing.

Smiling at her deviousness, he promised himself he'd speak to her later regarding the scare she had just given him and what he thought she deserved for it. He lifted her and began to walk toward her room. And because her gown was open, allowing him to see all for just a moment, which was all the time needed, his tight control broke and his face buried itself on her breast.

Instantly, she responded. Her body jerked to the touch of his warm mouth upon her and she moaned with pleasure as his hot wet tongue slid across her skin, leaving a trail of fire.

Suddenly, he stopped, his mouth leaving this tender morsel.

Her eyes blinked open when she heard him swear in disgust. All pretense of fainting was gone when she recognized the grimace of pain that spread across his face.

"Steven, what is it?" she asked, sliding from his arms.

"Be careful of the broken glass, my love," he warned knowingly.

Her eyes left his and she moaned guiltily, "Oh no, Steven, I am so sorry." And as she spied the blood gushing from a deep wound at the bottom of his foot, she continued, "Can you get back to your room? Here, let me help you, lean against me."

When he finally reached the bed, she left, calling out, "I will be back in a moment," and returned quickly with a thick towel. After wrapping his foot, she left again to dress herself and send for the doctor.

Later after the doctor cleaned and closed the cut, she sat by the bed. "I cannot tell you how sorry I am my fainting caused you pain, Steven. It was so silly of me."

He knew she lied, but decided he'd not push her into admitting the truth now. Soon enough she would come to him. He almost laughed as he realized the end of the bargain was clearly in sight.

Chapter 36

She pushed aside the mosquito netting and stepped out onto the dark terrace. She breathed deeply. The night was still and airless. Nothing stirred. Here there was still no relief.

Angelina's solitary candle on her bed stand gave off only the smallest illumination from her room. Moments before, she had stood in her tub and poured cold water from a pitcher over her shoulders. Soaking wet, she slipped into her robe, tying it loosely at her waist and leaving it almost completely opened, unable to stand anything clinging to her.

The weather had been unbearably hot for days. She was thankful a storm was coming. Perhaps it would bring some relief. In the distance, she could hear an occasional clap of thunder and less often a bolt of lightning would flash across the black sky.

Already, she was completely dry. She stood

at the oranate railing, waiting, hoping for a breeze.

Suddenly she hit the railing in frustration with the palm of her hand a bit too hard and growled, "Damn!"

It had been a week since Steven had returned from another business trip. His temper remained so serene while she got bitchier daily. Good Lord, the man seemed to be made of steel.

Now rubbing her bruised hand, she thought, *there had to be a way*. But no matter how deeply his passion blazed, seething just beyond his grinning lips and laughing eyes, he always held it under control.

She couldn't seem to push him over the edge. He would not break his word. He waited patiently for her to come to him.

How could he be so calm about it? This craving for his touch was tearing her to pieces. Her body literally ached with desire. She began to pace nervously, walking the terrace only to the length of her room and back again.

Steven was awake. She could smell his pipe tobacco, yet his room was in total darkness.

Obviously he too was unable to sleep. She knew it was for the same reason. But still he waited. Waiting, watching, and waiting again. Damn him for his patience.

She desperately wished she had the nerve to go to him. It seemed the longer they were separated, the harder it was for her to do anything about it.

This whole situation was ridiculous and unbelievable. She was embarrassed to admit her needs to him. Admit she was young and healthy and desired him dreadfully.

Sweat was beading on her forehead; a fine sheen covered the top of her lip. Her stomach constricted in a knot as she allowed herself to remember the touch of his hands on her. It seemed so long ago. God! How could she wait much longer? She had to do something. Make a move somehow.

"Does something trouble you, love?"

Abruptly, she stopped her pacing, while jumping slightly at the sound of his voice. Her eyes studied the darkness and, as a flash of lightning illuminated the dark terrace, she found his shadowy form leaning against the wall, almost hidden from her by a large potted plant that separated their doors.

She longed to go to him, to beg him to take her in his arms, to touch her, to kiss her. Oh God, she was going crazy with need.

Quickly she turned away, facing the railing, holding on until her knuckles turned white.

"It is the heat," she answered hoarsely.

"Aye, love, shall I ring for a cool drink?"

"Nay," she groaned, "It will not help."

"Perhaps you would care for a walk in the garden. It may help to cool you."

"I'm afraid that too would not help," she said, barely above a whisper.

He was beside her. "I have a need to move about and stretch my legs. Would you be so kind as to accompany me?"

"Aye Steven, if it is your wish," she smiled cautiously.

Together, they descended the stairs and walked companionably about the garden. Her mind was plotting. Tonight was the night. She would wait no more. Somehow, she'd manage it.

Finally, the wind began, very gently at first.

He looked down at her, a streak of lightning illuminating the garden. For just a moment, he saw her partially opened robe. In that instant, he could see almost all of her breasts as the gown opened with a gust of wind, leaving her nearly naked to the waist.

She breathed a deep sigh of relief as the cooling breeze began.

His body was instantly tense, his voice strained but forcibly calm, "Are you all right?"

She stood staring up at him, silent, unable to put into words the things she longed to say. Unable to ask for what she desired most. She turned slightly, leaning against a small garden table, dizzy with awareness of him.

Clouds opened, allowing the moon's rays to bathe them in soft light for just a moment.

Naked to the waist, he stood close to her. She breathed in his male scent, a clean mixture of tobacco, cologne, and soap. She watched as his eyes moved over her, nearly moaning out loud as she saw desire for her grow and kindle to a flame in their depths.

She began to breathe heavily. She couldn't answer him.

Leaning towards her, he groaned out painfully, "Is there something you want?" while watching her throat and the quick pulsating movement he saw throbbing there.

Her mind screamed, *he's giving you every opportunity. Say it, say it, you fool. You know what he wants to hear.*

And gathering her nerve, she slowly nodded her head while forcing herself to answer, her face flushed at her boldness.

The sky went black again as heavy dark clouds once more covered the moon's silvery glow.

"Aye Steven," she answered softly, her breath warm and sweet teasing on his cheek.

"What, love?"

Her eyes searched for his face, trying to make out his features in the blackness while her hands opened the tie that secured her robe. The robe parted to allow him to view her. But it was so dark, he could see nothing.

Finally, her hands groped for his, and slowly she raised them, bringing them in contact with her breasts.

She heard a muffled groan of pain come from deep within his chest.

He hesitated for an instant as if he couldn't believe it was finally happening. And then suddenly his hands were all over her, sliding to her waist and thighs and back again to her breasts.

Finally, at last, at last, she was in his arms, pressed tightly against his cool hard body. She thought she must have a fever. She was so hot. Her flesh seared his. She was sobbing his name into his chest.

Now the wind began in earnest, bellowing in their ears and whipping their hair about their faces in a wild raging frenzy. And then the rains came, soaking them in a torrent of cool water, and yet both felt nothing but the touch and feel of the other.

His face was buried in her neck, when he groaned out, "Tell me."

A long moment followed when only the sounds of their gasping breaths could be heard.

He raised his head, bringing his mouth closer to her ear and repeated, "Tell me, you must say it."

She moaned, lightheaded with his long awaited touch, her blue eyes dark and pleading, her voice breaking and nearly lost in the howling wind. Her hands crept up his chest, touching him, caressing him, "Oh God, Steven, it's you! It's always been you. I want you. I don't care anymore what you are, or what you've been. I only know I love you and if you don't make love to me, I shall die of wanting, for I've never felt pain such as this before."

Lightning flashed about them, thunder roared overhead, and they stood staring at one another, transfixed in awe, each reading of the other's love, clearly written in their eyes.

He watched her face, his eyes a mirror of her own longing. "Aye love, I know the feeling well," he smiled grimly.

Her arms about his neck pulled gently, finding no resistance as his head lowered to meet her.

At long last, their waiting at an end, their parted lips joined in a wild tumultuous kiss. Groaning, searching, their mouths fused together while each greedily explored the other, wishing never to stop.

She couldn't stand. She clung to him, begging him to never let her go.

Finally he lifted her and took her to the house. Once in her room, he put her down and ran for towels. A moment later, she stood naked as he rubbed her briskly with the thick thirsty material. Discarding his own clothing, he dried himself.

As if in a trance, she stood silent, watching him move the cloth over his chest. Softly, she spoke his name, "Steven, Steven, I love you so."

Smiling gently, he stood before her, his mouth only inches from hers. "I have never before thought about my name but when you speak it thus, it takes on a whole new meaning. It sounds to my ears as if it were a word of love."

Her hands moved up his chest feeling the pounding of his heart beneath them. Her eyes moved to his face, adoringly, she looked up at him, "For many months I have thought of it as such."

He smiled softly, and nodded, "Aye, I have not been mistaken then."

He bent down; his arm slipped behind her

knees; she was in his arms. He walked to the bed. She trembled so in anticipation, he could feel her shivering against him. His mouth was at her neck, nuzzling against the throbbing hollow of her throat. His voice was thick and husky with emotion as he asked, "Cold?"

She couldn't speak, so caught up in the desire of the moment was she, she simply shook her head.

The instant their bodies lay side by side, they were wild for each other. All thoughts of tenderness vanished as they clawed hungrily, touching to no satisfaction, but returning to touch once again.

She was dizzy, lost beyond any control, ecstatic with desire, about to be fulfilled at last.

His lips were hot and moist, searing her breasts, spreading to her waist, leaving a trail of fire across her belly. "Nay, God, Steven nay, you're killing me."

Her hands groped for him, pulling his maleness to her and she cried out in broken sobbing breaths, "Now Steven, please? Don't prolong it, just this once. We've waited forever."

And when he moved against her, she moaned, delirious with sensual sensations. "Aye, Steven. Oh love, aye, aye." And just before the final glorious moment of release, she moaned, "Steven, I can't bear it, love me, love me."

And Steven in turn was caught up in a blinding mindless throbbing passion that threatened his very sanity. He knew there would never be a time when their spirits would part again. He kissed her eyes, her cheeks, her neck and all the while, he whispered, "This time, love, this time it's forever," until his mouth was covering hers.

When they could once again breathe with some degree of normalcy, he groaned out, "I cannot believe I waited this long for you." And as his finger traced her fine brow, his dark eyes glowed with adoration as he continued, "You know, there were times I thought this would never happen. I've wanted you for so long. I've loved you for so long. Was it too fast for you? Was it good?"

She stretched languidly beneath him, her eyes half closed seductively, her lips holding just a trace of a smile, and with a slight shrug, she remarked casually, "It was adequate."

Surprised, he repeated, "Adequate?"

Laughing now, she responded, "Aye Steven, adequate, for I fear that if the truth were known, your head would swell to thrice its size and then what would become of all your fine handsome hats?"

He laughed at her nonsensical statement and then grinned devilishly, "Be not afraid my love, 'tis not my head that swells when I pleasure you."

She giggled and lowered her eyes, feigning embarrassment, "Oh for shame sir, how can you be so bold as to speak to me thus?"

Teasing, he replied, "Shall I speak to another then?"

"I have not the slightest doubt, sir, many

would welcome your boldness, but," she warned with a sly smile, "were I you, I would not."

"Indeed madam, I shall not. You need have no fear, for there is not another to compare to you. I feel a love for you so overwhelming, it compels and controls everything I think and do; so intense, I fear for my sanity. I wonder if you have not bewitched me. Are your eyes really as blue as they appear to me? Would your skin be so silky and soft to another's touch? Are you really this exquisitely beautiful being my eyes see? Do you understand, I begin to doubt my senses? Is this the raving of a man lost in the throes of his first true love, or a lunatic needing the safety of an asylum?"

"You ask the wrong one, Steven, for I too have never loved before and I also suffer much the same ailments."

After a moment of silence, while each enjoyed the touch and feel of the other, she whispered, "Do you know I love you?"

"Aye love, I know," he groaned into her mouth as his lips covered hers again, "I know."

"Steven?" she moaned after their mouths parted.

"Mmmm," he replied, intent at the moment on exploring her once again.

"Do you think in the future, we could sleep together? I get so damn lonely in that big bed by myself."

Laughing, he answered, "Darling, it matters not at all where we sleep, but this I promise you, we shall never again have separate bedrooms. Wherever we sleep, it shall be together. Now my love, I think there has been enough talk. I have some serious business to attend to, so if I could ask my lovely wife to join me in silence, I shall set about this most pleasurable task."

"Aye Steven," she sighed as his lips slipped from hers and strayed to her breasts to linger, sucking and licking, until the tips rose hard. And then leaving them, his mouth worked its way down her belly, and then her thighs, and all that could be heard was her gentle groan, "Oh aye, aye."

Chapter 37

Angelina was singing softly in her bath. She was radiant. Thinking back to last night brought a smile of remembered ecstasy to her lips. It had been a delicious night of love, lasting well past the first hint of dawn.

She had been so tired, but she wanted more. Having been so starved for him, she couldn't seem to get her fill. And then at dawn, he finally confessed to exhaustion, yet her hands and mouth brought him once more from weariness to a mind exploding climax.

Carefully, only moments ago, she had left the bed, leaving him undisturbed. Leaning back, she smiled, her eyes closed, remembering. God, how she loved him. What a fool she had been to wait so long.

Now it mattered not at all that she and Steven were loyal to different sides. Her mind reasoned, if he was considered a spy, was she not also?

Suddenly she realized it had taken her a long time to separate the man and his work, yet Steven had known nearly from the first where her loyalties lay and it never mattered to him.

His voice brought her instantly out of her dreamy reverie. "Madam, I do not take it kindly being abandoned and left to my own devices. Searching for you is not my idea of what we should be doing upon awakening."

Smiling, she turned slightly. He stood before her, unashamedly naked and gloriously handsome. Her eyes glowed with appreciation as she studied his form, and then turned seductive as she teased, "No? Pray tell sir, what is it we should be doing upon awakening?"

With a sly grin spreading across his handsome face, he walked to the tub. She thought he was going to pull her out, but suddenly, wordlessly, he joined her in the bath. Water splashed over the sides, soaking the floor, as she laughed, "Nay Steven, there is no room."

Still without a word, he slid in behind her, moving so she was sitting between his legs.

She leaned her head back, resting comfortably against his warm body. Turning her face she nuzzled her cheek against his hairy chest. Her voice grew suddenly weak and breathless. "I've no time to dally. Mrs. Harrington is coming for luncheon."

He breathed in the heady sweet scent of her hair and sighed, "Mrs. Harrington will have to wait. You have other more serious wifely duties to attend to. Here," he continued while taking the cloth and soap from her, "let me help you."

His arms circled her and she moaned, "Oh aye, Steven," as he fondled her breasts under the pretext of helping her to wash, "everyone should always bathe thus."

It wasn't long before she was no longer leaning against him, but on her knees and facing him, kissing his mouth, heedless of his scratching beard. Her arms about his neck, she pressed herself close and then her hand slipped down his stomach until she grasped him and he in turn groaned in agreement, "Aye love, 'tis the only way."

And suddenly, each feeling a need for the other so intense and uncontrollable, they never thought to leave the tub but continued their lovemaking under the water. Not since that long ago night at the Indian camp did they do such things, but this time, being perfectly sober, she found to her delight that loving him was indeed possible and highly pleasurable in more than one fashion and pose.

Angelina ran down the wide stairs, bubbling with laughter, as her husband followed in hot pursuit. A devilish gleam flashed in his eyes, while a grin played about his mouth. It was impossible to guess what he might do next, and with that look in his eye, she trusted him not at all.

She ran to the door of the sitting room and

stopped abruptly. She was weak with laughter. Putting her hands against his chest as if to hold him away, she giggled softly, "Please Steven, we have company. Let us at least try to act with some degree of decorum."

He grinned down into her happy face, laughter trembling his voice. "I can think of better things to do than act with decorum. Let's go to bed." And then he grabbed her, tickling her into another fit of giggles.

At first she tried to retaliate, but her hands only brought a groan of enjoyment from him and a distinct murmur of "More." Finally, she gave up and breathlessly managed to beg him to stop while pushing weakly against his chest.

At last he nodded in acquiescence.

It took her a few seconds to compose herself before she dared open the door. Her face was flushed from recent laughter when she entered the room with Steven at her side.

As Angelina was about to wish Mrs. Harrington welcome, Steven, standing at her left and just a half step behind her, reached down and firmly planted his hand on her derriére, giving it a firm squeeze.

His action was so unexpected and startling, that Angelina jumped some inches off the floor and forward, with surprise, her eyes wide with shock, and the poor elderly lady nearly had a seizure of fright as her hostess shrieked out her name. Helplessly, Angelina finished the sentence caught once again in a fit of giggles.

Finally forcing her laughter under control, she begged the lady's pardon and explained, lamely, she thought she saw a mouse and became a bit startled.

From behind her, she heard a strangled laugh.

Mrs. Harrington, although a widow for many years, had been fortunate to marry a man she loved, and had not forgotten their young life together. Although she was ignorant of the exact cause of Angelina's merriment, she could well guess from the radiant smiles and intimate looks the young couple shared.

When Mrs. Harrington smiled knowingly, Angelina turned scarlet, which only convinced the lady that something was afoot.

Steven, still behind her, smiled quite innocently when she turned to face him with eyes flashing murderously while her voice remained soft and pleasing. "Steven, will you ring and tell Jenny we are ready for luncheon now?" And with her back to their company still, she whispered, "You are going to suffer for that."

He took her hand and brought it to his lips, his eyes glittering with undisguised joy as he whispered conspiratorially, "Indeed, I cannot wait."

During their meal, Mrs. Harrington remarked, "I was in Portsmith yesterday and I noticed your ship being loaded with supplies. Are you about to leave us again?"

"Aye madam, I fear I must."

Angelina's look of disappointment was obvious.

Steven grinned, "Will you miss me, love?"

Looking into his merry eyes, Angelina was about to retort with some highly personal saucy barb, when she remembered Mrs. Harrington was present. Instead, she colored slightly and smiled shyly, "Of course, Steven."

Knowing his wife, he could well imagine what she was about to say and he could barely control his laughter.

Mrs. Harrington was at a loss as to why he was laughing at all.

Glancing at the lady's puzzled face, he grinned, "You must excuse me, madam. In truth, I am seldom in my wife's company that she doesn't bring a smile to my lips."

The rest of the meal continued on the same happy note until Mrs. Harrington decided she had stayed long enough.

Later that day, as their horses plodded through the dense lush forest, they came upon a small body of clear water. Steven dismounted and helped her from her horse. The forest was cool and damp. Large heavy branched trees protected them from the harsh strong afternoon sunlight.

From behind his saddle, Steven took a package containing a blanket, wine, and glasses. Spreading the blanket on the ground near the water, he filled their glasses.

Lying on the blanket, his hand propped under his head, he smiled at her as she lay beside him and gazed up dreamily to the tree tops high above them.

"What might you be dreaming of, madam?"

She sighed and looked at him, "You. It's so lovely here. How could you ever leave?"

He laughed, "Had I not, I never would have found you. Would you care to join me in a swim?"

She laughed happily, "Nay sir, I fear a swim with you could have only one possible conclusion, and although it seems private enough here, suppose someone should come along. What a scandal that would cause."

He smiled devilishly as his fingers began to unbutton his shirt. "Have no fear of a scandal, Mrs. Spencer. Have you forgotten I am your husband?"

"Nay Steven, 'tis a fact that has haunted me in one fashion or another for some time." And then smiling demurely, she added, "Sir, it is apparent once an idea has formed in your head, no amount of persuasion can dislodge it."

"Aye madam, my father has often told me I was spoiled and willful."

She nodded and grinned, "I believe he was not wrong in his judgment."

He looked at her for a long moment, his eyes studying her face. Finally he said, "It is too dangerous for travel at this time, for the war not only rages in the colonies, but in many other parts of the world. When it is over, I think we shall do some traveling. I know you are anxious to see your father and brother again. We will go there first and then I will take you to see my family. My mother is eager to meet you. To hear her say it, she has waited an extraordinarily long time for me to marry, and hungers for grandchildren." And then with a sly grin, he finished, "Do you think we could concede to an elderly lady's wants?"

She laughed at his ogling leer. "Where in England do your parents live?"

He smiled, "They live in Spain. On a country estate outside of Barcelona."

Her surprise was obvious, "Spain?"

"Aye, my father is Irish. He met my mother as a young girl through mutual friends, while visiting Spain. It is said they fell in love and caused a great scandal for she was promised to another. But my father was insistent to have her for himself and whisked her away and married her."

She looked at his handsome dark face with a teasing grin, "Oh Steven, truly that is most difficult to believe. I seriously doubt anyone from your family would whisk a woman away and marry her." She added, while trying unsuccessfully to keep a grin from her mouth and rolling her eyes to the sky, "Although I must confess it does sound vaguely familiar. I wonder where I could have heard that before?"

He grinned at her teasing remarks while his fingers reached for the buttons of her blouse. As the garment opened and revealed her golden smooth skin, his eyes glowed with admiration and he whispered softly, "Madam, you tempt me sorely. Aye, I cannot conceive of a time when you will not. How can I be held at fault for whisking you away to marry you when you tempt me so?"

She laughed gaily, her eyes twinkling with merriment, as she retorted, "Aye Steven, how indeed."

Together their clothes fell to the ground and they walked hand in hand to the cool water.

She came up gasping for air. His laughter rang out through the forest. She swung her small fists at him, while he continued to laugh at her attempts to hit him. "A moment longer would have been the end of me. Could it be that you grow tired of being a husband so soon?"

She lunged at him, knocking him back with her unexpected attack. He was still laughing as he allowed her to push him under while pulling her along.

Beneath the water, his mouth caught and held hers; his hand tangled in her hair, holding her close. Her pointed breasts pressed tight to his naked chest. Her soft silken body slid teasingly against his flesh and once again, Steven's passions flared to life.

Picking her up suddenly, she squealed, "Steven, do not dare!" thinking he was about to drop her under again.

But his eyes didn't answer her laughter as he carried her to the edge of the water. She gasped at the sudden seething desire she saw in their sparkling depths as he allowed her body to slip from his grip and slide against him until her feet touched the ground.

Her hands moved, caressing his chest, and she could say nothing but his name before his mouth covered hers in a wild, demanding, possessive kiss.

She couldn't believe it. She thought herself satiated yet she was wild for him again. A kiss, a look, a touch of his hand, brought her instantly alive with desire. Under his moving hands, she moaned, wanting him to never stop.

His lips left a trail of fire from her mouth and she groaned out his name, wanting once again to experience all the sensual pleasures he offered.

It was a leisurely afternoon of love and desire, holding many hours of pleasure which neither would forget, nor would the dark haired beauty and the giant black man who watched through the thick tropical growth a short distance away.

She was wild with jealousy and hatred. She wanted him, needed him. His hands touching Angelina stirred her to where she could almost feel them on herself. Her breathing grew harsh and shallow with desire. She had to have him, she had to.

The black man beside her was equally stirred. She glanced at him. He was licking his lips, imagining the feel of Angelina's golden body beneath his hands.

"Do you want her, Jake?" Miriam smiled slyly.

He grunted, his desire so strong, he was

barely able to speak.

"Help me and you can have her. I promise."

"When?"

"Soon, I promise you the time will come soon." As she spoke, she was desperately stripping her own clothes from her, her eyes on the bulge at the black man's groin. "Now Jake, now it's time for me." She was naked, a climax almost upon her, as she helped him pull his clothes off. "Hurry, Jake, pleasure me now, now."

Chapter 38

Steven was leaving again. Since coming to Santa Louisa, he had left on numerous missions, and always, Angelina had been sorry to see him go, finding herself constantly longing for his return. Now that they had reconciled, she had grown happy and content, glowing with incredible beauty under his adoring gaze. She felt her life had at long last found meaning, and she was more than ever distraught at the idea of his leaving. Knowing the loneliness she would have to bear left her far from happy.

She knew these trips were related to his work, for he had never offered to tell her what he was about. She never asked, nor did she wish to know. Only recently had she been able to separate the man and his work and she was hard put to jeopardize this new found peace in her heart.

She sighed sadly while stepping into the

welcome circle of his arms. "I wish it were possible for me to accompany you, Steven, for I fear I shall find myself with little to occupy my time." And blushing prettily, she added, with a devilish grin, "and more exactly, my nights."

Throwing his head back, he laughed with joy. His eyes twinkled with merriment. "My sweet little Angelina, so lady-like and refined, appears to be as lusty as a kitchen wench and to my immense pleasure as insatiable as a common street walker."

She giggled, "Aye Steven, I admit it as truth, but only with you."

His knuckles brushed gently against her jaw, his eyes tender, "Alas, I am delighted to admit I love being the target of your passions, even if it be true I'm usually exhausted after a night spent with you." He grinned, "Exhausted and never happier." His mouth was only inches from hers. Her arms about his neck. She pressed herself closer to him.

He groaned, "You please me beyond all else in life. You delight my soul."

His mouth was on hers and she was responding fully, unmindful of the servants' smiles as they went about their duties.

Finally, he pulled his lips away and whispered, "I fear, should I delay any longer, I will miss the tide for a quick tumble with you. Indeed, you are nearly impossible to leave. I think upon my return, a short trip is in store for us. Would you enjoy some island exploration? We could take the smaller boat, just the two of us. Would that please you, love?"

She smiled sweetly, "Oh aye, Steven, it would indeed."

He left her then. With a smile lingering on both their faces, he gave her a quick wave from atop his horse and disappeared behind the trees and foliage that bordered the road.

No sooner had Steven left than did Angelina begin to wait for his return. A sense of loneliness overcame her, so intense it felt a physical malady. Restlessly, she wandered from room to room, unable to think of anything that could occupy her time. And the things she could think of suddenly did not seem important enough to bother with.

It was later that same day when the drums began and continued through the night. Not since Angelina's arrival more than six months ago, had the drums beat so continually and with such force.

The next morning, Angelina awoke with a throbbing headache which only seemed to increase in intensity as the day wore on. And as the sound of the drums grew in violence and volume, so did the torturous pain in her head.

After questioning the servants, she discovered the cause. It seemed a voodoo priest or houngan was about to take a bride. There would be days of celebrating, for this was a very important happening.

Three days later, the incessant beating had not stopped. Angelina had finally sent for Dr. Jenkin. She felt awful. She couldn't stop her head from pounding, and now she began to shiver and tremble. She knew she had a fever.

Dr. Jenkin arrived and, after a thorough examination, gave her a heavy dose of medication. Soon she was resting easier. Just before she slipped off to a deep drugged sleep, Cicely bid her not to worry, promising all would be well, for Mrs. Webb had brought her a special tea to mix with her medication. Mrs. Webb had promised it would ease Angelina's headaches and any other ills she might have.

Puzzled, her drugged mind tried to understand. Why would Miriam bring her medication? Miriam hated her and could only hope for her ill health. She had been sick for three days; could Miriam have caused this?

She tried to call out, but her tongue was thick from the medication and she could only manage to mumble her maid's name before she felt its full effect and slept.

Even in her sleep, she heard the drums beat. Hour after hour it went on, until she felt herself absorbed into the drumming. She was floating. She was the hands hitting the drums. She was the drums themselves. She was the sound, drifting away into the black night.

She was dreaming of Miriam. It was late. Someone was whispering something to her, helping her dress. She could not see who it was. Her head would not clear; her eyes would not focus. She was engulfed in a thick fog; she could hear nothing but murmurs and see nothing but shadows. A bitter drink was forced down her throat. She slid into blackness.

A most ridiculous dream. No longer a drum, she began to sway her body to its hypnotic rhythm. At least she wasn't sick anymore. Dr. Jenkin gave lovely medicine.

She was traveling some distance atop a horse. Someone was holding her around her waist. She hoped it was Steven and tried to turn to see. She couldn't see his face.

Miriam appeared before her again. Annoyed, she wondered why a person could not dream what they wanted. She wished to dream of Steven, yet Miriam was constantly there.

Suddenly they were facing each other and laughing. They were in some sort of a black room that smelled of dampness and earth. She looked down; the floor was brown and soft beneath her naked feet. Was it dirt? Were they outside?

Miriam still before her, slowly began to take Angelina's clothing from her. Angelina tried to stop her. Her silly dream was turning into a nightmare. She hoped she would awaken soon.

Helplessly, she stood naked while Miriam fondled her breasts and slid her hands across the flesh of her stomach. Angelina shivered with disgust, yet she was unable to stop her. Her arms were so heavy, she couldn't lift them.

Miriam was brushing something across her; starting at her face and never stopping until her feet were covered. Angelina watched as Miriam worked. The warm liquid appeared to be red. What was she doing? Why?

All around her were the sound of voices humming and chanting with the beat of the drums. Miriam laughed again and covered Angelina with a long black cloak, exactly like the one she wore.

Again a bitter drink was brought to her lips. A moment later she felt better. Much better!

Miriam faded into the black walls. Suddenly Angelina was surrounded by others also dressed in black. She smiled pleasantly as unknown faces appeared before her eyes and then, just as suddenly, disappeared.

She felt as light as a feather. She felt beautiful. She felt desirable, and then overcome with intense desire. She wished Steven were home.

She began to move, swaying with the dreamy rhythm. The others who stood about, circling her, stepped back to give her room.

After some time, she stopped dancing and looked about. She was so shocked! All who had stood around her were suddenly naked and coupled—each person delirious with lust, all moaning and groaning out loud. No one cared what another might witness, so intent were they on their own release and desire.

Angelina felt a moment's disgust. She had never dreamt like this before, nor had she imagined the things these people were doing possible. What utter nonsense!

She laughed at her own foolishness. Someone began to swing her about. She spun from the faceless stranger's arms and began to dance again. She moved swaying in a slow deliberate sensual movement—her arms raised above her head, her eyes seductive, seeing nothing and no one.

The robe parted. She smiled as she felt the soft material cling and then pull away as she moved. Never before had she felt so light, so free. She was whirling about. Her robe opened again.

A man stood before her, reaching for her.

She couldn't see his face. She was in his arms. She smiled and moaned, "Steven." He laid her upon a hard bed. "Steven." Her body was exposed to his admiring eyes. "Steven." He stripped off his cloak and stood black and shining in the candlelight that surrounded their bed. She raised her arms to beckon him nearer. He bent over her, about to lie on her.

Suddenly, the drums stopped. A flash of light lit up the room. A loud explosive sound nearly deafened her. The acrid scent of gunpowder permeated the air.

Steven was gone! Where did he go?

Chapter 39

Steven had left Angelina's company with great reluctance. He had wanted to have her with him, but the cargo his ship carried was ammunitions. If the wrong side should approach his ship, or should they be fired upon, *The Savage* would surely be blown to pieces. No matter how much he wanted her, he would not risk her life.

He sat alone in his cabin. His eyes scanned his navigational charts while his mind kept returning to her face—her laughing, sometimes teasing, sometimes seductive eyes; her mouth, her sweet hypnotic tantalizing mouth.

"Damn!" he growled, annoyed at his schoolboy reaction to the short separation he had so far endured. He was beginning to believe he was fast becoming useless at anything but spending time in bed with his wife, for that was, of late, uppermost on his mind.

He uttered another sound of disgust as he gave up his work, grabbed his jacket, and left the cabin.

He stood on the forecastle deck directly behind the wheel and gazed out to sea. It was obvious they were headed for a serious storm. Already the sea was high and the man at the wheel was having a hard time holding the ship on its course.

Overhead, the sun shone brightly giving off that special bone-warming quality possible only among the islands. But in the distance, the sky was darkened to the color of black ash and growing steadily closer.

Steven's first mate came to stand by him, "Captain sir, looks like we're in for a bad one."

"Aye, Mr. Johnson. Have the men make ready." And with a hopeless sigh he continued, "Perhaps, with luck, we'll outrun it."

"I think not this time, Captain."

"I tend to agree, Mr. Johnson."

An hour later, the sea was so heavy, the wheel had to be tied in place. Everyone who dared walk the deck did so secured with a rope in order not to be thrown into the wild raging water.

The bow cut deep as the ship pitched forward and down, slicing through the giant waves. The schooner's two main masts were bare of canvas, yet the ship was tossed about as if its rigging were unfurled to full sail.

Steven reasoned that this storm was surely as menacing as the typhoons he had witnessed during his early sailing years in the

China Sea.

The howling and roar of the ocean was nearly deafening. Nothing and no one was dry. Water had managed to find its way below and into every crack and corner of the ship. The crew was bailing, but as yet to no avail, as the sea water continued to move freely about with every toss of the ship.

It was ten long wet hours later that the top of one of the two masts splintered against the storm's fury. The roar of the wood ripping free matched the screaming of the wind and it wasn't until the next day that men could be sent up the mast to assess the damage.

Steven reasoned, being only two days out of Portsmith, they would return to make repairs.

On the fourth night since its departure, *The Savage* docked once again at the small tropical island.

Steven's hunger for Angelina caused him to leave his ship in the capable hands of Mr. Johnson for repairs. With extraordinary speed, he crossed the eight miles that separated Rose Manor from the dock.

When he finally reached home, he was surprised and a little worried to find Angelina gone. No one seemed to know her whereabouts. Cicely became terrified, telling Steven her mistress had been ill with a fever and insisting she should still be abed.

A quick search of the property found nothing. Steven soon joined the young maid in her terror. Pouring himself a brandy, he paced the library floor. Manuel was summoned to him.

"Have you seen the mistress?"

A quick shake of the black man's head brought Steven no consolation.

"What the hell is going on around here? I leave for four days, and upon my return, Mrs. Spencer is gone with nary a clue to her whereabouts. And what in God's name is all that noise about?"

"A wedding, sir," Manuel ventured, "a voodoo priest is taking a bride."

"Why then have you not gone to see it? Nearly everyone around here enjoys watching these native ceremonies."

Manuel shook his head vehemently, "A very evil thing, sir, no one from here will go."

Steven thought, perhaps Angelina had gone to the King's Inn. Although he had extracted a promise from her to never do so, he knew she could be stubborn and willful and if she thought it necessary, she could and would disobey him.

He went to the stables and checked with a few men gathered there. Had anyone seen Mrs. Spencer? Was the carriage gone? No. Were all the animals in their stalls? Yes. Certainly she wouldn't have walked. Someone had come to fetch her and without the servants' knowledge. Why? How?

There was no help for it, he could not bear to simply sit and wait for her return. He had to find her.

He ordered Manuel to gather three other men and ready a horse for each for a search.

After arming himself heavily, should there be trouble, each of the men were given a gun.

He covered the eight miles to Portsmith in the fastest time yet. Soon he was at the King's Inn questioning the owners. Mary and Joe Favor swore they had not seen her in months. On the way back home, he stopped at Mrs. Harrington's plantation. The same story there. No one had seen her.

Where in God's name could she be? Steven was frantic; on the verge of total panic. A slow steady icy dread was descending over him. Something was wrong, terribly wrong. Those damn drums were driving him crazy. They were penetrating his whole being with fear. For as long as he had lived here, he had never heard the drums beat so continuously, nor so wildly. Trying to shake himself of the nearly paralyzing fear he felt, he tried to think. Perhaps feeling better, his wife had gone to watch the ceremony? But how would she have gotten there? Turning his horse off the road and into the thick tropical forest, he moved towards the sound of the drums and reasoned, he'd soon see. He had not a clue as to where else she might be.

At last the five men came upon a large group of natives dancing about a roaring fire. Nearby was a cave opening where more natives stood apparently watching something that was happening inside. The drumming became louder and more intense. Something important was happening. A woman laughed. The sound unnatural and cruel, grated on

Steven's already taut nerves and sent chills down his spine. The men with him were terrified and Manuel had to threaten them to prevent them from galloping off into the night.

Steven had seen many native ceremonies before, but never one with this intensity. Something was wrong. Something evil was happening. People were dancing about in a wild frenzy, some obviously believing they were possessed by a loa or spirit. Two men danced in and out of the large fire. A woman was eating a burning stick she had taken from the flames. Smoke was coming from her mouth and Steven nearly gagged as she opened her charred lips to scream out a horrible laughing sound.

A magical bead-wrapped rattle was being shaken over one woman while others were being doused with water which Steven knew was supposed to act as a magnet for spirits.

Another woman came out of the cave and stood for a moment at its entrance. Her body was painted red and she wore nothing but gold bands around her neck and a white turban around her head. She walked unnoticed by the wild crowd to a cage of chickens. As if in a trance, she took a chicken and, holding its flaying wings still, bit into its neck. Her mouth sputtered feathers and the chicken tried to claw her in its frenzy to escape. Finally she began sucking at its neck and drinking its blood, continuing to do so until the animal was still and lifeless in her hands. Some blood dribbled from her mouth and she laughed as if a lunatic, showing red stained teeth.

Moving her hands seductively over her breast, she spread the blood about.

Steven was disgusted. His men pressed again to leave. He ran his eyes over the crowd, searching for his wife. He was positive Angelina would not stay willingly to see such a disgusting display.

He was about to leave when, for some reason, he was drawn to look in the cave. Dismounting, he beckoned the men to follow him and walked the few feet to the cave's opening and forced his way through the crowded entrance.

The cave was large. In its center was a small fire. He was startled to see black candles set every few feet along a black draped wall. They gave off a minimum of light. Around the fire was a large circle scratched deeply into the dirt. Inside the circle were drawings of triangles and animals. The air was sickly sweet with the mixed scent of unwashed bodies and incense.

He looked about in astonishment! Outside the circle were many people coupling on the dirt floor, each involved in every imaginable act of sex, and most of them were covered with blood.

Steven had seen many things in his travels, but never before had he witnessed such lust. For a long time, he watched, drawn against his will, feeling himself being caught up in the thick atmosphere. The drumming and dim light added to the movement and moaning of the couples, giving the scene a surrealistic quality. He almost imagined himself among them and it stirred him more than he liked.

Forcing his feeling aside, he realized this was no ordinary voodoo ceremony. This was a calling on Satan. And he trembled at the evil he felt surrounding him.

His thoughts, once again, returned to his wife. Where the hell was she?

Just before he was about to turn and leave, his eye caught a familiar face. Miriam! What in God's name was she doing here?

Apparently in the throes of a trance, she looked right at him with glassy unseeing eyes. The shadows and dim light played tricks on his eyes and his imagination, and he thought he saw her head move in a three-hundred and sixty degree turn. When at last their eyes met again, and she finally realized who he was, her face split into a grin so evil that, for a moment, it sent shivers down his spine.

She was moving toward him, laughing wildly with happiness. He had come for her. She pulled open her cloak to entice him, displaying her naked body for him. He had come. He had come at last. She would have him now! She must have him now!

Steven also began to move. Unmindful of Miriam's insane thoughts, he was bent on finding out why she was here. He never noticed her opening her cloak for the two steps he took brought him within clear view of the entire cave, and there, to the left of the center, was his wife! She was dancing, swaying her body as he had never seen before. The black robe she wore opened as she moved. She was naked and painted red with blood! Her eyes were glassy and unseeing. Was she drugged?

Steven was shocked into immobility. He did nothing but gasp at the sight of her for she had never seemed more desirable. Her dancing was so seductive and sensuous, he couldn't stop the feeling of desire that instantly grew in the pit of his stomach.

He stood for a long moment, his desire growing almost out of control. His blood hammered in his ears, matching the rhythm of the drums. He forgot others could see her. He forgot others were there. He stared at the temptress before him. He couldn't seem to stop her. He didn't want to. She was beckoning him to come to her and he was helpless to resist. He wanted her, now! And he was going to have her, here.

A giant black man stepped between them. He picked her up and put her on a shrouded wide slab that resembled an altar. The black's cloak slipped to the floor; he too was naked. His entire body was painted a light ghoulish green. Obviously, he was the houngan. The high priest was bending over his wife, opening her cloak, apparently ready to mount her.

Suddenly he noticed the bodies of two babies, one on each end of the slab Angelina lay upon. Protruding grotesquely from each baby's middle was a dagger. Steven turned white with shock. His mind cleared instantly. Had he too been caught up in a trance? This was horror and perversion such as he had never known before.

He could hear Miriam's crazed laughter through a haze.

Angelina was reaching out, motioning the black to come to her. The priest moved closer still.

Steven was close enough now to hear her mumble his name. Without thought, Steven's guns were freed from his belt and in his hands.

Miriam screamed, "Nooo!" and ran the few steps that separated them.

He fired two shots. The man bending over his wife was lifted and thrown into the air, landing face down on the other side of Angelina.

Someone was screaming an agonizing, shrill, horror-filled sound. He looked to his right to see Miriam twisted into an unnatural position on the ground, her face bloody. Obviously, she had stepped between Steven and the priest at the last moment for there was now a gaping bloody hole where her nose had been.

The exploding sounds of his guns startled the others in the cave out of their hypnotic trance. At first they stood motionless, surprised to find a stranger in their midst and interrupting their ceremony.

All sound stopped. The silence was total and eerie as it grated on Steven's nerves. The guns in his hands were still smoking, giving off the acrid scent of gunpowder; quickly he reloaded them. A murmur was beginning to spread throughout the crowd. They were angry that he had stopped their ceremony, and angrier still that he had killed their houngan. Steven felt apprehensive. How the hell were they going to get out of here? The murmurs of the crowd were fast building to rage.

"Manuel, give me your weapons and pick up your mistress," he ordered. "The rest of you surround them and aim your guns at the crowd."

Quickly, the terrified men did as they were told, forming a circle with Manuel and Angelina at the center. Steven threw Manuel's gun and the two packets of ammunition he carried in his coat pocket into the fire.

"Walk," he ordered quietly. "Easy now, easy. Stay calm and walk out of here."

Steven, with both guns drawn, brought up the rear of the small group. For a moment it seemed the crowd was not going to part and let them leave. Suddenly from the fire came the sound of an exploding bullet, then another, and still more. Terrified, the women began to scream thinking the men were firing into the crowd. All who did not throw themselves on the ground, turned and ran from the cave. There was wild screaming; people were hysterical to get out.

When Steven and the men reached the cave's mouth there was no one in sight. With Manuel's help, Steven got Angelina on his horse. Fifteen minutes later, she was home.

Immediately, guards were posted and word was sent to the garrison for help. In the next few days, many natives were questioned, but no one would admit to being a participant in the night's ceremony or even knowing of its existence. Without a leader, the group of believers were obviously at a loss as to what to do, and no retaliation was ever taken.

For the next two years Steven, reluctant to leave his wife again, continued his work from his home, and sent his ship out in the care of its new captain, his former first mate, Mr. Johnson.

Chapter 40

On an early morning in September of '81, Angelina and Steven were enjoying a cup of tea on the terrace of their home when a messenger arrived with a packet of letters.

Steven gave Angelina those addressed to her and began reading one of his own. Anxious, as always, for news from the colonies, she devoured two letters from her father in quick succesion. She was disappointed, for neither of them told her any information of the war's progress.

Glancing up, she noticed Steven had finished reading and having done so, leaned back in his chair and sighed.

"What is it, Steven?"

Expressionless, he remarked, "Madam, it seems your rebel friends, with the help of Lafayette, have successfully cornered Lord Cornwallis at Yorktown. With his back up against the sea, there seems to be little doubt among your countrymen that the war is close to its finale."

She came to her feet so fast that her chair toppled and fell behind. "Steven, is it true?"

"I fear so, my dear," he commented dryly while a smile of pleasure played about his lips as he watched the ecstatic expression on his wife's face.

"At last, at last it is over," she laughed while barely able to contain herself.

"I think not, love. True it seems your rebels have injured the great angry lion, but he is far from slain. You may believe the end is in sight, but I fear it will not be quite so simple. Aye, I believe there is still some way to go before victory." After a moment of thought, he continued with a grin, "Would it be to your liking, madam, if I were to suggest a visit to your beloved Virginia, for it appears I have some business to attend to in the colonies."

In a flash, she was in his lap, her arms securely about his neck, nearly toppling his chair in her enthusiasm. "Oh Steven, do you mean it? I shall pack immediately. When are we leaving?"

He grinned, "I take it then, you are not adverse to my suggestion."

Happily, she remarked, "Oh Steven, it pleases me so to be able to see my father and brother again for it has been nigh onto two years since I have laid eyes on them." Suddenly all her happiness vanished and she looked up at him seriously, "But Steven, what of you? Would it be safe for you to go there now?"

He smiled at her obvious concern, "Fear not love, I promise you I will be quite safe."

He laughed merrily as she bestowed dozens of kisses to his face. "Be gone with you, madam. See about your packing. I too have much to do. If all goes well, perhaps we shall leave here within three days."

Her happy shrieks of laughter could be heard throughout the house as she raced up the stairs to her room, calling Cicely as she ran. There was so much to be done, she was at a loss to know where to start.

She was thankful she had not as yet told Steven she was again with child. Remembering how he had hovered over her like a mother hen the last time, left her with no doubt as to his inevitable attitude if he knew she was already three months into another pregnancy. She would wait until they arrived at her father's home before she told him.

Steven's ship entered the Chesapeake Bay on the fourteenth of September and rode up the Potomac, docking at Alexandria on the evening of the fifteenth.

Unbeknownst to him, he had by ten days missed a major sea battle as the British fleets of Admiral Thomas Graves and the French under Count de Grasse thundered at each other behind curtains of smoke. After the sea fight, Barras's fleet from Newport joined de Grasse. With thirty-two ships-of-the-line, the combined French fleet was too strong for the

British and Admiral Graves sailed for New York, leaving the harbor secure in the hands of the French.

In Virginia, the months of September remained excessively hot, allowing off duty soldiers, both American and their French allies, to idle away the afternoon hours in comfort.

With the English cornered for the moment only twelve miles away, and the Patriots' strength growing, they were a confident army. Most everyone agreed the end for Lord Cornwallis was simply a matter of time.

Angelina was at her father's home more than two weeks when Steven handed her a letter. With a wry smile, he said, "Madam, I feel sure this particular piece of correspondence will do much to lift your spirits."

Joseph Mathis, a friend of Jim's had written to her brother:

Dear Jim,

All in our company are much excited at the orders, just now received, to march. I doubt not our old friends at Yorktown eagerly await our long coming visit. Certainly, were it up to them, they would have had us wait for a more appropriate time. But we, being a much younger and reckless people, not endowed with generations of solid breeding, decided that now, rude or not, was the best time to pay a call.

Indeed, as they profess to be the most civilized and polite people on God's earth, we are all hoping they show a reasonable degree of courtesy and welcome us. In truth, our morale is of such magnitude, it matters little if it be with or without musket in hand.

The rest of the letter pertained to personal matters between friends. Angelina handed the paper back to her husband and smiled. "Truly sir, had I need of lifted spirit, this would surely be the answer."

On the night of October 22 an express rider, Thomas McHean, on his way to Philadelphia to meet the President of Congress, passed through Alexandria and let it be known Lord Cornwallis had surrendered the garrison of York to General Washington on October 17.

The news brought much merriment and celebration. People partied and danced in the streets for joy.

General Anthony Wayne, a fellow Virginian and a long time friend of James Barton, followed Washington north toward Philadelphia. Passing through Alexandria, he stopped to pay his friend a visit.

Mr. Barton invited General Wayne to stay the night. Accompanying him was Jim's friend, Sergeant Joseph Mathis. It was an evening of much merriment and celebrating. Toast upon toast was offered for everything from victory to a long awaited clean soft bed.

The men could scarely talk for laughing and Angelina was delighted. Being the only female in their midst, she was continuously busy accepting their requests for dancing.

Later, Angelina's old friend and fellow conspiritor Joseph Crockett, paid a visit.

Immediately upon spying Steven's presence, he bellowed, "Primrose! Good God ,man, it's been some time since I have seen you last. Do you know I laughed for days upon hearing of your episode at the inn and that puffed up English Colonel?"

Steven replied merrily, "Sir, I confess I too found that situation more than merely amusing, but sadly it brought to a close my usefulness to our cause and some of the most exciting experiences I have ever encountered."

"Aye," Joseph Crockett nodded knowingly, "your infiltration among the Indians and your close work with the English proved invaluable to our side. But in truth, there was scarcely a time since that I have not appreciated your new line of work, and to my mind you have proven yourself even more useful. The help you have given in delivering supplies has been immeasurable. I have word you are to receive a personal commendation from General Washington."

Modestly, Steven remarked, "You give me too much credit. Surely another would have done just as well."

"Perhaps," James Barton chimed in, "but it was you and not another who did it." And beaming with pride, he finished, "I find much to be proud of in my two sons."

Angelina croaked out in amazement, "You

knew, father?"

"Aye, Angelina," he grinned, "from the first. It was Joseph who introduced us and recommended Steven use our home as a base for his work."

Steven glanced into his wife's shocked face. Her eyes grew steadily larger and stormy. By reading her face, he knew this war of independence was small in comparison to what he was about to face. Yet she gave not the least hint of her anger to the men in the room.

It was sometime later that she excused herself and, smiling a fond farewell to the soldiers, she retired. No one but Steven noticed how her eyes slipped icily over him and her lack of a smile.

By the time she entered their room, she was so furious that she slammed the door so hard, it was clearly heard downstairs.

Steven, with an audible sigh, knew he was in for a battle. Wishing his fellow compatriots a good night, he followed Angelina to their room.

He was not surprised when he tried the handle to the door to find it locked. Knocking softly, he asked for admittance.

From behind the door, he heard her reply, "Were I you, sir, I would step lightly, for the fury I feel frightens even me."

"Angelina, allow me to explain."

No response.

"Please Angelina, open the door."

Nothing.

Giving up, he went to his old room and, trying the adjoining door, found that also locked. From behind the door he shook the handle and ordered, "Madam, open this door immediately!"

A vase crashed against the door in response.

She was furious. She couldn't remember ever before feeling such a fool. Good Lord, even her father had known. Everyone had known but his wife had been told nothing. And Steven, the man who professed to love her, had done it. She was pacing the floor. Her dress was thrown carelessly into a heap in the corner and she wore only a robe. She would never sleep tonight. Normally when upset she would ride until she felt some calmness, but tonight she dared not leave her room. Steven was out there somewhere. And Steven was the last person she wanted to see.

The terrace door to her room opened and he entered unnoticed. Still she continued to pace while he leaned against the wall and watched her.

It was some time before she noticed him, and jumped with surprise to see him standing inside her room.

She grabbed a bottle of perfume and with a furious scream of, "Get out!" she hurled it at him.

Quickly, he ducked, and the bottle crashed and shattered against the wall.

A lazy grin spread across his handsome face. His teeth flashed white against his dark skin. He began to stalk her.

She backed away and threw a hair brush.

"You lying bastard. Hypocrite! Charlatan! I have no need of your explanations. Do not come to me sniveling your excuses."

He side-stepped the brush and laughed, "Madam, a bastard I may be, but I did not lie and I have never sniveled in my life."

She threw a shoe, "Get out!"

He ducked again and continued to stalk her.

She was raging and the madder she got, the more he laughed. Another bottle of perfume flew from her hand.

"Go ahead," she taunted, "tell me of your undying love. Liar! A man in love does not lie."

His eyes narrowed and grew serious and threatening as he continued to move. His voice warned, "I told you madam, I did not lie."

He was backing her to the bed. She hit him with a shoe. He smiled menacingly. Realizing too late his intent, she tried to lunge to the right, when the weight of his body knocked her back and the two of them fell across the bed.

Holding her struggling body and flaying arms still, he smiled, "Madam, do me the courtesy of hearing me out."

"I am not interested in anything you might have to say, Primrose," she sneered. "In any case, how am I to believe you? Let me be!"

"I have never lied to you, Angelina. I simply allowed you to believe what you wished."

"You are mistaken, sir, if you think that is an adequate explanation. You never denied you were a spy. Therefore, you lied!"

Grinning he responded, "On the contrary, madam, I was a spy, I could not deny it. It is just that you believed me to be working for the British, and in a sense I was. Only the Patriots knew it."

"I gathered as much from the comments downstairs." For a long moment she looked at him, her confusion apparent. Finally she spoke, "I cannot fathom this. Are you not British? How is it then you worked for the rebel cause?"

"Aye my love, I am British but not English. My father's family came from Ireland as you know. In one way or another, we Irish have been much like the colonists, fighting the control of the English on our soil for as far back as I can remember.

"Because of the English, my father and most of his family fled Ireland with no more than the clothes on their backs. His family were landed gentry and although they were far from rich, they lived well.

"It seems one day our eminent king took a notion that our family's lands would fare better in an Englishman's hands. Someone, no doubt, he found favor with at the time.

"As if they had never existed, my family were set aside and left penniless. Because they were Irish, and worse yet Catholics, no one listened to them.

"For a short time my father and uncles tried to resist but to no avail, for the British sent in troops to settle in the new owners of Primrose Manor. Most of my family were killed and my father and his brother fled to the home of a distant relative in Spain."

Her eyes showed clearly her amazement as she asked, "But how then did the English believe you, knowing of your background?"

He smiled, "With the English pride being such that they believe everyone would naturally wish to be English, it was not difficult. Some years ago I bought Rose Manor and from that time forward, it was naturally assumed I was a loyal subject to the crown. Later, a few words spoken over a tankard of ale against the troublemakers in the colonies, plus some pieces of useless information, soon convinced them I was what I claimed to be."

"You beast," she punched his arm and

stood up. Again she started pacing the floor while he sat and watched her. "And to think I was worried for your safety should you be found out. I feel such a fool. I could throttle you. Why did you keep the truth from me all this time?"

"Actually, it wasn't until I spoke to Joseph Crockett the night you were bitten by that snake that I found us to be working for the same cause. He was a mite upset to be losing two agents and didn't hesitate to let me know. When I professed to have no knowledge of your activities, it gave him a jolly laugh indeed.

"But by then your reaction to finding my papers had changed your heart toward me." He sighed deeply as he continued, "Let us say we both possess an extraordinary amount of pride, for I was determined to have you love me no matter where my loyalties lay. So I said nothing and waited for the time you could admit you loved me above all else.

"I was going to tell you the day Landen abused you, for I saw your heart softening towards me, but with all the terror and concern for your injuries, I completely forgot about it. Later, I knew you were ready at almost any moment to come to me and I was hard put to jeopardize your feelings. Later still, it seemed to matter not in the least.

"Indeed, I am sorry now that I did not tell

you. Yet in truth," he continued, while giving her a sly grin, "I am not alone in keeping secrets."

Righteously, she snapped, "Steven, you knew what I was about from the first. Simply because I never discussed it with you, does not classify me as being deceitful."

Catching her hand as she continued to pace, he pulled her to him, "Aye love, that is so, yet it is not of what I speak." Slowly, he untied her robe and his hands spread unhindered across her abdomen. Pulling her closer to him, he nuzzled his face into her belly, his voice slightly muffled against her skin. "When were you planning to tell me of our future parenthood?"

"I was going to . . . what? How did you know?"

He smiled tenderly, and continued to hold her close to him, "There is little that passes me unnoticed, my love. I have known for some time."

"I was going to tell you. I was only waiting for an appropriate moment." And then poking his chest with her finger, she continued bossily, "Do not try to squirm out of this by changing the subject. I presume our initial meeting was a result of some encounter related to your work and not your story of a jealous husband?"

"Aye love, there was a time or two when I

was close to being found out. The night you refer to, I had a rendezvous with a man from Colonel Tarleton's staff. He told me to meet another agent a few weeks hence at the Cherokee village for a report on the Indians' total strength. It was immediately after the first meeting that a sentry approached me and started shooting. Of course I could not allow him to capture me for I carried certain damaging documents. It was these gunshots you heard just before I jumped on your horse."

Pulling away from him, she retied her robe. Still her anger had not been abated. She busied herself by straightening some of the mess she had made. "I was never so shocked. All this time together and I suspected nothing."

Arrogantly, he replied, "In the end, it mattered not at all, you found you loved me regardless."

She snapped angrily, "Aye Steven, damn it, but it would have been so much easier had I known. For so long I felt myself a traitor to love you."

Coming up behind her as she worked straightening out her dressing table, his arms slipped around her waist and he pulled her tightly against him. His face was buried in her neck when he whispered, "What is it you feel now?"

"Steven, stop that! I am furious."

Ignoring her, he remarked, "You are beautiful."

She watched through the mirror as his dark head moved against her neck. His hand pulled at her robe, baring her shoulder. His mouth slid across her skin to nibble, sending chilling sensations down her back.

She asked weakly, suddenly breathless and as always hungry for his touch, "Is that how you listen to me."

Suddenly she was in his arms and he was walking to the bed. "In truth madam, I find you so adorable, I am hard put to resist you."

His mouth held hers in a long sweet kiss as he put her on the bed and lay down beside her. When his lips finally left hers, he smiled down into her love-softened face.

She smiled seductively, her hands moving up his chest, caressing his broad shoulders, "Indeed there are moments, sir, when I am most happy you refuse to listen to me."

Chapter 41

It was February of '82 when Steven received a summons to meet with Washington who was now quartered in Philadelphia. It was necessary to arrange for food and clothing for a full regiment and Steven was, due to previous service, asked if he could be of assistance.

He left the next day, promising to return within a week or at the very least, write and let Angelina know of his whereabouts. He left in the midst of a blizzard. No relief appeared to be in sight as the snow continued to fall, getting deeper by the minute.

He huddled under his heavy coat and wrapped the woolen blanket tighter around him. His vision was cut short as he pulled his hat low, trying to protect his face from the stinging snow.

He presented a dark sharp figure against a background of white, as his horse plodded through the deep thick fluffy moisture.

Two men waited in the snow covered brush that bordered the road. This was not the first time John Landen and his partner, for the time being, had evilly estimated the value of an approaching rider. But had Landen known the identity of his soon-to-be-victim, he would have done his best to insure his suffering to the maximum.

Steven never saw the men as his horse rode past, neither did he realize that the sudden pressure and burning in his chest was caused by a bullet, nor did he feel the cold as his body hit the ground and rolled to a stop.

The baby was due to arrive in three weeks, and Angelina was a little surprised that Steven had not contacted her since he left, knowing how anxious he had been. Reasoning he was probably too busy, she shrugged it off.

Two weeks passed before a letter arrived. She was in the library having tea with her father when a messenger delivered it. But instead of a note from Steven, the envelope contained the bold heavy writing of General Washington.

It read in part:

Madam,

It grieves me deeply to inform you that your husband, who has been a great friend to our cause and more often than not indispensable in regards to the supplies he has procured for our brave army, has been killed.

The letter went on to say, although she didn't see it because it fell from her limp fingers to the floor—

Two men, having been deep in their drinks in a public room of an inn in Philadelphia, had been heard to boast of their newly amassed fortune. When questioned by a member of my staff who was in residence at the time, neither could give just cause as to why they should be in such excellent condition financially.

After a search, papers belonging to one Steven Spencer were found in their possession. During the extensive questioning which followed, it was learned they had killed a man, robbed him, and left his body, nearly naked, in the snow.

As of this writing, the two men responsible for this abominable act are awaiting their just punishment. It is my sorrowful duty, madam, to further report to you we have not as yet recovered your husband's body, although every effort in this matter is being taken.

Please be advised, I remain your humble servant,

G. Washington

The words DEAD! DEAD! DEAD! kept echoing through her mind. She couldn't fathom it. She laughed aloud. Impossible! The war was nearly over. She laughed again and then before her father's astonished eyes, she followed the letter to the floor, in a dead faint.

The shock of Steven's death brought on her labor. The next day she gave birth to a son whom she named Steven James.

Two months had passed since Steven died, and as yet she had not shed a single tear. Within her chest existed a pain so severe, she never stopped smiling, fearful that if she gave into the pain, it would rip her to pieces.

Her laughter was shallow, her nerves stretched taut. She was on the verge of collapse.

Her father was very concerned. She needed release and he had no idea how to help her. When he attempted to console her, she brushed aside his attempts with an airy denial of any suffering on her part.

But each time Steven's name was mentioned, her whole body became rigid, her eyes growing huge and tinged with panic.

Again today, James Barton had tried to talk to his daughter. Soon, in despair, he had given up when, refusing to discuss it, she fled to the safety and solitude of the garden.

It was a warm sunny April day, flowers were beginning to bloom and the garden gave off a sweet clean perfume. Angelina sat on a bench and with a sigh, raised her face to the warming sun. The sun's bright rays brought tears to her eyes. She breathed deeply, trying to ignore the discomfort in her chest, desperate to staunch the flow that threatened. *No, no, do not think! If you think you'll cry and if you cry, it'll be true. He will really be dead.*

Finally, successfully blinking back the tears, she breathed easier and willed her tense body to relax. For a moment she was tempted to wake the baby from his nap and bring him outside, but decided against it as she felt discomfort begin to grow in her breasts. Soon enough he would awaken to eat.

Her eyes gazed out upon the garden, admiring the colorful array of flowers, but when she saw a group of primroses in the early stages of bloom, it was her undoing.

No longer able to will away the thought of him, she succumbed to the inevitable. Memories flooded her entire being. She saw as clearly as if he stood before her, his laughing eyes, his tender smile, his strong arms, how the sun shown in his black hair and could tan him as dark as an Indian. How incredibly handsome he had been in a simple white shirt, his touch, his tender words of love.

The tears came then. Heartrending sobs tore through her. She never realized she was capable of such tears, and still more tears came. She cried for a long time and then finally, as if washed away, the continuous pain she had carried with her for two months began to lessen.

At last, grateful and hungry for his memory, she greedily and purposely thought of their times together. Their wild fights, their tumultuous lovemaking, their laughter, the tenderness they shared, the sweet short love she had known.

Finally able to smile a genuine smile, she left the garden and went to tend her baby. Steven James was stirring in his cradle. Quickly she changed his wet clothes and brought him to a chair in the corner of the room.

Undoing her dress, the baby nuzzled her, sucking greedily. She smiled, watching him as he ate hungrily. "Easy, child," she crooned while caressing his tiny body, "not so fast, you'll choke."

Her bedroom door opened, she did not look up. "Lizzy, could you see if Steven's clothes are dry? Bring them up and I will fold them when he is finished."

"The babe is as beautiful as his mother. Indeed, madam, you have done well."

Her eyes flew to the door.

Her heart turned over in her chest as she watched that familiar lazy grin spread across his mouth. He leaned against the door and teased. "In some ways, the lad reminds me of myself. Especially in his present position."

It took her a full minute to realize he was standing there, speaking to her, and not a figment of her imagination.

His arm hung in a sling that tied about his neck. He was terribly thin. Deep lines of suffering etched his face. She could clearly see he had been grieviously ill, yet his eyes were as merry and sharp as always.

She smiled brilliantly, her happiness so great, she was unable to speak.

"Madam, I do not intrude if I join you for a moment?"

Suddenly she was swept back in time, to the garden of Rose Manor, to that romantic night they had danced in the silvery moonlight, and he had spoken those same words.

Her eyes glistened with happy tears. At last she was on her feet. They met in the center of the room and as she walked into the warm circle of his arms, she sobbed almost incoherently, "You, sir, could never intrude, for I find your company most agreeable as of late."